CELIA

By Sophia Holloway

Kingscastle
The Season
Isabelle
The Chaperone
Celia

CELIA

SOPHIA HOLLOWAY

Allison & Busby Limited
11 Wardour Mews
London W1F 8AN
allisonandbusby.com

First published in Great Britain as *Bless Thine Inheritance* in 2018.
This edition is published by Allison and Busby in 2023.

A CIP catalogue record for this book is available from
the British Library.

First Edition

ISBN 978-0-7490-3052-0

Typeset in 11/16 pt Adobe Garamond Pro by
Allison & Busby Ltd.

By choosing this product, you help take care of the world's forests.
Learn more: www.fsc.org

FSC
www.fsc.org
MIX
Paper | Supporting
responsible forestry
FSC® C171272

Printed and bound by
CPI Group (UK) Ltd, Croydon, CR0 4YY

For K M L B

CHAPTER ONE

Lady Mardham disliked her sister-in-law intensely, and the feeling was mutual. They sat on either side of the Chippendale tea table with forced smiles, and exhibited the degree of civility that only appears when people loathe each other. Lady Blaby remembered when the chinoiserie style had been all the rage and the table was new. Like everything else at Meysey, she thought it behind the times; she herself had a far more fashionable example with delicate sabre legs and satinwood stringing. Lady Blaby was the proud possessor of a rich and indulgent husband, and changed the decor of her town house with every vagary of fashion. She was several years Lady Mardham's junior, and relished the knowledge that not only was she done up in the latest style, but that the few grey hairs she possessed could still be disguised with ease, and that her figure, despite bearing three children, was still remarkably good.

'I do hope you are keeping in comparatively good health, Pamela,' she cooed, with patently false concern.

'I am in the most robust of health, I assure you, my dear sister. We Cossingtons are renowned for it. My own dear Mama never suffered a day of rheumatism or loss of faculties until the day she died, at the age of three and eighty.'

'How reassuring, then, that you have a few more years left of well-being, however you may look.' Lady Blaby's coo became a commiserating purr. She was well aware that Lady Mardham was still two years short of fifty.

Lady Mardham coloured, and changed the subject, 'How is Sir Marmaduke?'

'He is, alas, confined with the gout at present, poor man, but has assured me that I should go and visit Lavinia and Charles in any case. He does not like a fuss to be made over him. I am so looking forward to seeing the baby, though the thought of being "Grandmama" is quite horrifying. Fortunately nobody would believe it to look at me.'

'No, my dear, you never did look the least maternal.' Lady Mardham could not resist the chance to launch a barb of her own, but Lady Blaby seemed to ignore it.

'Anyway, since I am travelling down to Batheaston I thought I would break my journey for an hour at my own old home and see how you were all getting on.'

Lady Blaby stressed the 'getting on'. She paused for a moment, and then dropped her stone of information into the pool of conversation and watched the ripples. 'You know, time flies by so fast. It does not seem five minutes since Charles was a babe in my arms, and here we are, with him a father, and my little Jane already excited at the thought of her come-out in the spring.'

Whilst simple arithmetic would have prepared Lady Mardham for this announcement, she did not often think about her niece, and as Lady Blaby had anticipated, it came as a shock.

'Goodness, already?'

'Why yes. She is so very promising too. A few more months and her figure will have developed a little more, but at least she is not inclined to put on excessive weight. Dumpy girls cannot be shown off to advantage, whatever one tries. I did worry that she might be throwing out a freckle last month, but it was a false alarm, and besides, as disfigurements go . . .' Lady Blaby left the sentence hanging, and gave Lady Mardham a look of sympathy which was really smug superiority.

Lady Mardham's smile became more fixed.

'Celia's complexion has always been faultless.'

'Ah yes, but who considers her complexion, these days?'

'More tea, Aurelia?' Her hostess did not look her in the eye.

* * *

After Lady Blaby's departure, Lady Mardham was closeted with her lord for some time. He had carefully avoided meeting his sister, and had taken refuge in his library. His spouse found him sympathetic, but disinclined to hold out much hope of success.

'By all means, my dear, do as you think fit, but for all the good it will do . . . And are you sure poor Celia is up to facing company again?'

'She must be. I declare this news will bring on my nervous spasms.'

Lord Mardham pursed his lips. His lady's 'nervous spasms' always managed to set the house by the ears and ruin his peace. He was a man who liked a quiet but convivial life. Having guests again would be pleasurable, for he was naturally social, but he feared it would all be rather daunting for poor Celia. He thought she had come to terms with things remarkably well, for she was a level-headed and sensible girl. It was all rather tragic for her, but there was nothing more that could be done, and she accepted her prospects with equanimity. He sometimes thought his wife still thought of the whole thing as some bad dream from which they might waken if they only put their minds to it.

'I recommend that the energy that might be expended in spasms, my dear, be channelled instead into your preparations. You will be wanting to make up a suitable party.'

Lady Mardham responded to this gentle guidance and went away to write lists – many of them. It was lacking but an hour until dinner when she asked to see her daughter in the yellow saloon, where the late afternoon sunshine gave the room a cheering golden glow. Lady Mardham fiddled with the lace at the cuffs of her gown. The door opened, and her daughter entered.

'You wished to speak with me, Mama?'

'Ah, Celia, dearest.' Lady Mardham addressed her younger child, but did so without quite looking directly at her, blissfully unaware how much it hurt her daughter. 'Come and sit down, my poor child. I have something we need to discuss.'

Celia Mardham did as she was bid, coming haltingly across the room, and set her stick beside her chair. She was a little short of twenty years old, but months of pain and discomfort had made her look older. She folded her hands in her lap. She was without doubt an exceedingly pretty girl, with rich brown hair, delicately arched brows, a straight nose, generous mouth and the complexion which her mother had extolled. Lady Mardham had been confident of her successful come-out, for who but a man with eyes only for blondes or raven-locked brunettes could not fail to be charmed by her. It was clear that she would make an excellent debut in Society and be snapped up in her first Season, except that her Season never took place. On a cold February day, only a couple of months before they were to remove to London, she had suffered an accident in the hunting field. Her horse had stumbled upon landing after a ditch and rolled onto her, and it had resulted in a broken femur, from which at first it was feared she might not recover. The local surgeon, knowing the high morbidity of such an injury, had prepared her parents for the worst and sent for the bone-setter from Cheltenham. At that expert gentleman's hands she had endured much, but he had successfully aligned the ends of the bone as best he could, and splinted the leg tightly. Initially, her survival was so great a relief that any other considerations were set aside.

Only very gradually had she regained her health. Three months she had been bedridden, the leg held straight to mend, but the knee so immobile that thereafter it had remained stiff, and impossible to flex fully. This meant that when she sat, her left foot stuck out a little before her, rather than being hidden demurely beside the right under her skirts, and advertised her as 'different'. The leg itself was now scarred from the ulceration that had been the consequence of that immobility, but at least that was only known by her maid and closest of relatives. What was more important was that Celia also had a pronounced limp. For months she could barely put her weight upon the limb, and every step was a struggle. Her mama had clung to the hope that the limp would disappear as she grew stronger, despite the doctor telling her that the shortening of the leg by some three inches meant that this was an impossibility. Thereafter Lady Mardham found it difficult to watch her daughter walk. Every ungainly step shouted at her that she was condemned to spinsterhood, unable to ever take her place in a dance set, or glide across a drawing room floor. Her good looks counted for nothing when people only saw the limp, and a Season would be both a waste and an embarrassment. In view of Lady Blaby's news, however, 'something must be done' to try, just once, to find the poor girl a husband.

'Your Papa and I are going to invite a few guests to stay.'

'Do you wish me to remove to Grandmama in the Dower House?' Celia frowned slightly. She could think of no other reason why her mama should look so embarrassed at disclosing this news. They had not invited anyone to Meysey in the eighteen months since her accident, and she had seen nobody outside the family except one of her brother's friends who had come into Gloucestershire with him after New Year.

'No, no, my dear.' Lady Mardham's confusion increased. 'You see, I . . . your papa and I, think it only fair that you do get the chance to meet people again. It is terribly unfortunate that . . . not that we blame you in any way, of course . . . and with your cousin Jane coming out next Season . . .'

Her daughter's frown remained, since none of this made a lot of sense.

'Forgive me, Mama, but when you say "meet people", do you mean gentlemen? I assure you that I have become perfectly accustomed to the idea that I will not marry, and Richard has assured me that I will always have a place in his home when he weds, or that I can, in time, have the Dower House.' Celia smiled, a little wryly, at her mama. 'I have no wish to be paraded as an object that some man might pity, and I can do none of the things a gentleman would expect in a situation where courtship is involved. I cannot dance, or ride, or even stroll. The situation is hopeless, but I do accept it.'

'You do not fully understand, my love. Richard is a dear boy, but marriage is the mark of success for a woman in this world. It gives you freedom. To make no effort at all to see you established would be neglectful, and . . . you will not know about your Grandpapa's will, for you were still playing with your dolls when he died, but he made provision . . . and none of us, even Grandmama, understood why . . . but there is a considerable legacy to whichever of his granddaughters weds first, and before her twenty-first birthday. Jane is being brought out next year, and of course you will reach that age next September.'

'You think I need the security of an inheritance? Am I to be indigent?'

'My dear Celia, the legacy is considerable. We are talking thirty thousand pounds, and seeing it go to *her* daughter would be the outside of enough.' Lady Mardham's tone became acid.

'Ah.' That, thought Celia, was the nub of the issue. Aunt Aurelia was loathed by both her brother and sister-in-law, and not popular even with her own mama, from what she had gathered from Grandmama, who regarded her daughter's second marriage as wilful disobedience.

Sir Marmaduke Blaby might have been well-heeled, but old Lady Mardham castigated him as a 'snivelling worm'. 'So you want to make a push to get me married off to spike Aunt Aurelia's guns.'

'That is not a lady-like term. I assume you picked it up from young Wakehurst when he came home last. Please do not use it in front of our guests.' Lady Mardham spoke repressively, but Celia knew she was just trying to avoid admitting the truth.

'So have you anyone in particular whom you think would not object to me?' Celia's smile was now fixed, and her eyes challenged.

'"Object"? You are not objectionable, Celia, but we have to be pragmatic. Sir Marcus Cotgrave told me last year how much you reminded him of his late wife, and that he could learn to ignore your deformity.'

'How generous of Sir Marcus. He is, by the way, five and forty at the least.'

'Mr Wombwell is not yet thirty, and his mama, with whom I correspond regularly, as you know, is very keen that he marry and settles down.'

'That is because he is rackety beyond belief. He is hardly a paragon of virtue. In fact you yourself have said how very wayward he has become. Indeed you told me that some of his recent exploits were not for delicate ears, so I can only assume that he is some form of libertine.'

'But he is the right age.'

'If there is the chance of thirty thousand pounds, Mama, why not let it be known and have all the fortune hunters who missed out this Season flock to our door?' Celia's sarcasm was obvious enough, but her words were again ignored.

'There is a stipulation that the gentleman must himself be solvent, with at least five thousand pounds of his own in the Funds, a regular income, and able to support a wife. Also the bequest is invalidated if used as an inducement; it may only be revealed once the betrothal is agreed.'

'What was Grandpapa thinking of?'

'He had a sister who died years ago, an unmarried sister who was determined not to marry. He saw her life, and was, apparently, keen that his granddaughters did not follow that path. He thought all women needed a husband to guide them.'

'I cannot see Grandmama being "guided" very often, even by him.' Celia gave a wry smile, for Grandmama was a force to be reckoned with, and her relatives treated her with utmost respect.

'Very true, but I think he clung on to the idea that he could guide her, even though he did not.'

'And why not simply divide the sum and make it available to Jane and myself upon marriage, not turn it into a race, and winner takes all?'

'Oh, do not ask me that, my poor Celia. Do you not think we have all of us wondered at it over the years? Whatever we think, that is as it stands, and . . . I have given it some thought, and so as not to make it too obvious, I will invite the Corfemullens, and get Richard to bring one or two of his friends, and you could invite

16

that girl you were at school with, the one who writes all those meandering letters.'

'Marianne Burton? She is a nice girl but, Mama, you know full well her father came up from trade.'

'And is a Member of Parliament, and knighted, so it does not mean we may not invite her, but of course she will not be eligible so no threat to you, my dear. And your papa says Sir Thomas is a very decent man.'

'Poor Celia' ignored the implication that any other woman in the party had to be married or ineligible through birth.

'When last we met she showed every sign of becoming very pretty.'

'Yes, but you were but sixteen dear, and she is younger. And she is not married yet so perhaps that came to nothing.' Lady Mardham looked upon the bright side.

'And I gather Sir Thomas is a man of wealth and she his sole heiress.'

'Yes, well . . . He is in the stoutest of health at present, as far as we know.' It was Lady Mardham's turn to ignore an implication. 'I shall write to your brother and see if he can find someone.' She rose, already formulating phrases in her head.

Celia remained seated some time. What she had said was truthful. She had accepted that her future was not the one she had always imagined. She also knew that what Mama said was equally true. Marriage was a freedom, and being the dependent relative was not. Everything about the bringing up of a daughter was focused upon the aim of 'seeing her established', from how she looked to the list of her accomplishments. The seminary had taught French, and Italian, and Celia, whilst not revealing such a thing to Mama for fear of being denounced as a bluestocking, had even cribbed a little Latin from her brother's school books. She had learnt to draw, to paint watercolours, to set a sleeve and embroider, to sing and play the pianoforte; there had been a dancing master and hours spent upon deportment. Even arithmetic had been taught so that she, as mistress of a house, could look over the quarterly accounts. As her brother's pensioner she would never see an account book. She had been condemned, in one moment of misfortune, to missing out on the practical advantages of marriage, and also that other side. She, like her peers, had dreamt of a handsome man falling in love with her, and she with him, followed by some vague matrimonial idyll. Well, no man would look at her now, other than with pity, and how she had come to hate pity. She gave herself a mental shake. Self-pity was the worst form of all. She had resolved to make the best of things, to be grateful for what she did have, but sometimes it was so very hard.

'And now I am to be exhibited in the hope that pity will win me a husband, and a fortune.' Celia voiced her thought aloud. 'What foolishness, and how very, very lowering.'

'Well, if that don't beat all,' the Honourable Richard Mardham, resplendent in what he considered a tasteful, deep purple, paisley silk dressing gown, and with a forkful of rare beef poised between plate and mouth, put down the missive he had received from his mother and heaved a sigh.

His friend, Lord Deben, who was a rather earlier riser, and had discovered him still at his breakfast, raised an enquiring eyebrow.

'Can't say one way or the other if you don't tell what it is, my dear fellow. Not a nasty shock, I hope? '

'Not exactly, but . . . my mama has decided to invite a load of people down to Meysey to try and . . .' He suddenly thought that telling his friend his family were downright desperate to get his sister married off was not quite the thing, and ended, lamely, 'cheer my sister up.'

'Er, is your sister blue-devilled? I mean, must be dashed unpleasant for her, hobbling about and whatnot, but last time I saw her she seemed remarkably stoic. Brave girl, I thought her.' Lord Deben was a young man without an excessive intelligence, but possessed of a very kind nature.

'Yes, well, Mama thinks she needs a fillip and has said she wants me to toddle down to the family seat and, mark you, to bring a couple of my friends with me.'

'Sounds very reasonable. I mean, not much fun being there with people you don't know or dislike. Much nicer to have a couple of your own friends about. Place might be packed with some very fusty old types for all you know. Not sure they would cheer the poor girl up very much. When is this to be?'

'Fortnight Wednesday. And I was thinking of heading

up to Yorkshire and staying with Rufus Leeming for some grouse shooting. Who would want to come into Gloucestershire with me?'

'Well, it will be the beginning of September, so there will be partridge. As I recall you do well for partridge, and if you want company, well, yours truly would be glad to oblige,' Lord Deben offered, diffidently. 'Not sure how my being there might cheer your sister up, but only too happy, etc . . .'

'Jolly decent of you, Debs. Sure you do not mind?'

'Not at all. To be honest, finding myself at a bit of a loose end at the moment, and I have no inclination to make a bolt for home. Father keeps asking what I am doing to occupy myself as if he thought I should actually do something specific. Just because he keeps writing long essay things, like one had to do at school, but all about some plant or other. Odd fish, my Pater, I sometimes think. I was complaining about it to Pocklington only yesterday evening. Now, there's a thought. What about inviting him too? Pocklington, not my father.'

Mr Mardham, ignoring the part of the letter which had suggested his friends be the sort hanging out for a wife in the near future, willingly assented to this idea. Lord Pocklington was a gentleman keen on outdoor pursuits, and had only remained in the Metropolis because his family seat was, in his words, 'infested with aunts'.

'At least you will be assured of good food, Debs.

Nothing fancy served at Meysey, but Cook has a way with patties . . .'

'I remember the last time I went down with you, and there was that raised pie. Melted in the mouth it did.' Lord Deben's mouth watered at the memory, and the whole idea suddenly seemed far more appealing to both gentlemen. Richard Mardham set aside his letter, requested his friend to await him while he dressed, and suggested they then go in search of Viscount Pocklington, via their club and Tattersall's ring.

CHAPTER TWO

Sir Thomas Burton was a man who knew his limitations. He was not ashamed of his comparatively humble beginnings as the son of a Bristol wine merchant, and exceedingly proud that he had risen to be an alderman of his city and then a Member of Parliament. He knew full well, however, that many of his aristocratic acquaintances tolerated him for his wealth and acumen, but yet looked down their noses at him for his origins. It did not bother him a whit for himself, but it did concern him that his only child, upon whom he had begrudged no expense at a very select Queen's Square seminary in Bath, might find her path to social acceptance blocked by 'trade'. That very 'trade' would one day make her, and thus her husband, very wealthy indeed, but for all the talk of young women who had risen above far more humble birth in the past, he had fears that his beautiful Marianne would end up a simple 'Mrs' when she ought to be a titled lady. Purchasing Embling Grange shortly after the death of his wife, he had gentrified himself to a degree where he frequently brushed shoulders with the aristocracy, but was not close. He was therefore quite surprised to find himself singled out by the Earl of Curborough in a Gloucester gunsmith's.

'Ah, Sir Thomas, thinking of acquiring a new gun for the shooting season, eh?' The earl's manner was that of a close friend, although they were but nodding acquaintances.

'Er, yes, my lord.' In truth, Sir Thomas, very much a townsman, had never owned a shotgun before, and was hoping his gamekeeper might take him somewhere out of the way and teach him what to do so that he would not disgrace himself in the months to come. 'Mr Prosser here has been checking what length of stock would suit me best.'

'Ah, yes. Let Prosser see you right and, well, perhaps I could offer you some shooting once the pheasant season begins.'

Sir Thomas blinked and mumbled his thanks, conscious that he would always accord the gunmaker the courtesy of 'Mister' because he respected the man's skill in his trade, just as the earl would never think of addressing the man with more than his surname.

'How is Miss Burton these days? Not "flown the nest" yet, has she?' Lord Curborough laughed at his own wit. This made up for the fact that it was extremely unlikely that anybody else would do so.

'No, my lord. She is a great support to me still, but I suppose it won't be long before some fine gentleman comes asking for her hand. She has just had a very kind invitation from Lady Mardham to stay with her friend Miss Mardham, at Meysey.'

'Has she, indeed. I know Mardham. The thing is, my boy Levedale needs to set up his nursery. Since my poor Laurence died, he is the last of our name and . . . Illustrious name of course, though we are not as plump in the pocket as once we were.' Lord Curborough sighed, but was watching Sir Thomas very closely. 'My elder boy was a little wild, though good at heart. Levedale was always the steadier of the two. Make a good, thoughtful husband.'

Sir Thomas was not sure how to respond. To agree would be to imply a knowledge of the young man he did not possess, and to disagree would be even worse.

'Quite so, my lord,' he managed, noncommittally.

'You would like having your daughter not too far placed from you, no doubt, mistress of a nice estate, and a countess.'

This was all going a little fast for Sir Thomas, but he nodded nonetheless.

'I shall see if Mardham will extend his invitation to Levedale, and you never know, perhaps it will be my boy asking for a private interview with you in the near future, what.'

Sir Thomas nodded again. He did not know whether to be delighted or worried.

* * *

Lord Curborough's ancestral seat was some twenty miles distant from Meysey, and he knew Lord Mardham through mutual acquaintances rather than being a close friend. In pursuance of his plan – and Lord Curborough considered it a very excellent one – he arranged to see several of these mutual acquaintances over the course of the week, playing upon the fact that he was a 'lonesome widower rattling about his home', and on the third foray found himself in luck, for the Mardhams were also dining. Some judicious eavesdropping led him to understand that the underlying reason for the house party was to show off Miss Mardham, though why they were bothering to do so eluded him, since surely she was some form of cripple.

It was a simple matter to engage in private conversation with the viscount, as they joined the ladies after the port.

'How is your son? Robert, isn't it?'

'Richard. He does very well. He is up in Town still, as the young bucks like to be, you know, but coming down to Meysey next week, which will please his mama.'

'Ah yes, my own poor wife doted upon our boys.' Curborough sighed, heavily. 'I am glad she did not live to see Laurence depart this life so young. But there. Arthur – Levedale as he now is – well, he's a sound fellow, but there is little to interest him at home, and he is kicking his heels rather.'

As a hint, it was not subtle, but Lord Curborough was not a subtle man.

'He is in Gloucestershire?'

'Why yes,' lied Curborough, unblushingly.

'Er, perhaps he might care to join the younger set with us then, from the eighth.'

'You know, that sounds the very thing.' Curborough managed to look as if this was a delightful surprise to him. 'He is at low ebb, you know, not having found any filly up to his weight, so to speak, this Season.' That, thought Curborough, ought to be the clincher. No need to say that he would not be taking a second glance at a 'filly' that trotted out lame.

'He would be very welcome to spend a few weeks with us. Not that we have anything more than some fishing, a little shooting, and some jolly company. I shall get my lady to send an invitation.'

Lord Curborough's delight was not feigned, and he returned home to write, that very evening, commanding his son and heir to return forthwith to the family seat as a matter of urgency.

'I am not sure we do not need another lady, after all, you know.' Lady Mardham looked down her final list of guests. There were several names with lines scrawled through them, and scribbled superscriptions. 'The Corfemullens cancel each other out, if you see what I mean, and Richard does not count of course, but he is bringing Lord Pocklington and Lord Deben, and Sir

Marcus Cotgrave has accepted, and Mr Wombwell, and his mama is coming as my own friend, and now it seems we are to have Lord Levedale also, but the good news is that Curborough has hinted he is on the lookout for a wife, so . . . That is five gentlemen and only two young ladies. Oh dear! I cannot think of three more. No, wait! We could invite the Darwens' daughter. She is back after an unsuccessful first Season.'

'That might be because she has a very uncertain and spiteful temper, Mama. You have described her as "that awful girl" on several occasions.' Celia did not sound delighted.

'True, but that was before her come-out. Besides, if it is true, do you not see that as to your advantage?'

'No, since for the majority of the time I will be the one having to entertain her.'

'Nevertheless, she evens up the numbers a little, so I will send out an invitation. Oh, now what about my cousin Cora's girl? If she is anything like her mother in her youth she will not turn heads. Very average, was Cora. Came as a total surprise when she married Colonel Clandon. I am sure Cora would be delighted for her to have the opportunity of mixing with the right sort of people. Now what is her name? Sarah, or Susanna, or is it Sophia?'

Celia said nothing. After all, her mama was talking to herself more than to her. For her own part she was not looking forward to a house full of gentlemen before whom Mama would expect her to use wiles, which she did not even think she possessed, to catch one as a husband. It was embarrassing, for her and for them. She would far prefer to live quietly where everyone, except Mama, had got used to her limp. The guests would either stare at her, or do as Mama did, and look away, pretending not to notice. At least everyone except Lord Deben. He had come down with Richard while she still felt very unused to her bad leg, and was rather overwhelmed by it, and he had treated her in much the same way as Richard himself. She could happily treat him as she did her brother, but the thought of him as a suitor was perfectly ridiculous.

Viscount Levedale drove up the curving drive towards the house in which he had been born. He had happy early memories of it, before his brother Laurence, and then he himself, were sent off to school. He smiled, recalling how enormous even the small formal gardens had seemed to them, as they played chase, hid from Nurse, or pretended to be hunting dragons. It was as if that was another world, for in later years everything had changed. Laurence and he had grown apart after his elder sibling was sent down from Oxford and given himself up to a life of gambling, loose women and frequent inebriation. Mama had grown hollow-cheeked and ill, ravaged as much by worry as disease, and since her death, three years past, her younger son had only been home the once, and that was six months ago, when his brother had been interred in the same family vault. Now he came because he was summoned, and an air of melancholy and slight dilapidation clung to Silvertons.

His groom jumped down to take the chestnuts' heads, and his lordship climbed down, thanked him, and went to ring the bell that he heard echo through the house. A stooped and elderly butler opened the door after some minutes, and looked up at him with rheumy eyes.

'Good afternoon, Pawston.'

'My lord! You were not expected until tomorrow.'

'I am early, yes. Will that discommode everyone?' He gave the butler a smile, and Pawston, as always, fell under its charm.

'Not at all, my lord. His lordship is not at present at home, however. He is gone over to Squire Huxtable this afternoon, but is due home to dine. May I say as how it is a great pleasure to see you home again, my lord.' Pawston positively beamed at him, as befitted a butler who had been in service in the house since before his lordship had made his entry into the world.

'Thank you, Pawston. It is good to be home.' This was not entirely true. There were sad ghosts in Silvertons, and Levedale was at a loss to understand what his sire had considered so important that he had commanded – and it was no less – that he come up from Devon immediately. He had always been a poor second in his father's eye, largely because Laurence was so like his father in looks and temperament. 'Young

Arthur' had been more in his mother's mould – quiet, thoughtful, and completely uninterested in those things in which Laurence had found entertainment. Not for him a life of tawdry women, high stakes gambling and heavy drinking.

Lord Curborough seemed to have regarded his heir's lifestyle as one of which to be proud, and his younger son correctly assumed that it was the same he himself had followed in his youth. That in itself ought to have been a warning to Laurence, for Lord Curborough was florid of face and large of girth, and the Romney which hung in the long gallery showed him a rakish, dark and handsome young man of lithe build. Laurence had once looked so similar that his mother described him as a walking portrait of his father.

That his debauchery would ruin not just his figure but his health and empty what little remained in the family coffers had been obvious to everyone except father and son. Arthur, living within his allowance, was castigated by his father as 'boring', and when he had inherited a neat little Devon property from his maternal grandparent and chosen to go and live there, Lord Curborough had gone so far as to question his paternity. 'Why any son of mine should want to play farmers in the middle of nowhere I cannot imagine. Almost I might have imagined your mother had played me false.' This had been an unfounded slur upon his countess. Lady Curborough had been accounted something of a beauty in her youth, with glossy chestnut locks, and near perfect features, if with rather too tall and slender a figure. From her, Arthur had inherited colouring and inches, for he was an inch or two over six foot, whilst his brother and father were of a very average height. The bond between mother and son had been close. When in adulthood he understood the reasons for his mama's gentle melancholy, his relationship with his father had deteriorated to the point where he came to Silvertons only to see her, and usually when his father was away. Her death had grieved him deeply, whilst it was the death of Laurence from a disordered liver that had nearly broken Lord Curborough. His grief was exacerbated by the discovery that his heir had been far more deeply in debt than even he had thought possible, and the discharge of those debts, on top of the earl's continued extravagances, had resulted in much of the estate being mortgaged or put out to long-term lease.

Stepping into his brother's shoes had not given the new Lord Levedale any pleasure, nor improved his relationship with his father. The urgency of the missive demanding that he return to the family seat meant that he had obeyed it, but without any enthusiasm. Now, as he looked about him and mentally reviewed all that the house needed in renovations, he became quite despondent. He settled himself in the library with a volume of Juvenal which had clearly not been taken from the shelf in decades, and a glass of what he had to admit was a devilish fine burgundy which cleared the dust of travel from his throat, and waited.

It was some two hours later when Lord Curborough arrived home. Levedale heard his blustering voice in the vestibule, and his terse comment that he would see his son when he had changed for dinner. The Juvenal was replaced, and the viscount made his own way upstairs to the chamber he had occupied since late adolescence. There were signs of moth in the curtains, which had faded from a rich green to a muted drab, and the paint on the window embrasure was yellowed with the sun, and cracked. It was not a room much used, but he had seen that even the public rooms were little better. He compared it to his own modest residence, a neat house of local stone with a simple stuccoed facade and of seven bedchambers, which was amply served by a butler, cook, two serving men and two maids. His only extravagance had been to increase the size of the succession house in the kitchen garden to provide his household with earlier produce and exotic fruits.

His man, Welney, had laid out his evening clothes in readiness, and called immediately for hot water, since his lordship liked to shave before dining, being a gentleman whose chin could lose its smoothness in the course of the day.

'I regret that this chamber being so far distant from the kitchens, my lord, I cannot vouch for the water being as hot as you would wish it.'

'Oh, I am used to that, Welney, do not worry.' His lordship rubbed his jawline and grimaced.

'Will we be remaining long, my lord?'

'I cannot say, until my father has disclosed the reason for his summons. I think I will stop off in Bath on our return journey for a few days. You have been muttering over the state of my shirts and I could invest in some new ones.'

Welney made a noise which was both a denial that he did anything so impolite as mutter and yet was also approving of this plan.

Until such time as the servants withdrew, Lord Curborough confined his discourse with his son to platitudes, which that gentleman found frustrating. However, the food, whilst far too much for one of Lord Levedale's abstemious appetite, was very good, and he sent his plaudits to the cook. Eventually, Lord Curborough nodded dismissal to Pawston, the staff withdrew, and father and son were left alone.

'So, sir, what is the reason for your hasty summons?' The viscount's tone had an edge of challenge to it.

'You are my heir. I am not as young as I was, and we need to discuss your nursery.'

'My what?' The viscount choked over his port. 'Good God, Father, even if you had notice to quit, which I doubt, having seen you enjoy a more than sufficient dinner, there is no urgency for that. I am not yet seven and twenty.'

'You never know how long you have. Look at your poor brother.'

'There are no guarantees, I will concede, but Laurence's lifestyle is not mine. I say again, there is no rush for me to get myself leg-shackled.'

'There is every need. I will not disguise from you that the state of our finances is . . . weak. A good marriage will bolster our position, keep the creditors from the door.'

'From your door, sir. And I thought that Laurence's debts had been paid off.'

'Since then luck has not been on my side.'

'You mean that after all that we went through, you have not curtailed your own . . . entertainments?' Lord Levedale looked horrified.

'Don't come over all puritanical, Levedale. A man must have distractions, especially after the misery of bereavement.'

'Not if they make a dire situation even worse.'

'It is academic why we have reached this position. Suffice to say if you make a good match the bank will hold back on any foreclosures.'

'That far gone? And stop saying "we". This is your mess.'

'And you are all the family remaining to me, so it is "ours". I had thought of remarriage myself, but the thought of some chit maundering about the place trying to change everything is too much.'

'So you expect me to go heiress-hunting like some cheap fortune-hunter.'

'No need to hunt. I have found the ideal girl for

you, and she is the heiress to a cool fifty thousand. You should applaud my foresight. I met with Sir Thomas Burton and discovered his daughter is to be one of a house party at Mardham's place, from next Wednesday. Got you an invitation. She is considered a good-looking girl, so I am not making things difficult for you.'

'Thank you, sir, for that. Not that you would have held back if she were cross-eyed and bald.' Lord Levedale was not appeased by this information.

'Don't be ridiculous. I would not expect you to marry a freak. And for that matter nor would I have suggested a cripple, even if she had a good sum coming with her.'

'A cripple?' Lord Levedale frowned. This seemed very specific.

'Yes, Mardham's girl. All I ask is you turn up at Meysey, do the decent by the Burton chit, and she will accept you. You don't possess Laurence's good looks and charm, but you are not ill-favoured and you are the heir to an earldom. Her father is mighty keen to see her go up in the world.'

'If she is so pretty, why wasn't she snapped up during her London Season?' Levedale was now suspicious.

'She wasn't presented.' Lord Curborough did not look his son in the eye.

'You mean her papa is some cit.'

'Sir Thomas Burton is a Member of Parliament.'

'Doesn't stop him being a cit.'

'And your grandfather married the heiress to a "tin baron" so I do not know that you should turn your nose up at money. Besides, the girl has been raised properly. She won't disgrace you and smell of the shop, you know.'

Lord Levedale's brain was reeling. He had no inclination to marry for several years yet, and here was his father, not only demanding he marry, but lining up the prospective bride.

'I won't do it. It is the outside of enough. Economise, sir, and the bank will . . .'

'The bank won't, I tell you. You may not care if I am dragged off to a debtor's prison, and everything is sold off, but would you have our name dragged through the mud, the Earls of Curborough become landless objects of ridicule?'

'Pity you did not think of this earlier, sir,' remarked Levedale, running his hand through hair. 'Why you didn't show some sense after Laurence died I will never know, and do not spout that "diversion" flummery at me again. If you had but made an effort, kept things steady, it would have saved a lot of trouble.' He sighed. Whilst he might harangue his father for his stupidity, he could not improve matters except by doing as he requested. Like it or not, and he liked it not at all, he was in a difficult position. 'Alright. I will agree to go to Meysey, and I will see if this Miss Burton and I could make a match of it, but I make no promises, mind you, none at all. I'll be damned if I marry a woman I have not the slightest *tendre* for, simply to save your skin.'

'You'll be saving your own, and that of your own heir, and without a good match you are damned too, my boy.' Lord Curborough gave a grim half-smile.

The sad truth was, he was right.

CHAPTER THREE

Lady Mardham had known Maria Wombwell from the time of their first Season, and if her friend had not married a title, then she had certainly married a gentleman with lineage and money. The two ladies were frequent correspondents, though they met less often. Mrs Wombwell had withdrawn from Society upon the untimely death of her husband a dozen years previously. She had been a devoted wife, and had thereafter channelled all her energies into being an even more devoted and doting mother. Her son, at an age where doting parents of either gender were a source of embarrassment, had taken full advantage of her ever open purse whilst simultaneously doing as many things as possible to prove he was not the paragon she fondly imagined. He went about with a rackety set, of which the then Lord Levedale was a member, but his fondness was not for cards, or blue ruin, but rather the fair sex. He ran a succession of expensive mistresses in the way many gentlemen ran a string of racehorses, and interspersed this with leading eligible young ladies into falling head over heels in love with him, only to disappoint them at the last. He had developed a reputation as 'dissolute and dangerous', but, as his mama wrote to her 'dear friend Pamela', all he needed to steady him was 'a good sort of girl who would not expect too high a degree of permanent devotion'. Lady Mardham thought Celia sensible enough to see him for what he was, and grasp any opportunity that presented itself.

It was shortly after luncheon on the eighth that Mr Wombwell, with what his parent described as a sick headache, and Lady Mardham privately considered to be 'in a bad mood', arrived at Meysey. Mrs Wombwell arrived in a very stylish travelling carriage and he was driving his high perch phaeton. He was scowling, his thick, dark brows beetling, and his lips compressed in a pout, and his mother glanced at him with patent concern even as Lady Mardham advanced, smiling, to greet them. Fortunately for Mrs Wombwell's nerves, her son could not resist getting even matchmaking mamas eating out of his hand, and the scowl was replaced with a charming smile as he bent over his hostess's hand.

'Lady Mardham. How kind of you to invite me. I am sure I will have a perfectly splendid time.' Voice and look won her over, and she actually blushed. She seemed quite unconscious that he had cut his parent out of the greeting entirely.

'I hope we may entertain you, Mr Wombwell, tolerably well. There is quite a young set here, so you need not fear to be kicking your heels among the older generation. My son is coming down with Lord Deben and Lord Pocklington, and my dear Celia has her cousin Miss Clandon, and her friends Miss Burton and Miss Darwen coming to stay.'

'Then both entertaining and charming company is assured, ma'am.' His eyes danced, and as they worked the magic he expected, Lady Mardham was blissfully unaware that it was not from delight but the knowledge that she was ignorant of his deception. He was some four or five years older than the other young gentlemen and of a very different set. He considered himself far more polished, and a proper man of the world whilst they 'paddled' at the edge of excitement. They would bore him. He also had little doubt his mama had persuaded him to join her so that she could parade another line of mediocre and simpering maids before him. Any young woman worth noting he had already seen during the Season. None of the four young ladies named conjured up any image in his mind.

He would not have come, had it not been prudent to remove himself from London and his creditors until after Quarter Day, and remaining with his parent obviated the need for any day to day expenditure. Furthermore, if any tradesman sought to dun him, they would find the trail very cold if he and his mama were not at home. She would, of course, pay up, but the sighs and Tragedy Jill looks were always so very wearing. He had come into his inheritance upon reaching full age, but although it had been ample it had been frittered away, so that whilst he had initially complained at how large a jointure his father had reserved for his mama, he now had reason to be very grateful for it.

Celia, who had been showing her cousin to her allotted chamber and generally trying to encourage the very shy Sarah Clandon to look less as if she wished the ground would swallow her up, appeared at the head of the stairs with that damsel. Mr Wombwell looked up, and was dazzled for a full half-minute, right up to the point where Celia laid her hand carefully upon the bannister and began to descend, one stair at a time. His amazement turned to fascinated horror, and Celia reddened. Miss Clandon, waiting to come down a little behind her cousin, frowned. It seemed very rude to stare in that manner.

Fortunately for Celia, it was at that moment that hearty voices were heard outside, and distraction arrived in the form of her brother and his two friends. They had spent two days on the road, breaking their journey at Speenhamland, and had engaged in a light-hearted 'race' between Lord Deben and Mr Mardham, who was driving himself and Lord Pocklington. Lord Deben had won by the slimmest of margins, and the other two gentlemen were trying to declare it at worst a draw, since their vehicle had been carrying the greater weight. It was three very jolly young men who entered the hall, with Mr Mardham leading the way, and greeting his mama with more affection than politeness, giving her not only a peck upon the cheek but thereafter an exuberant hug, and complimenting her upon her looks.

'We had a fine run down, Mama, and here are Deben and Pocklington come to eat you out of house and home.' He waved an arm in the direction of his friends, who came forward more respectfully, and bowed over her ladyship's hand with words of thanks and assurances that their appetites, whilst healthy, would not lead to this calamity.

As they did so, Celia came down the stairs unobserved, as she thought, but Lord Deben, in advance of Lord Pocklington, looked to her and smiled.

'Miss Mardham, your servant, ma'am.' He bowed. She made the sketchiest of curtsies, for it was something else she could no longer do with grace, and then extended her hand. He came to take it in a firm clasp. He had an open, pleasant countenance, and spaniel brown eyes that were twinkling.

'I trust we find you in tolerably good health. The weather has been quite stultifying up in Town and if it has been so here, then you might feel a little jaded.'

'Ah, but my lord, in the country it is a little cooler. We have more breeze.' She dimpled, and added, 'Had you not been "loitering" in the Metropolis, you would have discovered this.'

Lady Mardham frowned, but his lordship laughed, comprehending the bantering tone.

'Got me there, ma'am. I cannot deny it, but I can blame Mardham. If he had not remained, then I would have bolted for the verdant pastures.'

'Hey, don't lay the fault on me!' Mr Mardham grinned at friend and sister and then held out both hands to Celia. 'You look very well, my dear. Shall I apologise straight away for bringing Deben to tell you faradiddles?'

'Not at all, Richard. I believe every word he tells me.' Her eyes danced. 'Unlike yours.'

'Dash it, I didn't expect to return to the bosom of my family and be abused.' He feigned horror.

'No?' Her eyebrows rose further, and he laughed.

Lord Pocklington, still engaged in pleasantries with his hostess, looked across to the source of laughter. Having been told by his friend Mardham of his sister's situation, he was surprised by how she could be so at ease. The poor girl must be virtually housebound, and he could think of nothing worse.

Mr Wombwell, who found himself, most unusually, not the centre of attention, interrupted the sibling exchanges, and Celia retreated instantly within her shell of cool politeness. He made his bow with grace, said all the right things, but she was distant, even vaguely disapproving. This took him by surprise. He was used to young women doing everything to encourage him, whatever their mamas might have warned. To find one patently uninterested dented his pride. How dare she treat him in such a manner. He scarcely listened as Lady Mardham invited her guests to divest themselves of their travelling raiment and meet in the drawing room for tea.

Whilst Lord Pocklington, a tall, rather loose-limbed young man, lacked Mr Wombwell's grace, his introduction thawed Miss Mardham's iciness. Miss Clandon, who had made a very good attempt at being invisible, was introduced, and the arrivals were conducted upstairs. Lady Mardham escorted Mrs Wombwell herself, wanting the opportunity to speak with her friend in private.

Celia looked at 'Cousin Sarah'. Miss Clandon looked rather overawed.

'Shall we await everyone in the drawing room, Sarah?'

'Yes. Cousin Celia, I do not think Mr Wombwell liked the way you . . . I mean he seemed a bit put out that . . .' She stumbled over how she might phrase her thought.

'I confess I have not met anyone quite like him before, but if he expects everyone to admire him, then he is in for a sad shock. Did you like him?'

'Oh no. But then it does not really matter what I think.' Miss Clandon did not sound perturbed by this, but Celia frowned. 'Mama told me that she "did not think anything would come of it", my visit she meant, and that I was to learn, and observe, and be grateful.'

'Goodness, that makes you sound like "the poor relation".'

'But that is exactly what I am, Cousin.' Sarah gave a twisted smile.

Celia, who had thought her very shy relative was simply one of those girls who were naturally excessively self-effacing, felt a wave of shame rise to her cheek. Sarah might be quiet but she was not lacking in understanding.

'I am sorry. Since I do not consider you in that light, the thought had not occurred to me.'

'You can be sure Mr Wombwell will. I could tell from his manner at our introduction. It was dismissive. But I disliked him before that, for the way he stared at you coming down the stairs.'

'He did. I can only suppose Mrs Wombwell had not warned him in advance.'

'He should not need "warning". You are not some freak of nature to frighten him. I far preferred your brother and his friends. They seem much nicer, true gentlemen.'

Celia could not but giggle at her brother as a 'true gentleman', but acknowledged that the three friends compared very favourably with the polished Mr Wombwell.

'And we still have the "delights" of Lord Levedale, and, oh dear me, Sir Marcus Cotgrave, who, I must warn you, sees in me an image of his late-lamented wife.'

'Oh.' There was not much else Miss Clandon could say to this, so she simply added, 'And Miss Darwen and Miss Burton are yet to arrive.'

'Yes, the fair Marianne.'

* * *

The gentlemen appeared in the drawing room a little before her ladyship, and Celia assumed the temporary role of hostess, ringing for tea even as her brother suggested something 'less brown'.

'Oh, I am sorry, should you wish for wine?' Celia felt a little foolish. She was not au fait with the requirements of gentlemen.

'Not at all, ma'am. Tea would be just the thing.' Lord Deben quelled the look of disbelief on his friend's face. 'Long journey and all that. Very . . . invigorating, is tea.'

Richard Mardham, having never offered his friends any non-alcoholic beverage other than coffee, nearly choked. Lord Pocklington, taking his lead from Lord Deben, avowed himself equally delighted to take tea with the ladies, and when Celia then asked her brother if he would take wine or tea, he gave in with a show of nonchalance.

'Oh tea will do very well. I forgot we are not in Town.'

'It must be so difficult, when one looks out of the window too. Vastly similar views, no doubt.' Celia bit her lip.

'You ought not to roast me. I am your older brother and deserve some respect, miss.' He strove to sound serious, and failed.

'My Grandmama will not drink any tea but that which she blends herself, as though it were snuff,' mused Lord Pocklington. 'Not that she sniffs up tea leaves, you understand. Whenever she travels, and it is rarely these days, she takes her tea with her, like her dressing case, and her own china.'

'My Aunt Augusta always takes her own sheets. In fact my mother claims she takes an entire linen cupboard with her.' Lord Deben, following his friend's lead, thought this would be a suitable topic to discuss in front of young ladies 'taking tea'. He did not possess sisters, and was not one for the muslin company. In fact he generally found the fair sex a little daunting. Miss Mardham was perhaps the only damsel who did not cast him in a fluster, and that had been because when he had met her at New Year she was scarcely more than an invalid still, and he had fallen in with her brother's easy manner with her, trying to make the abnormal situation seem normal.

The exchanges upon the vicissitudes of elderly female relations continued until Lady Mardham and Mrs Wombwell joined them, thereby embarrassing Lord Pocklington, who was at that moment giving a mildly exaggerated impression of a deaf and addled old relative who kept pointing at guests and asking why they had come, even if she had invited them. His lordship straightened up, colouring.

'I . . . er . . .' Words were not his strongest point, and now they eluded him completely.

Mrs Wombwell, with a wave of maternal understanding, stepped nobly into the breach.

'I had hoped Stephen would be downstairs also by now. Perhaps it was too hot whilst he was driving. I did ask him to come in my carriage, but he says that being driven, rather than concentrating upon the road himself, makes him feel unwell.'

Lady Mardham sought a sympathetic phrase, and her lips parted. What she had been about to say was lost, however, as the door was opened to admit Miss Marianne Burton. Her ladyship was transfixed, and simply stared. Her son let out a long admiring breath; Lord Deben whispered something unintelligible; Lord Pocklington's jaw dropped, and he blinked several times.

'Oh, my poor girl,' whispered Lady Mardham, under her breath, and glided forward as Celia, marginally less astounded at the apparition before them, took her first step towards her erstwhile schoolfriend.

Miss Burton, apparently either unconscious of the effect she had upon everyone, or used to being stared at, came forward, her hands held out, and her beautifully shaped lower lip trembling.

'Oh, Celia, my dear friend, how terrible! And you used to be the best of dancers and so very pretty.'

Her tactless comment made Celia wince, but it was made with total sincerity and genuine sympathy. Lady Mardham was prey to the uncharitable wish that Miss Burton might be nothing more than a nightmare of her own imagining. Not only was she ravishingly beautiful, but clearly liable to add to poor Celia's discomfiture by advertising her disability at every turn.

'Good afternoon, Miss Burton. I do hope you have not been wearied by your journey. I am sure that you will be glad of the opportunity to rest before changing for dinner.'

Marianne Burton made her hostess a very pretty curtsey, and blithely denied any feeling of tiredness, but agreed that she would be pleased to change her dress.

'I will show you to your room,' offered Celia.

'Can you manage the stairs?' Marianne was all concern.

'Why yes, of course. I am not as swift, but quite capable you know.' Celia concealed her dislike of the sympathy.

Before they had reached the door, the overdue Mr Wombwell entered. Being rather more used to comely feminine company, he did not succumb to the incoherent admiration of the other gentlemen. Only by the briefest widening of his eyes might it have been seen that Miss Burton made a favourable impression upon him. He bowed and awaited introduction very calmly, and did not watch her as she left the room. Lady Mardham heaved a sigh of relief. Perhaps he already knew of Miss Burton's origins and would treat her with indifference.

Lady Mardham did not know Mr Wombwell in the slightest.

Sir Marcus Cotgrave lived not more than eight miles from Meysey, across the Wiltshire border, and was expected to arrive a little before the time when everyone would change for dinner. Lord Corfemullen and his wife, who was one of Lord Mardham's cousins, arrived several hours earlier, with her ladyship very voluble as to the appalling state of the road from Oxford. Miss Darwen was equally loquacious, complaining about the cast shoe that delayed her arrival as though the horse had lost it on purpose.

Lord Levedale was announced just after both ladies had retired to rid their persons of the ravages of travel, and made his bow to his host and hostess and Corfemullen, whom he did not know. His manners were good, and not by the least twitch of a muscle might one have guessed that he was regretting giving in to his parent's demand. He had no knowledge of who else might be making up the party, and wondered whether the presence of younger guests, other than 'the Heiress', had been his sire's invention. Lady Mardham soon made all clear, however.

'You will be delighted to hear that my son, Richard, and his friends Lord Pocklington and the Viscount Deben, are also staying with us, and Mr Wombwell, and an old friend of the family, Sir Marcus Cotgrave.'

Levedale had never met Sir Marcus Cotgrave, was a couple of years older than Mr Mardham and his cronies, and knew them little more than by sight, and regarded Mr Wombwell as another example of a man gone to the bad in the manner of his brother. It did not bode well for an entertaining stay. He said something appropriate, however, and enquired as to the dinner hour, after which he withdrew to make his preparations.

Lady Mardham thought him pleasant enough in form and manner, perhaps a little tall, and for one who was reputedly hanging out for a wife, lacking a little keenness. She had expected someone more effusive, though she had no idea why that should be.

Miss Clandon, at least, fulfilled many of her hostess's expectations. She was a very quiet girl, inclined to speak in barely more than a whisper, and blushed with surprise whenever addressed. In fairness, Lady Mardham admitted she was prettier than her mama had been at the same age, but this was damning with faint praise.

'You cannot know just how delighted I was to see her, my lord,' she declared, when that gentleman entered her dressing room as her maid completed the arrangement of her hair for dinner. 'Quite a shy dab of a thing, she is, and I would have to be honest and say her ears stick out a little. If I had been Cora I would have had her wear a tight band about her head at night in the hope of them growing more normally. I have placed her next to Mr Wombwell and Lord Pocklington at dinner this evening. Celia is next to Sir Marcus and Lord Levedale. I have no idea why Richard brought Deben with him. He is a nice enough young man but patently not interested in setting up his nursery as yet. I thought it safest to place him next to the awful Burton girl, with Richard on her other side.'

'Awful? I would not say that, my dear. Pretty thing, I thought her.'

'Pretty? My lord, she is stunning. Had poor Celia not been . . . They would have been much on a par, but as it stands . . . I wish I had never let Celia persuade me into letting her come.'

Lord Mardham, unaware of the truth, merely nodded in conjugal agreement.

'Does not help.'

"Does not . . . ?' It mars all. What man would take a second glance at poor Celia with that girl in the room? And what is worse, the tactless innocent keeps saying things which highlight our daughter's plight. I admit I would have happily strangled her this afternoon when she asked whether Celia was able to climb the stairs. What did she think? That we have her sleep in the morning room upon a truckle bed?'

'She was just being solicitous, I am sure, my dear.'

'But it was in front of the young men, all except Levedale. Oh dear, this is going to be a disaster.' Lady Mardham's voice trembled.

'I think that it will only be a disaster if everyone is bored and miserable. You know, hoping that somehow Celia might receive an offer is aiming for the moon, my dear. We both know it, but the attempt is worthy.'

With which thought, Lady Mardham had to be content.

Their 'poor Celia' was at that moment thinking the opposite. It was not worth the attempt at all. Had her cousin and her schoolfriend come to visit without any gentlemen, she might have anticipated some pleasure. Marianne was far too inclined to pity, and Celia hated pity, but she was kind-hearted and might learn not to treat her as incapable of anything. Sarah was so overawed that it was difficult to know what to make of her as yet, and Celia would no more have invited Lavinia Darwen than the Tsar of Russia. The problem lay in the presence of men whom her parents were hoping she might attract. Well, she would not, or rather could not, with the exception of Sir Marcus, who sighed whenever he looked at her. Whether this was from pity or because he saw again his lost wife, it was hard to say, but both made Celia cringe.

CHAPTER FOUR

Celia came downstairs early for dinner. Not for her could there be the grand entrance to show herself off. It was far better, advised mama, that her 'problem' not be advertised more than necessary. Celia agreed, though from rather different motives. At least the guests, with the exception of Lord Levedale, were now all aware of her situation. She wore a gown of simple cut, with little embellishment, but of a deep straw colour which showed off her colouring to advantage. Lady Mardham had entered her room as she was dressing, and frowned, suggesting something rather more decorated, but Celia had shaken her head.

'Knots of ribbon and a vandyke hem will not distract them, Mama, you can be sure. Let us be honest. I have a severe limp, and there is an end to it. Now, ought I to wear the pearl set, or the peridots Grandmama gave me last birthday?'

'Would you at least wear the patten, Celia, so that when you are standing . . .'

Celia pulled a face. She hated the wooden patten that made her look level but, even with a suede leather sole, made a peculiar clumping noise as she walked, and not only failed to conceal the distorted manner of her walking but made her shortened leg ache as much as did the good one, which bore additional weight and strain.

'Mama, I—'

'I understand you cannot bear to wear it all day, my poor child, but at least you can appear more normal in the evenings.'

'More normal' she had said, and Lady Mardham had no insight into how lowering, demeaning, were her words. When even her parent looked upon her as abnormal, what hope could Celia have of being treated as a woman, not a cripple or a freak?

Marianne Burton came down with Sarah Clandon, and the beauty of the one highlighted the very forgettable appearance of the other. Miss Burton had access to the finest dressmakers in Bath, ladies who were almost falling over themselves to dress her, since she showed their creations to such advantage as had other ladies imagining that they might look as good in similar gowns. She had taste, and was well aware that money was not best shown off by gewgaws. Her muslin was pearly white, and delicately embroidered all over the bodice, subtly drawing the eye to her curvaceous bosom, and the little puff sleeves showed off the pale slenderness of her arms for the brief inches before her long gloves. She wore pearls, as fitting for so young a lady, but they were of impressive dimensions and graded perfectly for size. When they entered the room, Lady Mardham only really 'saw' Marianne Burton. Everything about her was, admitted Lady Mardham to herself, and with great reluctance, perfect.

Sarah Clandon's gown was similar in colour, and there the similarities ended. It had an edging of lace to the sleeves and neck that had been taken from an old gown of her mama's, and she had applied it herself with neat little stitches. About her neck was clasped a pendant with a prettily cut aquamarine that successfully deepened the rather pale blue of her eyes, but she had neither bracelet nor hair ornament, and she wore no earrings. She would not be remembered for being ugly, but then it was doubtful that she would be remembered at all.

Lord Levedale walked in almost upon the heels of Richard Mardham, and for a moment he wondered if his father had inadvertently done him the greatest favour of his life. The young lady was beautiful, breathtakingly so, and he did indeed catch his breath even as he advanced further. Then he saw Miss Burton. To a dispassionate observer there was no doubt who was the most to be admired, but even as she turned towards him, a shy smile upon her cupid's bow of a mouth, he dismissed her as 'typical diamond of the first water'. His gaze was upon the young woman in the straw coloured silk, who looked at him questioningly. No man had ever looked at her like that before. Celia smiled, but wryly. *Wait until he sees you move*, she thought to herself, and then watch his expression change. Part of her wanted to stand still longer, to enjoy the feeling his gaze gave her, but she was an honest girl. She stepped forward, her stick made visible from among the folds of her gown, even as her mama tried to distract him by speaking to him, making introductions. He only half attended. For a moment his eyes registered surprise, and then, yes, the pity. Celia could have wept, but instead the twisted smile merely remained fixed.

'Miss Mardham.' He made his bow as his hostess introduced her. She sketched a curtsey, but with the hated and little used patten there was a wobble to it, and a moment's unsteadiness. His arm went out and she laid her hand instinctively upon it.

'I am sorry, my lord.' She lowered her gaze, blushing in shame, and withdrew her hand.

'There is no need, Miss Mardham.'

'It was clumsy of me.'

His father had said that the daughter of the house was 'a cripple'. Somehow he could not associate the term with the vision before him. The problem was that he had no idea what to say that would not sound patronising, or even offensive. He therefore said nothing, but shook his head.

Lady Mardham was making the other ladies known to him, whilst giving Celia a look which was half remonstrance and half disappointment. Celia ignored it.

Lords Pocklington and Deben entered, clearly in good humour, and the atmosphere lightened. They were evidently awestruck by Marianne Burton's face and figure, but both were well-brought up young men and attempted manfully to disguise the fact, with, however, limited success. They were certainly not distracted by Miss Darwen, who was a strong-willed young woman who disregarded the sage advice of her maid, and liked to deck out her person with as many items of jewellery as possible. Mr Mardham whispered to Lord Deben that the 'clanking' of her bangles and bracelets reminded him of convicts sent to the hulks.

It lacked but five minutes to the dinner hour when Mr Wombwell made his entrance, and it was 'an entrance'. Country hours it might be, but he was as resplendent as at a Mayfair dinner, his dark locks brushed to a glossiness that owed little to oils and much to the hard work of his valet, his linens spotless and snowy, his coat moulded to his elegant form. If Miss Burton was the 'belle', then he was most certainly the 'beau'. He knew it, and had an air which indicated he expected to be treated as such. It made Celia's hackles rise, and the look she gave him was far from admiring. He resented it. Miss Burton, however, was once more suitably impressed, and he rewarded her with a winning smile

'I can only say I am very glad you are not a horse, Miss Mardham.' He spoke lightly, for it struck him that expressing sympathy would alienate her.

'No indeed, my lord, since you would be hard pressed to explain leading a horse in to dinner.' She felt a little light-headed, and responded instinctively.

Lady Mardham, hearing the laugh behind her, assumed it was some joke between her son and his friends.

If Lady Mardham had thought her arrangement of the diners about the table had been safe, she was disabused of the idea in short order. For some peculiar reason it had not occurred to her that her son might be as bowled over by Miss Burton as the other young men, and the sight of him patently trying to impress her quite put his mama off her white soup. On the opposite side of the table Mr Wombwell, clearly affronted at being placed next to 'the nobody', was as good as ignoring Cousin Sarah, and devoting himself to flattering Lady Corfemullen, to that lady's pleasure and her lord's irritation, whilst sending occasional glances across to Miss Burton signalling that he would infinitely prefer to be flattering her.

Lord Pocklington, not a ladies' man, was attempting to entertain Sarah Clandon with tales of hunting, to which she listened with little understanding, having never ridden to hounds, and Miss Darwen, who declared herself, with crushing finality, allergic to horses. Lord Deben, across the table from them, divided his time between trying to edge into the conversation with Miss Burton, and offering to pass dishes to Miss Clandon, since he could think of no other means of showing she was not forgotten. Sarah wondered if he thought her emaciated.

Meanwhile, Sir Marcus Cotgrave was not to be put off, just because he had not secured the position as Celia's escort into dinner. He divided his time politely between Mrs Wombwell and Celia, and most certainly did not monopolise her, but what he did say made her long to hit him with the dish of fried sweetbreads that was placed nearest to her. Lord Levedale even overheard him ask her if she could manage to pass him the entrecôte of veal, as if it might be too much of an ordeal.

'Miss Mardham, without wishing to appear rude, I feel I ought to tell you that I do not think that passing the buttered carrots would be beyond your powers,' murmured the viscount, in a tone of exasperation.

'Thank you, my lord. Vegetables are so much less tiring, are they not?' Her reply was little more than a whisper.

'I am amazed that you can retain a sense of humour, ma'am.'

She glanced at him then, seeing the sternness in his face.

'I . . . can pretend to do so, sir, and one becomes habituated.' She gave him her twisted smile once more. 'Now, if you, my lord, are sufficiently strong enough to place the sauce bearnaise within my reach . . .'

Their eyes met, held, and then mutual embarrassment made them look away. The degree of attraction was so unexpected, so confusing, that they pulled back from it in incomprehension. Their conversation thereafter was stilted and their body language stiff, which Lady Mardham noted. She sighed. That Woman looked ever more likely to see her Jane inherit thirty thousand pounds.

When the ladies withdrew, Sir Marcus managed to knock Celia's stick from where it hung on the back of her chair as he rose, drawing further attention to her predicament, and his eyes followed her as she left the room. His expression was one of mournful sympathy. Lord Levedale studiously avoided watching her depart, even though the sound of her halting steps was clear.

The gentlemen settled to their port, and the talk turned to the sport they were likely to enjoy. Lord Pocklington became quite animated, and a bantering discussion followed on the merits of particular fishing flies. Lord Levedale, who enjoyed fishing, nevertheless remained on the periphery of the conversation, and appeared to be studying the contents of his glass with such intensity that Lord Mardham asked whether it was not to his taste, or was he rather attempting to deduce its exact origins.

In the drawing room, the party had divided by age. The senior ladies were enjoying an exchange of gossip about their peers, whilst the young ladies were talking about the latest fashion in bonnets.

Celia played her part in this, but felt it a very superficial thing, and also realised that for Sarah, the idea of buying a hat upon whim would be unthinkable. In fact she had little doubt that her cousin would rejuvenate hats with a change of veil or ribbon. Marianne, by contrast, guilelessly described a variety of very expensive-sounding hats she had tried on in Bath when she had last visited. It was not that she played off her wealth, but rather that she took it as normal. Lavinia Darwen trumped them all by discussing hats she had seen in the windows of the finest milliners in London, though Celia noted that she only spoke of one which she had purchased.

The conversation drifted from head to toe, from hats to silk stockings, and both their price and liability to wear into holes so very easily.

It was while Marianne was speaking that the gentlemen joined them, and Levedale heard her slightly high-pitched voice as he came into the room.

'Oh yes, and do you recall how you wore out your dancing slippers, Celia, when . . .' There was a short silence and then Miss Burton continued, hesitantly. 'I am so very sorry, Celia. You really were the best dancer in the class and . . . now . . . it is so unfair . . .'

'No, now I cannot dance.' Celia stated it flatly. In her head she added 'nor ride, nor walk among the bluebells in the woods in spring, nor even walk from room to room without conscious effort.' She felt guilty at the jealousy she experienced watching others do what was taken for granted. Only when one could not walk without a struggle did the simple act of placing one foot in front of the other become something about which one even gave a thought, and the things denied to her were things she did miss.

Lord Levedale caught the tension that flickered across her face for but a moment. Marianne Burton was trying to make things better, and thus made them worse.

'Of course dancing is not everything. We do not dance every day, do we? I mean, I most certainly do not. There are so many other things to do. Papa has encouraged me to visit the needy in the hamlet by our house, and says one ought to have serious occupations for the day beyond pleasure. I have even been taking instruction upon housekeeping, for when I must take those duties in the future.'

Celia could not 'visit the needy' without very obvious assistance, and the chances of her running a household seemed remote.

Lady Mardham winced.

It was Lady Corfemullen who came, rather unexpectedly, to the rescue.

'A good housekeeper is worth her weight in gold. I sometimes think they are more vital to the good running of the house than the butler, for who else sees to it that one has enough candles, and the sheets are aired and in good order and . . .' She continued with a varied list of important domestic duties, which only ended when her lord made an harrumphing sound in his throat, which she rightly took as a signal that she was 'rattling on'.

Mr Wombwell took a seat beside Miss Burton before the other young men had a chance, and feigned an interest in her tale of taking a pig's cheek and a good round cheese to a widow with six children. Lord Pocklington and Mr Mardham were in deep discussion over a shotgun, and Lord Deben, seeing Sarah Clandon sitting very quietly as if expecting to be alone, took it upon himself to do the decent thing. That she nearly jumped out of her skin when he asked if he might be seated in the chair next to her, seemed to prove the fact.

Lord Levedale hung back, and let Sir Marcus Cotgrave engage Miss Mardham. The pull of attraction was so unexpected and strong he doubted himself. One heard, of course, of the *coup de foudre* but it always sounded a bit far-fetched to him. Yet here he was, having never clapped eyes on the girl before this afternoon, having to fight the desire to look at her all the time. It was madness.

'My dear wife loved to paint in watercolours, Miss Mardham, and even when ailing, used to sit upon the terrace and paint the flowers. She knew all the names, you know, such a retentive memory.'

'Alas, Sir Marcus, I am one who is always forgetting where I have put things,' murmured Celia, trying her best to be the antithesis of the late and much lamented Lady Cotgrave, 'and my watercolours were always described by the teacher as "insipid". I think I made everything too . . . watery.'

He was boring her, and she resented it because it

66

made her feel guilty. Had he been merely avuncular she might have been a little sympathetic to him, for he was patently a lonely man who missed his wife, but he was not. This made her feel both uncomfortable and angry. On top of which she wanted to think, and do so alone.

'. . . and a little regular practise will increase proficiency, I am sure.'

She blinked at him.

'With the brush and paints, my dear Miss Mardham.'

'Oh, yes, perhaps so, sir.'

'Forgive me. You seem a little preoccupied. Does your,' he paused, wondering if 'leg' were to indelicate a term to use, 'limb give you discomfort at the end of the day?'

'I cannot claim it as an excuse, Sir Marcus. One becomes used to a degree of discomfort so that it is perfectly normal, and today has not been an especially difficult day. I fear I am simply a little tired. It is you who must forgive me.' In truth, her uninjured leg and hip ached with the additional stresses put through them, and the weight of the patten seemed to drag upon her bad leg.

He made much of forgiveness not being necessary, and she itched to be able to withdraw. After the tea tray had been brought in, she looked several times at the clock. Sarah, noticing, claimed to be weary, and begged permission to retire, although she had found Lord Deben's gentle anecdotes most entertaining, and could have happily lingered. Celia gave her a grateful look, for it meant she did not have to be the first and look weak. Marianne would have followed, but for Mr Wombwell leaning slightly closer to her and saying something which made her cheeks take on a slightly pinker hue.

As she made her way, slowly, towards the stairs, Celia thanked her cousin.

'It was kind of you, Sarah. I had no desire to be seen as "the weak cripple".'

'It is nothing. I understand. One is marked by generalisations, like being "the poor relation". One becomes used to it, but need not like it.'

Celia laid her hand upon her cousin's arm, not for support but in support.

'Our circumstances are both very different, and yet similar, Cousin. It is good that we shall be friends, and we shall, yes?'

'I would like that very much.' Sarah smiled, and the two young women went upstairs arm in arm.

When Celia lay in her bed, willing the ache in her good leg to ease that she might sleep, she tried to make sense of the day, or rather the evening. Lord Levedale was not a Sir Marcus Cotgrave, an older man seeking a younger wife to fill a space in his life. He was – and she felt her colour rise – remarkably good-looking in an unostentatious way. He did not parade himself as the saturnine Mr Wombwell did, patently expecting admiration, feeding upon it. He was tall without being gangly, his features were serious but he clearly had a sense of humour, and the look of pity she had dreaded had appeared, but only very briefly, as if he were caught unawares by it. From the other things he had said she was persuaded he was keen to let her know he did not regard her simply as 'a poor crippled girl', and that first glance had been admiring. She told herself that she was a fool to hope for the impossible, but she went to sleep with the hint of a smile upon her lips.

CHAPTER FIVE

Lord Levedale awoke to a dewy September morning, and the prospect of a good breakfast and a day's fishing. He was glad of it, although more from the fact that it would keep him from the ladies than a desire to net a splendid fish. He had been sent, most reluctantly, to 'land' a wealthy wife, and in view of the previous evening this was now even more distasteful to him. Miss Burton could not be faulted on her looks, though he found her charms too obvious. She did not appear, on first impressions, to be the sort of girl who had tantrums, unlike the repellent and overbejewelled Miss Darwen, and she did not tease men with her beauty. On the other hand, she did not possess that certain something that had drawn him instantly to Miss Mardham, though he had no idea as to what that something might be. It was disquieting of itself, let alone in conjunction with the knowledge that his duty was to engage the affections of The Heiress. It was very tempting, he thought, to remain for as short a time as possible, send a missive to his house in Devon, and have them send an urgent letter recalling him home. It was cowardice, of course, but very tempting.

He went down early to breakfast, confident that the ladies would not put in an appearance until rather later, and found Lord Deben, the naturally early riser, partaking of gammon and eggs.

'Morning, Levedale. I tell you what, the gammon here is something else. No idea how they cure it, or whatever they do, but it is far better than in Town.'

'Good morning, Deben. The receipt is probably some secret passed on from generation to generation, and perhaps also in the breed of the pig. Old Spots are the local breed.'

'They are? Well, you learn something every day of your life. Are you, um, interested in pigs?' Deben looked a little concerned, wondering if Levedale's interest was like his own sire's obsession with things botanical.

'I find them more interesting than cattle or sheep. Quite clever, are pigs, and on the Home Farm my man swears blind that a happy pig makes good pork.'

'But how,' enquired Deben, reasonably, 'does one tell if a pig is happy or not? They cannot mope or dance jigs or . . .'

'Certainly they do not dance jigs.' Lord Levedale laughed. 'But you know, you can tell if a dog is miserable, and pigs are, I am told, more intelligent than dogs.'

'Wouldn't fancy having a pig at my feet of an evening, though, and my younger brother Jack was bitten by a sow once. Fearsome teeth it had, and he could not sit down for a week. Now, try this,' Deben pushed the platter of gammon towards Lord Levedale. 'This one must have been very, very happy, in fact positively euphoric, if what you say is true.'

Lord Levedale sat down to enjoy his breakfast.

Marianne Burton was an inveterate letter writer, although she wrote as she thought, with little punctuation, and was liable to muddle her topics together in such a way that the recipient had to read the letter several times to comprehend it. She was very unsure about commas, and worked upon the principle 'if in doubt – leave it out'. With Lord Mardham offering to frank her letters, she did not feel the need to cross the pages, for which her fond Papa was most grateful. He had sent her with instructions to tell him all about her stay, which in effect meant hearing about any suitors in the offing. Sir Thomas was confident that anyone invited to Meysey would be suitable for his little girl.

She wrote her first letter before going down to breakfast, so that he might be assured of her safe arrival, and that she had received a kindly reception.

Beloved Papa,

The new upholstery in the carriage meant that I arrived here not at all bumped up and down or wearied. Meysey is a nice house but some of the furniture is rather old and has many passages and I got lost on the way up to my room to change for dinner which included a positively delicious compôte of plums. I think it is all the wooden panelling which looks just the same except for the pictures. I now know that my room is to the left after the portrait of the lady with the sweet little dog in the huge hat.

Marianne paused, read the sentence again, and applied arrows so that Papa might not think the dog was wearing the hat.

Lady Mardham is very gracious and Lord Mardham is like Uncle Joshua except that he does not sneeze snuff over one and is rather taller and more polished of manner and has darker hair and a slow smile but does not laugh. I was terribly upset to see poor Celia. Although I knew about her tragic accident it was only upon seeing her in person that I realised how much it has RUINED her life. She hobbles to a most marked degree even with her old lady's stick and can only walk very slowly and with a strange rocking and rolling motion which make me feel quite seasick. At least I think it is how I would feel had I ever been at sea which thankfully I have not. I am quite glad that travel to The Continent is impossible because of The War. She is in other ways a most beautiful girl but her life is positively blighted, and she is dependent upon others. In order to stand about before dinner last night she wore a thick patten under one shoe and made a very odd noise as she walked.

Feeling that this might make her soft-hearted Papa dismal, Marianne added:

But she puts a very brave face upon her situation and has a healthy appetite.

The other ladies of the party are Lady Corfemullen who is of an age with Lady Mardham and has come with her lord Celia's cousin who is very quiet and looks impoverished judging by her gowns and a young lady called Miss Darwen who has been in London all Season and knows everything except how to dress. Oh Papa, if you had seen her come down to dinner positively jangling with bracelets you would have laughed. I am so glad you employed such an experienced maid as Tackley to guide me over the finer points of dressing for Miss Darwen illustrates how one may otherwise make

*the most horrible mistakes. I am sure she is very
nice really but she is not as open and approachable
as Celia and we have not spoken much together.*

This was not quite honest, and cost Marianne a pang.
In fact it was quite obvious that Miss Darwen held
herself to be superior to the other young ladies, and did
not so much engage in conversation as deliver lectures.
However, Marianne was a person of positive outlook,
and hoped that over time Miss Darwen might thaw.

*Mr Richard Mardham has come and brought
his friends Lord Pocklington and Lord Deben
with him. Lord Pocklington is very tall and likes
shooting horses and fishing.*

Marianne contemplated a comma, but the more she
wondered the less sure she became, and so omitted it.

*Lord Deben is not short but not as tall and is very
kind. He talked to The Poor Relation for ages after
dinner so that she might not feel ignored. I imagine
he has many elderly aunts. He too liked the plum
compôte.*

*The other gentlemen are Sir Marcus Cotgrave
who is a widower and sad Lord Levedale who
arrived last of all in a very pretty waistcoat and Mr
Wombwell who is a very splendid London beau.
He is terribly well dressed and immaculate of*

person and perhaps a little haughty but he sat by me after dinner last night and was very amusing. Lord Levedale does not seem impressed by him but I found him quite droll.

The gentlemen are going out fishing today for the weather is fine.

Marianne pondered what else to say.

I will bear what you told me very much in mind Papa and learn from being in company with ladies of distinction but they are in truth very little different to the Misses Hopton or Jane Mytchett other than in the range of their accomplishments. Miss Darwen plays the harp but she did not bring it with her to Meysey and says that she likes to perform songs in Italian and French.

I shall write to you often dearest Papa with all the news from my sojourn here. Lord Mardham is franking this for me.

Your loving daughter,

Marianne

Pleased with her efforts, Marianne folded the letter, made out its direction, and slipped it into her reticule so that she might pass it to Lord Mardham when she saw him.

Sarah Clandon knocked on Celia's door, and called her cousin's name. Celia responded by inviting her within, and Sarah found her at her dressing chest with her maid threading a riband through her hair.

'Good morning, Cousin. I wondered if we might go down to breakfast together?' Sarah smiled, a little diffidently. She did not want to be seen as pushing.

'Why yes, as long as you do not say "and please lean upon my arm".' Celia gave a wry smile at the mirror, being unable to turn her head without her maid remonstrating with her. Sarah saw it as a reflection, and grinned.

'Well, I shall not, but neither will I skip down the stairs as I have no doubt Miss Darwen would do, just to prove her agility.'

'She is insufferable, is she not? What odds she spends the morning telling us how her days were spent "at the Hub of Society".' Celia was a good mimic, and pitched her voice just slightly off key.

Sarah laughed.

'I could not tell,' continued Celia, 'whether she was unable to see that she set up people's backs, or whether she knew and enjoyed doing so. To be fair to Mama, she knows Lady Darwen, who is a pleasant enough lady, but the Awful Lavinia has not been encountered since she came out. I am sure Mama had hoped for an improvement and regrets her invitation.'

'Probably, but . . .'

'But what, Sarah?' Sarah coloured. Celia thanked Horley, her maid, and dismissed her. 'Tell me.'

'Do not think I am not very grateful for the invitation here, Cousin Celia, but I am very obviously here to make up the numbers for dinner and such, whilst not in any way drawing attention. I would guess Lady Mardham selected Miss Darwen for the same reason, since she clearly did not "take" during the Season. In that way she is the ideal guest. Unfortunately, in all others she is simply ghastly.'

'Oh dear. I fear you may be right, Sarah.' Celia was again made aware that Sarah Clandon was no fool. 'That is just how Mama would have planned it. She was certainly disappointed when she saw how very beautiful Marianne is become.' Celia sighed. 'This whole party was designed to show me off, as though any man in possession of his wits would look twice at me. It is embarrassing.'

'I do not see why they should not.' Sarah was pragmatic. 'You are very pretty.'

'And very lame. What man would want to marry a girl who cannot dance, cannot even be a châtelaine capable of walking round his house with the housekeeper?'

'A man who sets greater store by who you are than how you look.'

'Oh Sarah. I should have you with me always to stop me wallowing in self-pity. Now, let us go down and be admired forthwith.' Celia stuck her chin in the air with a look as ridiculously haughty as Miss Darwen's, but ruined the effect by giggling.

* * *

They arrived in the hall just as the fishing party left the breakfast parlour. Richard Mardham came and gave his sister a brotherly hug, and told her he would catch her a lively brown trout for her luncheon.

'I am all anticipation, Brother-dear. How shall I pass the morning other than by day-dreaming about fish?'

'If you are rude, miss, I shall give my catch to Cousin Sarah.'

Sarah murmured that she very much enjoyed fresh fish.

'Of course, if we are successful, Miss Clandon, you may be faced with eating fish at every meal for the next three days,' remarked Lord Levedale, drily.

'Trout fillet, trout pâté, trout, er, soup?' Celia suggested.

'Exactly, Miss Mardham.'

'Well, I draw the line at trout sorbet.' Celia pulled a face.

'I should jolly well think so,' declared Lord Deben. 'Only a really "odd fish" would like that, eh. Mind you, I had an uncle whose favourite dish was lampreys. Revolting! Er, the fish, not the uncle, you understand. My mother said the cook nearly resigned when asked to prepare them.'

'I think some king died from eating lampreys.' Lord Pocklington frowned, dredging up this fact from the recesses of his memory.

'Not surprised. Did not kill my uncle though. Influenza did for him.'

Lord Levedale's lips twitched, as much from the expression on the faces of the two young ladies as from Deben's diversion on his relative. Miss Mardham's lips were compressed, and her eyes danced. Miss Clandon looked amused but indulgent.

Mr Mardham, slightly shocked at Lord Pocklington exhibiting a knowledge of history, recommended that the gentlemen be upon their way, and the two ladies wished them 'good hunting', although Celia murmured that 'hunting fish' sounded most irregular, and rather primaeval. The ladies entered the breakfast parlour, and Celia's appetite dwindled instantly, for it was occupied by Miss Darwen and Sir Marcus Cotgrave. Miss Darwen smiled at the new arrivals.

'Ah, there you are at last. I was saying to Sir Marcus that so few ladies have the ability to rise from their beds with any degree of celerity, although of course, you do have a reasonable excuse, Miss Mardham.'

The smile lengthened. In one succinct sentence she had accused Miss Clandon of sloth, and highlighted Miss Mardham's disability. It did not, however, have quite the result she was expecting from Sir Marcus Cotgrave.

'It is very courageous of you to come downstairs so early in the day, Miss Mardham. Do you perhaps take a rest in the afternoons?' He gave her a look which combined solicitousness and unwelcome admiration.

'Courageous? I hardly think the term applicable, Sir Marcus. I am not suffering from some debilitating disease which curtails my strength. I shall not faint from exhaustion because I rose before nine of the clock, and I most certainly shall not need to recline for the afternoon to restore myself for the evening.'

He looked relieved, and yet, she thought, vaguely disappointed. It struck her that he wished to see her as unbelievably fragile so that he might control her every moment in a cloying despotism. Perhaps his late wife had come to depend upon him so greatly that recreating that situation made him feel at ease. It did not appeal to Celia in any way at all.

'Being "brave" is not a ladylike attribute,' asserted Miss Darwen. 'A degree of stoicism is to be admired in the face of adversity, but an active bravery, as opposed to the passive form, smacks of hoydenism. It is the prerequisite of the male to show courage and protect "the weaker vessel".'

'My choice of words might have been unfortunate, ma'am,' conceded Sir Marcus, though without conviction, and Celia despised him the more for not standing up for himself. Miss Darwen accepted his surrender with a gracious inclination of the head.

'Are you not fishing with the other gentlemen, sir?' enquired Miss Clandon, seeking to divert the topic.

'I enjoy fishing, Miss Clandon, but in peace and solitude. The "young bucks",' and he smiled in an avuncular fashion, 'would not find me good company, nor I be happy amongst them. I am thus at the disposal of you ladies, to direct upon any quest that might assist you.'

'What a pity dragons are completely extinct in Gloucestershire, Sir Marcus.' Celia could not resist picking upon his offer, 'for a "quest" for a missing volume of a novel, or a skein of silk that has slipped within the depths of a sofa, sounds so terribly mundane.'

'Dragons are a complete fabrication, you know.' Miss Darwen commented, as though Celia thought that dragons might still linger in far flung shires such as Yorkshire. 'One hears of large bones being found in rocks, but I give no credence to it, for it makes no sense. How could a bone get inside a rock?'

There being no obvious answer to this conundrum, the other three persons gave no reply, and Miss Darwen was contented.

It was at this juncture that Miss Burton entered, her smile sunny, her attitude one ready to be pleased, at total variance to Miss Darwen.

'I do hope I am not too late to breakfast,' she said, eyeing the table. 'I am such a sleepy-head as a rule, but this morning I rose betimes and have been writing to my papa.'

'The cupboard is not, Miss Burton, bare.' Sir Marcus indicated the sideboard with a ponderous flourish.

'Oh good. Have we a plan for the morning? It is such a lovely day we are surely not to be cooped up indoors?'

'The weather is decidedly clement. We might take a turn about the gardens and then essay a little sketching, if there are materials enough for everyone.' Miss Darwen saw herself as the senior young lady, and thus in charge, regardless of the fact that it was neither her house, nor her gardens, and she was the guest.

'But Celia . . .' Marianne Burton glanced at her former schoolfriend, 'you will not be able to come with us.'

'Has Miss Mardham a conveyance, a Bath chair or some such?' Sir Marcus looked about him as if one might be concealed in the breakfast parlour. 'I am perfectly happy to offer my services to push, rather than utilise a servant.'

Celia did possess a Bath chair, which had its uses, but was remarkably uncomfortable to sit in for any length of time, and was very bumpy when moving. It was used sparingly.

'If you cannot come out with us it will spoil our morning,' sighed Marianne, as Celia wondered if she might deny any method of getting about the gardens.

'There is a Bath chair, but I would prefer simply to take my time walking to the end of the terrace, and set up my sketching materials ready for when you return. You must remember that the gardens are familiar to me, and not to you. Should you find any particularly fine specimens of flowers or leaves which we might draw, then bring them back to me.'

'That sounds an excellent scheme.' Sir Marcus was contemplating not having to entertain the other young ladies and devoting himself to Miss Mardham. 'I shall give you my arm and carry your pencils, and remain with you, Miss Mardham, to fetch anything you might have forgotten.'

Celia's heart sank, but Marianne beamed at her with such unaffected delight that she felt guilty for wishing she might take back her suggestion.

By the time the trio of young ladies joined Celia beneath the spreading boughs of a beech at the end of the terrace, half an hour later, Celia could have cheerfully requested that the attending footman should strangle her unwanted companion.

Instead of letting her walk with her stick at her own pace, he had taken it from her, with a tolerant smile, telling her that his arm was far more secure. He had then not so much walked as crept along the path at a pace which left Celia convinced they had been overtaken by a snail, and which she actually found more awkward, since his crooked arm was not at the level she could lean upon with any ease. When they reached the shade of the trees, where the footman had been instructed to place a seat and some chairs, he almost pushed her onto the seat, where he could sit comfortably next to her, or rather uncomfortably, as she saw it. He then went back himself to bring sketching books and pencils, and set them upon the small table.

'You see, Miss Mardham, I know just what you require, since my dear Clarissa had just such equipment for her artistry. Myself, I was never adroit with pencil or brush, but they are accomplishments which young ladies study, are they not, and so I was forgiven. My own accomplishment was, and is, an ability to recite verse.'

To Celia's utmost horror, he then proceeded to recite stanza upon stanza of Alexander Pope in a dull voice which was not a monotone, but managed to give stresses in the most unexpected places which ruined any rhythm in the verse. He was still droning on as the other girls drew near.

'Ah, Pope!' declared Miss Darwen, '*Eloisa to Abelard*, is it not? I prefer his *Ode on the Spring*. 'Lo! Where the rosy-bosomed Hours, Fair Venus' train appear, Disclose the long-expected flowers, And wake the purple year!"

'But that is Thomas Gray,' murmured Miss Burton.

'Oh no, you are wrong. It is Alexander Pope.' Miss Darwen shook her head at Marianne Burton, secure in the knowledge that what she thought was always so, and that Miss Burton was an empty-headed doll.

'I am sure it is Gray.' Miss Burton did not back down, although her voice had a trace of doubt which made Miss Darwen smile.

'You may be sure that I am—'

'You know, it is Gray, ma'am.' Sir Marcus, frowning in concentration as he attempted to recall the poem, did not see that Miss Darwen would brook no opposition.

'Are you telling me that I am wrong, Sir Marcus?' Miss Darwen looked at him as if his temerity was boundless.

'I think I would rather say "mistaken", ma'am.' Sir Marcus gave her one of his rather patronising and paternal smiles. Whilst Celia had curbed any response upon receipt of one, Miss Darwen pursed her lips and gave him a stare that had wilted stronger men. He wavered. He was sure that he was correct, but this frightening young woman unmanned him. His smile faded. 'However, I make no claim to being always correct.'

Miss Darwen took this as surrender. Celia, meanwhile, had spoken quietly to the footman, who absented himself, and returned a few minutes later with a slim leather-bound volume, and presented it to her with a bow.

'Thank you, Joseph.' Celia opened the book. 'I think this ought to be easy to resolve. Yes, here we are. *Ode on the Spring*. This, by the by, is a book of the poems of Thomas Gray.' She spoke sweetly, and placed the book upon the table in front of Miss Darwen. Sir Marcus gave her a look of profound gratitude, which she did not want, but Miss Darwen gazed at it as if it were a poisoned chalice, and then glared at Celia.

'It is the height of rudeness to place a guest in the wrong.'

'But I have placed a guest in the right, have I not, Sir Marcus?'

Sir Marcus made an indeterminate noise which he hoped would appease both ladies, and showed him as lily-livered to each.

'I have brought yarrow and bear's breeches to draw,' announced Miss Clandon, in an attempt to change the subject.

'Those are the common names,' responded Miss Darwen. 'You mean achillea and aconitum.'

'Acanthus,' mouthed Celia, whilst Miss Darwen was staring at Miss Clandon, and grinned. Sarah Clandon kept a straight face, but it was a struggle.

The ladies began to draw, and Sir Marcus, not daring to spout more poetry lest Miss Darwen begin another onslaught, felt superfluous. He sat, making the occasional comment comparing his late wife's style with Miss Mardham's, but was clearly out of place. Had there been but Celia, her cousin, and her friend, the morning would have been spent in light-hearted chatter, and been most enjoyable. As it was, it was dominated by Miss Darwen instructing them upon how they might improve their work, though she kept her own at an angle where it was not easily seen by her companions. It was with no small degree of relief that Celia finally announced that it must surely be time for luncheon, and they ought to go and see if there was fresh fish upon the table.

CHAPTER SIX

In fact the fishermen did not arrive back at the house until mid-afternoon, though bearing a good display of trout, which was to be sent down to the kitchens. Lord Pocklington had caught the heaviest, and Mr Mardham had caught the greatest number. Lord Levedale claimed to have 'let a few escape' so that the ladies would be spared the trout sorbet, which made Miss Burton giggle.

'But we may ask the other gentlemen whether these escapes took place before or after the number of fish caught reached a reasonable number, my lord.' Celia smiled at him, and he felt his stomach give a little flip. He smiled back, instinctively.

'What's that?' demanded Richard Mardham, who had been attending more to Lord Deben's description to Miss Clandon of a particularly long 'fight' on his line.

'Did Lord Levedale permit any of the fish that took his hook to escape before you all had a fine catch, Richard?'

'I don't know about that so much, Celia, but there was a brute of a fish quite early on, on the first beat we tried. It must have been at least six pounds, but he got away just before he was landed.'

'He would have been tough,' declared Lord Levedale, with a nonchalant gesture, but his eyes were dancing, 'and there must have been a hole in the net.'

'A net without holes, sir, is not a net,' riposted Celia, with a prim smile.

He grimaced, acknowledging the hit. Just for a moment he forgot anyone else was in the room.

'Pedant,' he murmured, appreciatively.

Celia's smile came very close to a grin, and then, suddenly, she looked startled, and blushed. Her heart was beating far faster than it ought. She looked away.

'Would someone kindly remove these dead creatures before I have to leave the room?' Miss Darwen pulled a face.

'Almost a reason to keep them here,' muttered Celia, under her breath, and Lord Levedale, who caught her words, frowned. He wondered what Miss Darwen had done to upset her.

'At least Levedale caught only trout,' disclosed Lord Pocklington, ignoring Miss Darwen. 'Deben here pulled something devilish ugly out of the river.'

Lord Deben covered his face with his hands in mock horror.

'The shame of it. I had hoped you would keep that secret, Pocklington.' He lowered his hands, revealing a rueful countenance. 'I dare not even describe the thing in front of ladies.'

'It was a fish though, my lord?' Sarah Clandon had been largely silent, but was curious.

'It had a head, tail, gills and fins, and it swam, so I suppose it counted as a fish, Miss Clandon, but not one I would care to eat, or indeed meet again.'

'Was it huge?' Miss Burton shuddered.

'Oh no, no more than about six inches long, but its head was too big for its body and—'

'You said you would not describe it in front of ladies, sir,' Miss Clandon reminded him, with a soft smile.

'Oh Lord, so I did, My apologies. Shows just how much it cuts one up, catching a thing like that.'

'Deben is talking about a bullhead, Celia. Remember when you came with me once, years back, and I got one on my line? You screamed for ages.'

'I recall the incident distinctly. I was, I hasten to say, but ten years old, and my wicked older brother here, tried to drop it down my neck.' Celia did not wish to appear too pusillanimous.

'You did not, did you, Mardham? Dashed unpleasant thing to do.' Deben shook a finger at his friend, but was grinning.

'My little sister.' Richard Mardham shrugged, as if that were reason enough.

'My brother Bovington once put a spider in my bed.

He was berated most vehemently for it.' Miss Darwen disliked being on the periphery of conversation, and her mouth opened to continue.

'I never possessed a sister,' Lord Levedale interjected. 'Tell me, Mardham, are there open and closed seasons on baiting them?'

'Oh, there was never a closed season, Levedale, and they rise to almost any bait you care to use.' Brother looked at sister, and grinned, mischievously.

'Unfair,' declared Celia, 'and do not think I was in every case the victim. One night Richard put a sheet over his head and came to my bedchamber making frightful ghostly noises. It gave me a terrible fright, and I threw the water glass from on top of my nightstand at him.'

'It gave me a black eye, and then smashed and we had the house in uproar. What was more, my father took his hand to me in the morning.'

'For frightening your sister. Quite right too.' Lord Deben nodded, approvingly.

'Er, no, for waking him up and giving Mama hysterics. It was only a jape, and I paid a heavy penalty for it.' It clearly rankled, even years later.

'I, on the other hand, was given a glass of warm milk, and a bag of sugar plums next day,' dimpled Celia. 'The rewards of virtue.'

'The rewards of courage, Miss Mardham.' Lord Deben swept her a bow. 'Not many young ladies would dare throw things at a ghost.'

'Well, it was in some ways a very impractical thing to have done, for had it been a ghost, the glass would have gone straight through it,' admitted Celia. 'I confess I was most alarmed when I awoke to see this white phantom at the end of my bed, and throwing something was purely a natural reaction, as was the scream.'

'Will somebody kindly remove the fish.' Miss Darwen's slightly off-key voice was raised in strident demand. Celia Mardham was far too much the centre of attention.

'Do you still obey your "natural reactions", Miss Mardham?' murmured Lord Levedale, and looked her straight in the eye. Her comprehension was instant.

'I have learnt to curb them, alas,' she whispered back.

'What a pity. It would have been worth seeing, especially using a fish.'

Celia suffered an inexplicable coughing fit.

Lord Levedale was seated opposite Miss Burton at dinner, divided from her by what he considered a singularly revolting piece of silverware depicting three very smug looking putti in unsustainable poses, each holding a cornucopia into which flowers from the Mardham gardens had been tastefully arranged. He was conscious of the thought that he hoped Miss Mardham had not been responsible. The young lady herself was at the further end of the table between Lord Corfemullen and Lord Pocklington, and Lord Levedale told himself that this was a good thing. Having decided to keep away from her, he had gravitated towards her far too easily after the fishing. On his own right-hand side sat Miss Clandon, and to his left, worryingly, Miss Darwen.

Miss Clandon did not put herself forward, and Lord Levedale, whilst normally commending quiet modesty in a young lady, tonight wished that she was the opposite. There might then have been a chance for him not to have been monopolised by Miss Darwen. As it was, when he did try and engage Miss Clandon in conversation, Miss Darwen interjected before any response was made, and dragged the subject back to herself, which was her favourite topic.

'Have you had any recent communication from your brother in the Peninsula, Miss Clandon?'

'Alas, my lord, he was always an infrequent correspondent, even when at school, and time has not improved matters.'

'I have never left a letter without a response for longer than three days, even when, as a child, I had the severest of toothaches and was in perfect agonies with it,' declared Miss Darwen. 'The importance of a prompt reply was impressed upon me by my governess, and how right she was.' She paused very briefly as she was offered more wine, and Lord Levedale took his chance and turned back to Sarah Clandon.

'The exigencies of campaigning, and the difficulties of sending any missive back down the lines of communication must stand as his excuse, ma'am.'

'Oh yes. I—'

'There is never any valid excuse for poor manners in the matter of letters,' pronounced Miss Darwen, authoritatively. 'I myself have castigated my brother, Bovington, for dilatoriness whilst up at Oxford, for he had our Mama in a perfect worry when he did not answer her epistle when he contracted the mumps.'

'It is a common childhood illness, I believe.' Lord Deben, seated on Miss Darwen's other side, had been talking with Mrs Wombwell. The strident tone of Miss Darwen had, however, distracted him. Catching the phrase 'perfect worry', he offered a consoling thought.

'"Common", Lord Deben?' Miss Darwen turned her pale green glare upon him. It was singularly unnerving. As many men before him had done, he crumbled.

'Er, as in frequently suffered,' he gabbled, 'or rather, many people get it. Had it myself at Eton, and the infirmary was positively packed with boys.'

'My brother was not a schoolboy.' Miss Darwen said the word 'schoolboy' as if it were a lower form of life. 'He was educated at home, by tutors, and was considered an exceptional student at the University.'

Mr Richard Mardham, who had been a year above Lord Bovington at Merton, choked over a mouthful of buttered crab. He remembered the young gentleman as having indeed been exceptional, but rather for the inventiveness of his escapades rather than his intellectual ability.

Much as Lord Levedale wished to ignore Miss

Darwen, he thought it only fair to come to Deben's aid.

'Such contagious complaints flourish wherever people live in close proximity, ma'am, and school is where a majority of boys are likely to encounter it.'

'My father,' added Miss Clandon, bravely re-entering the conversation, 'said that recruits in his regiment seemed more prone to ailments than those soldiers of some years service.' It earned her an encouraging smile from Lord Levedale.

'Soldiers,' sniffed Miss Darwen, evidently setting them even lower than schoolboys. She then, to the consternation of her unwilling auditors, brought the subject back to her views on the epistolary art. 'Most soldiery are illiterate, of course. The ability to correspond with clarity and on diverse subjects is one of the things which marks a gentleman, or a lady. My governess, a most superior woman, was used to write me three letters each week as an exercise, letters covering many topics to which I was expected to construct suitable replies, and if I fell short of her high standards I had to repeat the attempts until she was satisfied. I well recall one which discussed the poetry of Mr Wordsworth, the efficacy of lavender in cases of headache, and how to express condolences to a bereaved person whose distant relative has deceased. The degree of sympathy is quite awkward. I was reminded by my preceptress that whilst in most cases the loss occasions practical inconveniences, the wearing of black gloves, or abstention from dancing, there are some relationships that are closer than the mere family tree might indicate. A beloved great aunt who has been as a grandparent might be much mourned. My own Great Aunt Theresa . . .'

Miss Darwen was apparently inexhaustible, and a great believer in the benefit that the wisdom of her nearly twenty years of life would be to others. Lord Levedale glanced at Miss Clandon, and saw her bite her lip, her eyes twinkling. He had put her down as the sort of girl who was quiet because she had nothing to say, but revised that opinion. She was, perhaps, simply an observer more than a participant, through habit or inclination.

Lord Levedale was about to find out there were worse things than having to listen to Miss Darwen. He was about to be hunted by her.

Lavinia Darwen had arrived at Meysey feeling suitably superior, being the only young lady to have experienced a London Season. That it had not ended as her parents would have hoped was evident from the absence of the announcement of her impending nuptials in the *Morning Post*, but she chose to overlook this. The invitation to Meysey had been seen by her mama as an opportunity to seize victory from the jaws of defeat, and she was on the strictest of instructions to bite her tongue and try her hardest to attract some interest from among the gentlemen of the party. Privately, Miss Darwen thought this unlikely, since she had seen the gentlemen in London, and had found them all 'wanting'. It was not that she did not come up to scratch with them, she had decided, but that none had been worthy of her hand. Lord Deben she dismissed as a dolt, Mr Mardham was a 'thoughtless boy', Lord Pocklington was sports mad to the exclusion of all else, and 'That Man Wombwell' was rude and unpleasant. By this Miss Darwen meant that he had actually avoided dancing with her.

Lord Levedale had not been in Town and was new to her. She assessed him, in the manner of a wolf selecting a lamb. He was a little too tall for her liking, and if she had a preference it was for fair men with a greater wave or curl to their hair, but his figure was good, his manners appeared to be guaranteed to please, and he was available. Miss Mardham was beneath her consideration as a rival. Lord Levedale's apparent desire to please her must spring from an excess of pity and gallantry, since no man in his right mind would choose a cripple over a woman strong of mind and limb. It was unfortunate of course that the Burton chit was such a pretty little empty-head, but Miss Darwen knew that her own strengths lay in the sharpness of her mind, and the decisiveness of her actions. The less well-disposed towards her, of which there were many, would have said rather that she was marked by the sharpness of her tongue, and a total lack of consideration for anyone else, but of course she did not listen to such people.

Having decided upon her course, Miss Darwen made her plan with a near military precision which would have won plaudits in Horseguards.

In pursuance of her prey, Miss Darwen had to isolate Lord Levedale from those upon whom he might otherwise focus his attention, and divert it to herself. The most obvious way in which she might achieve this was by hovering in his vicinity, so that she could intervene, or more accurately, intrude, at will. She was a young woman for whom the term 'self-doubt' had no meaning. That her methods had scared away potential suitors in London, and ensured that she had come away without making friends among her peers, did not occur to her.

When the gentlemen joined the ladies after dinner, Lord Levedale went to sit beside Miss Burton, and began to entertain her in a gentle fashion. He felt as if he were talking to a child, for she was a wide-eyed innocent, and very naïve. She must be about the same age as Miss Mardham, for he had overheard that they were friends at school together, and yet he could not jest as he would with Miss Mardham. Marianne Burton would have looked blankly at him. She was easy to please, unaffected despite her amazingly good looks, and did not interest him. He told himself he must try, must apply himself. After all, many men married young women for whom they had no wild passion.

He wondered at himself. He had never actually suffered 'a wild passion' for any female, so why had that thought hit him now?

'. . . and Papa says that he would not care for me to waltz, unless I was a married lady and my partner was my husband.'

'I have waltzed at Almack's.' Miss Darwen, seeing her opportunity, sat upon the chair nearest to the sofa. 'Of course I only did so when one of the Lady Patronesses, the Countess Lieven, said that I might do so. It is not, as some fear, a fast dance at all, and my mama had no objections to me learning it. I should not care to see it at public balls, however, not that I attend them, because those of less gentlemanly upbringing might try and take liberties.'

Lord Levedale thought that any man who actually wanted to take liberties with Miss Darwen ought to be carted away to Bedlam.

'Almack's,' breathed Marianne Burton, reverently, which was just what Miss Darwen wanted. 'Oh, it must be wonderful.' With little hope of a London Season, Marianne turned it into the stuff of dreams.

'It can be crowded, hot, and with too many mamas,' remarked Lord Levedale, prosaically.

'There speaks the man.' Celia joined the conversation, to Miss Darwen's annoyance.

'You, of course, will not have entered its portals, Miss Mardham.' Miss Darwen's lip curled.

'No, and it would be pointless if I did, since I can

neither waltz nor stand up for the cotillion or any other dance,' Celia snapped at her.

The curl increased, because Miss Darwen felt superior, and had, she decided, made Miss Mardham show herself in a poor light, as well as highlighting her disability.

'And Celia was ever such a good dancer,' added Marianne, which did not help matters.

Lord Levedale saw Miss Mardham cringe, ever so slightly, and her hand upon her stick gripped it convulsively. He did not blame her for her intemperance, but rather wished there was something he might say that could help. There was nothing. His expression hardened, for he felt impotent when he wanted to be supportive.

Miss Darwen saw the look, and misread it as disapprobation. When she retired, she did so confident that she had bested both The Ninny and The Cripple, and was half way up the stairs when she stopped, and listened intently.

Mrs Wombwell and her son were in the hall, speaking in low voices, or rather Mrs Wombwell was speaking, and the words floated up, just sufficiently audible to be made out. Miss Darwen held her breath.

'. . . she assures me that although the girl is perfectly respectable, properly educated, and of course very beautiful, her father comes from trade, my dear, *trade*!' Mrs Wombwell's voice went up an octave on the repetition. 'He is a Member of Parliament now, though that need not mean so very much. I recall another such who was . . . well, anyway, he has a knighthood and a little estate, and perhaps to some that might make her acceptable, but Lady Mardham said the girl was not for the likes of those with good lineage and "nice" requirements. She is most certainly not for the likes of a Wombwell, with connections to a dukedom and two marquessates on the distaff. Imagine having a man who sold things as your papa-in-law!' She made it sound as if Sir Thomas Burton sold vegetables in the street. Lady Mardham had not, obviously, intimated to her dear friend that Marianne Burton was the heiress to a fortune of fifty thousand pounds. It was an irrelevancy, unless one was short of money, and the Wombwells had always been perfectly well-heeled.

'Then if she is so tarnished, why was she invited in the first place?' Mr Wombwell sounded cheated. He had no serious intentions, of course, but even playing with a young woman others knew to 'smell of the shop' was too much.

'Oh, I suppose because poor Celia cannot get out to make friends with other girls now, and they were friends at school. She is a really lovely girl, such a pretty face. Poor Celia.' Mrs Wombwell cast her son a furtive glance.

'She would be lovely, but for that disgusting limp. It is repellent. She cannot even sit with grace. It is not her fault, I admit, but she will end her days a spinster, and understandably so.' Mr Wombwell, having been treated with coolness by Miss Mardham, was not disposed to think of her in a generous manner.

Thus Mr Wombwell dashed the silent hopes of his parent that he might take to Celia, and she be the catalyst for him ameliorating his wild lifestyle. It had not been a very strong hope in the maternal breast, but she sighed, nonetheless.

Miss Darwen could have laughed out loud with delight. Here was just the proof, as if proof were needed, that she was right to dismiss Celia Mardham as a rival in any way, and ammunition, should Miss Burton's looks trump her lack of incisive wit.

CHAPTER SEVEN

Lord Deben, who described Miss Darwen to Lord Pocklington as 'terrifying in the extreme', tried to keep out of her way for the next couple of days as much as possible. This led to him advancing cautiously into rooms, and either withdrawing upon some very flimsy excuse if she were present, or placing himself as far as possible from her and sitting very quietly. Sarah Clandon observed this behaviour, and found it amusing. She was alone in the blue parlour on the Saturday morning, writing a letter to her brother, when Lord Deben peered round the door, and breathed an audible sigh of relief.

'She is not here, my lord, not under the table, nor lurking in an alcove.'

'Oh dear! Dash it, Miss Clandon, am I that obvious?'

'To me, sir, yes, but then I am renowned for being

sharp-eyed.' She smiled at him.

'Ah. I beg you will not reveal your observations to everyone else. If "She" found out . . .' He shuddered. 'You must think me a very cowardly specimen, ma'am, but I assure you I am not as lily-livered as I seem. It is just I have no idea how to . . . deal with a young lady of her ilk.' He looked a little crestfallen.

'To be fair, sir, I doubt many of us know, for she is . . . most unusual.'

'You appear sanguine enough, Miss Clandon.' There was a touch of admiration in his voice.

'But that is easy when she has rarely spoken to me, or rather at me. I am too insignificant.'

'Surely not!' Lord Deben, who had actually noticed Miss Clandon more than anyone else over the last few days, was shocked. She was a quiet young woman, restful, and with a very gentle smile that made him feel, most peculiarly, as if everything in the world was all right.

That smile grew now.

'Oh, I assure you that I am. Terribly insignificant. And especially to Miss Darwen.' It was the first time the lady's name had been mentioned, but it had not been needed.

'I . . . you are busy, and I ought to leave you to your letter.' Lord Deben wanted so much to remain in the room he just knew he ought to leave.

'I am writing to my brother, although it may be months before any reply is forthcoming. Please feel free to remain, sir. I am sure that sitting in the same room, as long as we are, of course, on opposite sides, could not be seen as inappropriate, and this room has the definite advantage of not containing Miss Darwen.'

He blinked, smiled, and sat, at first a little stiffly, in a large wing-backed chair. Sarah Clandon resumed her letter, initially conscious of being watched, but soon lost in her epistle. As she relaxed, so to did Lord Deben. His gaze rested easily upon her in profile. She had a straight little nose that had the veriest hint of turning up at the end, and a smooth brow. Her hair was fine, and looked soft. It was a mousey sort of colour he could not describe, but he liked it. He liked everything about her. He had never looked at females, having been in awe of every one of them since his redoubtable nurse, and his mama. They were impossible to predict, like an unbroken horse, and would be as likely to burst into tears as berate one over something omitted or committed that had been entirely unintentional. The nearest he had come to treating one as friendly was Miss Mardham, having encountered her as barely beyond being an invalid, and somehow not as a woman. Miss Clandon was friendly but he was also, much to his surprise, very aware of her femininity. It made him feel confused, excited, protective and several other things that he had not previously experienced. Had it been explained to him that these were the signs of falling in love, he would have panicked, but since he had told nobody, he remained in blissful ignorance.

The silence was amicable, but eventually Miss Clandon set aside the pen, and folded the letter.

'There. Lord Mardham has offered to frank it for me, and it will soon be on its way to Spain. I worry about my brother very much, though I know that it is pointless. I am so very conscious that news is tardy. I am writing to him today, but perhaps he was in battle three days since and . . .' She bit her lip.

'If you are close, might I suggest that somehow you would sense if anything . . . untoward had happened to him, Miss Clandon.' Lord Deben was unsure if this was possible, but it was the best he could offer in solace.

'Perhaps. It is foolish of me to have such a feeling, let alone admit it out loud.' She sighed.

'I think it not at all foolish, and can only say that I feel honoured that you have made me privy to it. I shall not breathe a word to anyone about it, I promise you.' He felt the mood was too sombre and serious, and suggested that they ought to join the other members of the party, in case their joint absence occasioned remark. In order to prevent any scandalous thoughts, he opened the door for her, and did not follow until he had counted to forty, which seemed a decent number.

Since the morning was inclement, and the gentlemen had no inclination to go out in the rain, everyone was confined within doors. Marianne was sorting out skeins of muddled silks for Lady Mardham, and Miss Darwen was expounding upon the efficacy of crushed cucumber for the complexion. Celia was sat with a book, but could not read it in peace. Her mama and Lady Corfemullen were nearest to the fire, which cheered an otherwise damp, grey morning.

Sarah Clandon entered, which gave Miss Darwen pause for but a moment before she continued her lecture, for that is how it sounded, and smiled at Marianne, surrounded by knots of colour. She offered to help, and had just sat down when Lord Deben entered, and found no other gentlemen to be present.

'Oh,' he exclaimed.

'My brother and Lord Pocklington have gone to play a game of billiards, my lord, if you seek them,' offered Celia, looking up from her book.

'Thank you, Miss Mardham.' There was relief in his voice, and he withdrew with a brief bow to the company of ladies.

He found his two friends, and also Mr Wombwell, who, since he no longer desired to flirt with Miss Burton, had no entertainment on offer among the ladies. He did not look very interested in the game, nor was he included in the conversation, which centred around Lord Pocklington's newly redecorated hunting box in Leicestershire. Lord Pocklington looked up from his shot as Lord Deben entered, and enquired where he had been hiding.

'Got lost,' lied Lord Deben, determined not to reveal he had been in the same room alone with Miss Clandon.

'Lost? Here? Good Lord, Debs, do you need a map?' Richard Mardham was incredulous.

'Well, I got lost to begin with, and then I . . . er,

got to looking at your family portraits. There are some very pretty women among them, but a couple of very rum-looking chaps in breastplates. They did not look at all clubbable.' Deben was thinking of one particular painting he had noticed about the house.

'"Clubbable"? I should say not. That was probably Sir Rufus Mardham or his son, Edward. They sided with Cromwell in the Civil War, and by all accounts were the most miserable types, who disapproved of dancing, and sang psalms a lot. I really ought to apologise for them.'

'No point in apologising for dead ancestors,' remarked Lord Pocklington, sensibly. 'Live ones are a different matter. I have an uncle, and Mama is always apologising for him. Cannot take his wine, and always falls asleep under the table after the first bottle. Snores too. She tried not inviting him, but he is her only remaining brother, so it became difficult.'

The conversation broadened to embarrassing incidents the young gentlemen had witnessed, and Mr Wombwell stalked out.

'Well done, Debs,' declared Mr Mardham, laughing. 'We could not ask him to leave, but all he did was stand there and look down his nose at us. Most off-putting it was. I am sure I missed a cannon because of him.'

Mr Wombwell was beginning to wish he had not accompanied his mama to Meysey, for all the advantages of eluding his creditors. The other men were not of his set, and the women could be of no interest to him. He had no great love of shooting or fishing, and the rain pattering down the window panes echoed his mood. He met Lord Mardham emerging from his book room. Lord Mardham did not like his guests to look dismal.

'What is the matter, Wombwell? You look as if you had dropped a guinea and picked up a farthing.'

'I . . . dislike the rain, my lord. It depresses spirits.' Mr Wombwell did look suitably depressed.

'Well, do not look at it. Here we are with pretty girls in the house, and Miss Burton worth a tidy sum at that, and you are looking miserable? I thought you quite a hit with her the other night.' Lord Mardham, in total ignorance of his lady's machinations, simply sought to make his guest the happier.

'Tidy sum?' Mr Wombwell raised an eyebrow, and something in his look made Lord Mardham suddenly wary.

'Well, you know, she is not some penniless orphan upon whom we have taken pity.' Lord Mardham appeared a little flustered, and Mr Wombwell could see he was back-tracking.

'Ah, I see.' He saw far more than Lord Mardham would have liked, and resolved to find out more. Miss Burton had become unworthy of his attentions by her birth, but a sufficient financial inducement could see him overcome his scruples, most unscrupulously.

* * *

Miss Burton herself had by this time ceased untangling threads, having been handed a letter from her father. Excusing herself, she went to sit in the window seat and read the paternal missive.

My darling girl,

I received your letter and was delighted to hear that you have settled in well with Lord and Lady Mardham. I know that you will conduct yourself with propriety and do your old Papa proud.

Actually seeing how 'showing off' gewgaws is detrimental is far better than merely being told about them, and to find that it can happen amongst the most well-bred young women should be a salutary reminder. You will never fall into that error, not that I thought it very likely, for you were ever a good and obedient girl. Far better to wear a little and of the best quality than festoon oneself with trumpery, like an overdecorated mantelshelf.

Marianne giggled, imagining Miss Darwen as a mantelshelf. At least if she were, she would be silent.

What you say about poor Miss Mardham is distressing, for I know you hold her in affection and have a soft and kind heart. Since, however, she is being strong, so too must you be strong, and remember that however calamitous her accident, it did not, thank the Heavens, prove fatal.

Sir Thomas had taken some time considering his next words.

This Mr Wombwell, whom I discover from consulting with Sir Hamilton Tyne, is a connection of the Dukes of Bedford, has, my dear, somewhat of a reputation, and not a good one. His habit is to single out innocent young ladies, and try to make them fall enamoured of him, whereupon he casts them aside. It is distasteful for me to have to warn you, my child, but be very cautious how you take what he says to you. A man of sweet words need not be one of sweet nature.

Of the other gentlemen you mentioned, I cannot say that I know much, except that Lord Levedale is reputed to be a steady young man, not given to excesses, and is the heir to the Earl of Curborough.

Saying any more looked a little as if he were pushing the viscount at her, and Sir Thomas hoped that singling him out in a mild way might show Marianne that here at least was a gentleman she might encourage in a modest manner. Sir Thomas felt a little aggrieved that the Mardhams had invited a man who was, to put no finer point upon it, a rackety rake, to stay with them whilst his Innocent Lamb was in residence. Since Marianne was so beautiful she was the most likely to receive Wombwell's dangerous attentions. Sir Hamilton Tyne had not minced his words, and given such a lurid account of the man's seductions, and reports of his deceptive good looks, that Sir Thomas had suffered a most dyspeptic night and in the small hours had even contemplated setting off next day to rescue his only child from Meysey.

The morning had brought calm good sense, and so Sir Thomas restrained his paternal impulses, and restricted himself to a letter. Sir Thomas sighed. He missed his daughter's presence in his house, and although he was keen to promote her achieving a good marriage, he secretly wished that the event might not take place in the too near future.

For myself, I have been taking lessons from Preston, the gamekeeper, and can report that not only have I not shot any person, but that I brought down a woodpigeon on the day of your departure. Your Papa will never be an outstanding shot, but it is to be hoped he will not disgrace you, and may even be bringing pheasants home from the shoots. I know that roasted pheasant is a favourite of yours.

Enjoy your visit to Meysey, my dear child, and do not forget your papa at home. I await your next letter with interest.

Your ever loving,

Papa

Marianne hugged the letter to her bosom. She was not only a dutiful daughter, but close to her sire, and although she had got used to being apart from him during her schooling, she did not like to think of him rattling about their house on his own. His warning upon Mr Wombwell was timely. Marianne was very inexperienced, and Mr Wombwell made a girl feel very honoured when he sat and talked with her. At the same time there was something about him which Marianne could not describe, but it had tempered her liking of him. He was most entertaining, and of course a very dashing man of the world, but once or twice she had seen something in his expression which almost frightened her. That he had dropped her the past two evenings had been a mixture of regret and relief. Lord Levedale, who had for the most part replaced him in entertaining her, was far less intense or – she had no other word for it – predatory.

'I will be careful, Papa,' she whispered to the letter.

There was another letter delivered from father to progeny, and this one was received with far less pleasure. Lord Levedale had groaned inwardly when he recognised his father's angular hand upon the direction, and gone to his bedchamber to read it in private, fearing that his face may betray his emotions as he read the contents. It was also a way of avoiding Miss Darwen, who seemed to appear out of the woodwork wherever he went in the house, like some malevolent spirit, ready to talk at him, and, even, which was far worse, simper.

As he set his foot upon the first stair he heard the rustle of skirts and winced, but then came the tap of a stick, and he turned with relief. Celia was shutting the door of the yellow saloon behind her. Her brows were slightly drawn together.

'Miss Mardham, are you in some discomfort? I ask because my groom broke his arm a few years ago, and he says it aches when the weather turns damp.'

'I confess that it is not the best weather for me,' she admitted, 'but if I am honest, the main reason for my poor humour is not an aching bone, but a collection of bones in a living person.'

'The Darwen.'

'Yes, my lord, just so. She has just suggested that as soon as it stops raining "everyone goes for a walk to clear the cobwebs" and liven them up. She looked at me so smugly, too.'

'You must miss the freedom. I know you were a horsewoman, but did you also enjoy walking, Miss Mardham?'

'Oh yes. I like the open air, and would frequently walk across the park to the Dower House to see my grandmama. Now I have to order the carriage and there is no spontaneity.'

'If you would like spontaneity, Miss Mardham, I am sure your brother would lend me his tilbury. That has a canopy to it. It is not raining sufficiently for you to become very wet, and it would not take long to make ready. I put myself at your disposal. You might visit your grandmother and still be back for luncheon.'

'That is a very generous offer, sir, but you have a letter in your hand. You must have been about to read it.'

'And I may still do so. I can send round to the stables and have learnt all that the letter contains before the tilbury is at the front door.'

He saw her waver.

'Be spontaneous, ma'am.'

'Yes, I will. Thank you. I must ask Mama of course, but . . . fifteen minutes?'

'I shall speak to your brother, and fifteen minutes sounds a sufficient time.' He smiled at her, and she smiled back, then opened the door into the saloon again. The sound of Miss Darwen's discordant voice just reached his ears. He went in search of Richard Mardham, and thereafter sent a message to the stables before taking the stairs two at a time. He rang for his valet once he reached his chamber, and then sat at the dressing table to read his sire's letter. His mood changed as he broke the seal, and the appellation made him pull a face.

My dear boy,

I hope by now you have made yourself popular at Meysey, and especially so with the beautiful Burton chit.

'Good Lord, has he no scruples?' exclaimed the viscount. It also occurred to him that the way to be popular might be by ejecting Miss Darwen from an upper window, but that was a wicked thought that only Miss Mardham might fully appreciate. He shook his head. She was there again, in his thoughts, even as he tried to be unemotional and sensible. He read on, and his expression grew dismal.

I had a damned unpleasant interview with Ruyton yesterday. I nearly turned the man off, however many years he has been the family man of business. His animadversions upon what courses of action are open to us were lacking in respect, and unspeakably forthright. Our situation remains awkward in the extreme. The Bank has been put off until Christmas, but if we cannot pay them at least the interest in the New Year, they are threatening to call in their loans forthwith. The acreage is already mortgaged up to the hilt and there will be nothing for it but for us to sell up the house and contents. What your poor dear mother would say I cannot bring myself to think.

'Oh yes, bring Mama into it. Trust you to do so, when you ignored her for years and went your own way. Very rich, Father, very rich!'

This estate has been in the family for centuries, and it grieves me that we have come to this pretty pass.

At this point Lord Levedale nearly tore the sheet in two. The persistent use of 'we', 'our' and 'us' bound him tightly to the situation, although it was grossly unfair. It was clearly used to apply pressure, and Lord Levedale resented it. Deep down, however, there really was a duty, not to his father, or to his brother, but the ancestors who had built the manor upon which Silvertons now stood, who had built the Jacobean house which had been the precursor of the house reputedly designed by a student of Hawksmoor a century ago, and had made the estate flourish. If he had been in love with another young lady it would have been different, but he was not. Miss Burton would solve at least all the immediate problems, and if he was circumspect, and took all control of the estate from his father, they might yet come about in a few years. A small voice in his head questioned the premise that he was not in love with another, but he dismissed it. He told himself firmly that he was no more in love with Miss Mardham than with Miss Burton, but knew it was a lie. They had met but a few days previously, and he could not be in love with her upon such a short acquaintanceship. It was rather that he had a propensity towards her, an inclination to love her, one which he must overcome. It would not, perhaps, be easy, for there was a mutual understanding that sprang from he knew not what.

'I must treat her as a friend, not as a lover would treat her.' Even as he said it, he wondered what it would be like to hold her in his arms and see her smiling up at him, and the spark of desire for her flickered as if to prove it would not be easily snuffed out.

I intimated to Ruyton that an advantageous match might be in the offing, and he thought this might be our salvation. I did not name the young lady of course, nor the exact figure, but it was enough to keep the man from wringing his hands like a Cassandra, and foretelling doom and insolvency.

I am trusting you to do the right thing, Levedale.

Your loving father,

Curborough

'Begins with a lie and ends with a lie, and the middle part full of duty. Damn it all!' Levedale ran his hand through his chestnut hair and swore, long and hard. It was a devil of a fix, made the worse by the presence of a young lady with a lame leg.

CHAPTER EIGHT

Celia was ready before the fifteen minutes had elapsed, and Lord Levedale found her seated in the hall, in bonnet and pelisse. She looked quite excited, and he thought how sad it was that something as simple as going across the home park upon a whim should be a cause of such delight. He did not, of course, know that it was as much the company as the outing which made her glow with pleasure.

'Behold me, ready on time, my lord. Never let it be said that ladies are always late.' She hoped she did not sound pert.

'Not all ladies are prone to tardiness, but there are those who dawdle, or spend an inordinate time before their looking glass.'

'You speak from experience, sir?' she quizzed him.

It seemed so natural to engage in gentle verbal jousting with this man.

'Not very much, Miss Mardham, but enough to make me applaud your promptness.'

She stood, and as she walked to the door, he came to walk at her side, on the opposite side to her stick, and offered his arm, not as vital support, but as a gentleman to a lady. He looked down at her, as she looked up, and yet again a frisson ran through him. Was there a hint of a blush?

The rain had diminished, but it was still wet.

'Now, here is our conveyance.' He paused. 'I am sorry, but will it prove awkward for you, getting up into the tilbury.'

'Yes, but it does not signify. However I travel, there is awkwardness.'

Beside the tilbury, Celia reached up her hand, and put her weight onto her good leg, raising the shorter limb carefully. For a moment she would be balanced upon it on the step. Without thinking, Lord Levedale, put his hands, lightly, to her waist, in case of any loss of balance. She stiffened, made the step, and sat down, using the arranging of her skirts as the excuse for not looking directly at him.

'Thank you.'

'No. I am sorry, Miss Mardham. I acted precipitately, but the step was damp. If you had slipped . . .'

'My thanks are genuine, sir. I merely regret the need.' She spoke quietly.

'I understand. Now, I promise to drive at a sensible pace, and not treat you to some exhibition of reckless driving.' He climbed up beside her, nodded to the groom to leave the horses' heads and climb up behind, and set off at a steady trot, requesting directions where the drive bifurcated. She gave them, and pointed out specimen trees planted by her great-grandfather that now made visual statements in the landscape.

'You walked this route, Miss Mardham?'

'Well, I generally took short cuts by walking paths. The carriage route is about half as long again, because it tends to skirt about the park. It is no more than a mile, on foot.' She sighed. 'It is so good to be out.'

'Even in autumnal drizzle?'

'Even in autumnal drizzle, sir. It is very kind of you.'

'Not at all.'

'And it does keep you away from You Know Who.' With the groom sat immediately behind them, Celia did not wish to name Miss Darwen.

'I had not thought of that, ma'am.' Lord Levedale sounded surprised, rather too surprised, she thought.

'You had not? Hmmm. I am not sure that I believe you. It saves you skulking about.'

'Me, skulking?'

'Yes, my lord, skulking.'

'I deny it, totally.' His lips twitched.

'How else would you describe your behaviour this morning?'

'Circumspect,' he answered, quickly.

'Cowardly.' She turned her head and looked at his profile. It was not the profile of a Greek god, for which she was thankful, having always thought they looked mean-spirited or haughty. His nose was not perfectly straight, having a hint of the aquiline, his chin was firm, and his mouth, currently trying to disguise a smile, was one which she thought could show resolution as well as humour. 'But if you did not offer to drive me from motives of self-preservation, then I am even deeper in your debt.'

The smile evaporated in an instant, and the lips thinned.

'You are not in my debt, Miss Mardham. Not at all.' His voice was suddenly stern.

'I . . . I am sorry if I have offended, sir.' She sounded deflated, and he cursed himself.

'Forgive me, ma'am. That is not the case. I am merely unable to consider such a trifling service as putting you under any obligation. And besides, it has, as you say, freed me from being haunted.'

They swept round a bend in the roadway, and before them, squat and square, but neither small nor unfriendly, was the Dower House, a building of warm, Cotswold stone in the Queen Anne style.

'Very nice,' murmured Lord Levedale, approvingly.

'Yes. I have always thought so. My brother has said that one day I may live here, and the thought pleases me.' There was only the slightest hint of melancholy in her tone, and she was smiling, but her words struck him like a blow. This was all the future she saw for herself: a girl not yet twenty, a beautiful girl of entrancing charm and a ready wit, looking to life in the Dower House. He almost felt the need to rail against it out loud, and it took an effort of will to remain silent.

He slowed the horse to stand four square before the house, and the groom jumped down.

'We shall not be more than half an hour, my lord, but best your groom takes the tilbury round to the stables lest he and Claret get cold.'

'Claret?'

'That is the horse's name. He is a good old boy.' Celia made her preparations to dismount, and found Lord Levedale before her.

'It would be simpler, ma'am, if you let me . . .' He held out his hands to lift her down, and place her safely upon the gravel. There was no doubting the increased colour of her cheek.

'Thank you again,' she said, and added quickly, 'Grandmama will be most surprised.'

Her grandmother's butler was certainly surprised.

'Miss Celia! Well, here's an unexpected turn up, to be sure. How good it is to see you, miss. Her ladyship will be that pleased to see you too. And whom may I announce, sir?' He looked at Lord Levedale.

'This is Lord Levedale, Chorley, who is one of the party staying at Meysey.'

'Welcome, my lord.' Chorley made his bow. 'Thomas will take your coat.'

123

The footman took hat, coat and Celia's pelisse, and then, tenderly, her bonnet.

'If you will be pleased to follow me, my lord. Miss Celia of course knows the way.' Chorley led them through a spacious hall, where a wide oak staircase swept up to the upper storey, and into a light and airy room where a fire blazed and gave off such heat that Lord Levedale wondered if they might give off steam. Celia went forward as quickly as her halting gait would permit, and bent to kiss the old lady's cheek.

'What's this? I had no notion you were coming to visit. Your Mama never mentioned it.'

'It was . . . spontaneous, Grandmama.' Celia beamed at her grandmother.

'And you, I did not catch the name, for Chorley mumbles so.'

Chorley had announced Lord Levedale perfectly clearly, but the Dowager Lady Mardham was not going to admit she was hard of hearing.

'I am Lord Levedale, ma'am.' He bowed, and there was a hint of a smile.

She frowned.

'Curborough's boy. Hmmm.' It was not an approving 'hmmm'. 'Mended your ways, I hope.'

'Er, no, ma'am, but I think you are mistaking me for my brother, Laurence. He was Lord Levedale until . . . his demise.'

Lady Mardham did not look at all put out by this. Her eyes narrowed as she scrutinised him more closely.

'You look like your mother.'

'Thank you, ma'am. I take that as a compliment.'

'As you should. Curborough was a witless popinjay. Never fathomed why she married him.'

'Grandmama!' Celia was mortified that her grandmother would openly insult Lord Levedale's father, but Lord Levedale did not bat an eye.

'I think she might have been the happier had she not, I agree.'

'You do?' Lady Mardham looked taken aback.

'Yes, ma'am.' He did not elaborate, and there was a short silence, which Celia curtailed by launching into a description of the house party.

'Sounds an odd set to me,' snorted the dowager. 'Maria Wombwell was a drippy sort of girl, and I hear her son is a libertine.'

'Where do you get all your information, ma'am?' Lord Levedale was intrigued.

'I have my sources, young man. Just because I live in the middle of a field does not make me a cow.' Lord Levedale choked, and Celia covered her face and laughed, which earned her a reprimand.

'But Grandmama, the park is lovely, and not at all like a field.'

'It is green and goes on for as far as I can see, and nobody comes to see me. Might as well be a field.'

'But it is a very fine house, ma'am.' Lord Levedale was not using flattery.

'Too many draughts, and not all the sweeps in the

shire can cure my bedchamber chimney of smoking.'

'You might move into another?'

'Why? It is the best bedchamber.'

Lord Levedale decided it would be best not to become embroiled further in a conversation that might become an argument he was bound to lose. He looked rather beseechingly at Celia, who took pity on him. Lady Mardham noted the look between them and she wondered, just a little.

'We must not stay long, Grandmama.'

'No, for it will be time for my luncheon, and Cook has only made a meal for me. I doubt you would enjoy sitting watching me eat it.'

'We would be pleased that you enjoyed it, Grandmama.'

'Pretty words, miss, pretty words.' She looked at Lord Levedale. 'Has she tried them on you?'

If she had hoped to put him out of countenance, she failed.

'Actually, ma'am, on the way here Miss Mardham accused me of cowardice, so I think she can be acquitted of doing so.'

It was Celia's turn to choke, but he turned a bland gaze upon her. The old lady felt there was some secret joke to which she was not privy, and it disgruntled her. She listened to the tale of Miss Darwen and the poem, which amused Lord Levedale, and then came to a decision.

'I am going to throw you out. I am hungry.'

'May we come again, Grandmama, without warning?' Celia smiled lovingly at her grandmother.

'As long as is it not when I am about to eat, you may. Now, kiss me like a dutiful girl, and be gone.'

She proffered her cheek, and Celia did as she was bid. Lord Levedale, not to be outdone, lifted a gnarled hand and his lips brushed the back of her fingers in a courtesy Lady Mardham appreciated, though she called him 'a jackanapes'.

'I think that went rather well,' announced Lord Levedale, assisting Celia into the tilbury. The grin on his face lasted all the way back to Meysey.

After luncheon Lord Levedale ignored the continuing drizzle, and wandered over to the stables, where he was greeted with some consternation.

'Are you wishful to be a-going out again, my lord?' His groom had hurried from the tack room as soon as a stable boy alerted him, and still had a half polished bit in his hand.

'No, no, Jeb, I was actually wanting to speak with Lord Mardham's head groom, and not in complaint.'

'I'll fetch him to you, my lord, but come out of this here mizzle. There's only me and Lord Pocklington's man cleaning bridles in the harness room.' Jebediah Knook ushered his employer into a room redolent of leather and saddle soap. Lord Pocklington's groom was caught mid-spit as he polished a cheekpiece, and choked as he stood up. Lord Levedale apologised for intruding and smiled, but it could not be said that the groom relaxed.

Thankfully, it was only a couple of minutes later that Lord Mardham's head groom came in and touched his cap to Lord Levedale.

'You wished to see me, my lord.'

'Yes, I did, er . . .'

'Harrop, my lord.'

'Well, Harrop, do you have a pony cart in the stables?'

'A pony cart, my lord?' The head groom looked stunned. A humble pony cart was not for the likes of Quality.

'I know it sounds an odd thing to ask, and I am not about to try and set some ridiculous fashion. It is just that I have had an idea, and before I approach Lord Mardham, I thought I would find out what the stables could provide.' Lord Levedale did not elaborate until he and Harrop were alone among the assorted equipages of host and guests, and then he explained his purpose.

'So you see, whilst a bespoke carriage would be the ideal, in the meantime, and for basic work, an even-tempered little pony and a good, stable conveyance are what we would need for teaching purposes.'

'Well, my lord, I can see as how that would be a grand idea, and Miss Celia . . . ah, what happened was an awful mischance. A good rider she was, and understanding of her horses, and I would lay a month's wages she never crammed her horse at that fence where they came down. Pure bad luck it was and . . .' He sighed. 'Howsoever, what's done is done, and if his lordship is agreeable . . . Trouble is, my lord, the only pony cart in the stables is the one that one of the lads drives when Mrs Howsell, the housekeeper up at the House, has need to go into Cirencester. It's in good condition, I wouldn't have anything rickety here, but it is not fitting for the likes of Miss Celia or yourself to be seen in.'

'Show me. We would be working within the estate for the most part, and in the circumstances, how it looks has to be pretty immaterial.'

Harrop passed along the line of visitors' vehicles, her ladyship's barouche-landau, the travelling carriage and then to the outmoded and more lowly transport. There was a serviceable, if unfashionably styled gig, in which young Mr Mardham had first tooled the reins before he bought his tilbury, the tilbury itself, a dog cart, and the pony cart. It was most certainly not something which Lord Levedale would have imagined himself driving, but he consoled himself with the thought that none of his friends would see him do so, and the cause was good. It would mean initially teaching Miss Mardham to drive seated sideways, but that was no matter. What was of importance was making access easier and the seating, which was bare board, more comfortable.

'Could the local blacksmith add an extra step, one

which could be bolted on for while it is needed? It would make it much easier for Miss Mardham. And we will need a cushion affair for the seat. I doubt there is a great deal of comfort normally.' He looked at the fairly basic springing.

'I can send over to Jacob Twiston, the smith, and for something temp'ry like, Mrs Howsell will be able to provide an old window seat cushion, p'raps, my lord.'

'Excellent. Do nothing until I have Lord Mardham's permission, however. He may be dead set against such a scheme.'

'If it makes Miss Celia's life the happier, I would doubt it, my lord, but he'll be thinking of her safety first and foremost.'

'As am I, Harrop, as am I. Thank you.'

Lord Levedale next sought out his host, but since he wanted private conversation with him, this proved awkward. Lord Mardham was in the billiards room with the other gentlemen, watching in some amusement as Lord Pocklington systematically beat his son.

The atmosphere was light-hearted, and although keen to share his idea with Lord Mardham, Lord Levedale gave no outward sign of impatience. Instead, he offered himself as scorer as Lord Corfemullen took on Sir Marcus. This proved a less entertaining game, and Mr Mardham took his two friends off part way through, very obviously not including Mr Wombwell, who was left to making desultory conversation with Lord Mardham, and was caught between pleasure that the young sprigs realised he was above their touch, and irritation at being consigned to boredom. He would have far preferred seeking out the ladies, but on his own this would appear odd.

Lord Levedale took the opportunity to study Sir Marcus Cotgrave at a time when the man was not setting up Miss Mardham's back. His initial impression had been that the widower must be a little slow, since he seemed totally unaware of the prickliness of the young lady whenever he offered to assist her or make overt allowances for her disability. He appeared, however, perfectly able to conduct a sensible and serious conversation with Lord Corfemullen upon the state of the post roads in Oxfordshire whilst deftly potting the ivory balls. His witticisms were on the ponderous side, but he was not some blundering idiot of a man. Why could he not see how his manner alienated the young lady?

With the conclusion of the game, the billiards room party broke up, and Lord Levedale was able to request a private conversation with Lord Mardham, who looked a little surprised but assented willingly enough.

'By all means, Levedale. Let us adjourn to the library, where we are unlikely to be disturbed.' He led the way to that chamber, and invited his guest to be seated. Once ensconced, he enquired how he might be of assistance.

'Well, sir, I was wondering . . .' This was not going to be easy. 'You see, I have been observing Miss Mardham, and hearing too that if she as much as wishes to take the air upon the terrace she has to avail herself of a rather uncomfortable Bath chair, and the assistance of a footman. She is, was, clearly an active young lady and it must be terribly frustrating for her.'

'There is little further that can be done.'

'Medically, I am sure that is true, but what about if she were able to drive herself about, visit her grandmother at the Dower House, that sort of thing. A degree of independence would be a boon to her.'

'I am afraid she has great difficulty getting in and out of carriages, and if there were to be another accident . . .'

'I am not talking some fashionable turn-out, my lord. I am talking about something practical for her use. My mama had a low phaeton some years ago, and one designed for Miss Mardham specifically would be low enough, with one permanent step, to enable her to get in and out with only minimal assistance, and a pair of twelve two ponies would be easy to handle. The centre of gravity would be so low an upset would be most unlikely, and she would have a groom up behind her.'

'If it gave the poor girl some freedom I suppose the expense would be worthwhile, but she cannot drive.' Lord Mardham frowned, considering.

'That is where I come in, sir. I am no nonpareil,

but I am a tidy whip, and do not flash about the countryside at neck or nothing pace. If you would give your permission for me to teach her, upon the estate itself, I would be pleased to do so. I had the temerity to take a look in your stables earlier, and there is a little pony cart which would not be too awkward for Miss Mardham to climb into, and that would be extremely safe. As a teaching vehicle it would seem ideal.'

'You seem to have thought this all through, Levedale.'

'I have given the matter most serous consideration, sir.'

'Well, I am inclined to accept your offer, but I think it would be prudent to ask Lady Mardham's opinion upon the matter first. If she is in agreement I will tell you after dinner.'

'Thank you, sir. I hope she will see the benefits outweigh the minimal risk.'

With which Lord Levedale accepted a glass of fine burgundy, and then departed, not unhopeful of a positive outcome.

Once Lord Levedale had taken himself off, Lord Mardham went to find his lady. She was in one of the smaller saloons, reclining upon a daybed with a novel, while Lady Corfemullen, in a similar posture, dozed lightly upon another chaise longue. She put her finger to her lips when he entered the room, and got up very quietly, coming to the door. Once in the hallway, she smiled at him.

'You find me heartily bored, my lord. That new novel Maria Edgehill recommended is perfectly atrocious.'

'I have some news that will interest you my dear, and may alleviate your boredom.' He took her by the elbow and guided her into the book room. 'I have been closeted with Levedale.'

Her eyes widened.

'Oh, do not say he—'

'In less than a week? My dear, be sensible. He wishes to teach Celia to drive.'

'But she cannot. I mean, she cannot climb in and out of carriages without the greatest difficulty and—'

'He has thought of that. In fact he has thought of almost everything.' Lord Mardham gave a wry smile, and explained what Levedale had said to him.

'The pony cart is small, and impractical for three, so if he did take her driving, there would be no groom. Having said which, they would only be within the park, and he is not the type to take liberties. I am much inclined to agree to his proposal and I beg you will not fly up into the boughs over the proprieties.'

'Fly up into the boughs? Why, my lord? It is of all things an excellent notion.'

'It is?' He looked confused, having been prepared for remonstration rather than approbation.

'Yes, of course. I had been worried that he was paying rather too much attention to the Burton girl, but perhaps he is playing a cautious game, and of course he is being almost hounded by the awful Darwen chit.

I only wish we had some excuse to send the girl home. It is all very well her not being any form of rival to poor dear Celia, but she is quite poisonous, you know. She ruins conversation at dinner.'

'Oh, I do not know. I was quite entertained last night, hearing her tell Gerald Corfemullen how to avoid being cheated by his servants. His face was a picture.'

'She cannot be stopped, that is the worst of it. You know she even makes Cora's girl look charming.' Lady Mardham shook her head. 'What a pity we cannot find an excuse to rid ourselves of her. However, what you say about Levedale is all to the good. Celia always appeared in a good light when with her horses. There is hope for us yet avoiding That Woman's daughter inheriting your papa's money.'

'More to the point, it might see Celia established, but we must not pre-empt the issue. Nothing may come of it in the end.'

'We shall see.' Lady Mardham was quite prepared to become involved if necessary. 'You just tell Lord Levedale he has our blessing.'

'That, my dear, sounds far too much as if we are treating the offer to teach her to drive as a proposal of marriage already. I shall inform him that you see no objection to his teaching Celia to handle the reins in form, even without the chaperonage of a groom, as long as they remain in the park itself and do not venture onto the public roads. Oh, and it will mean buying a pair of ponies and a low-slung phaeton.'

'It is her birthday at the end of the month. It would be a nice present.' Lady Mardham beamed at him, and returned to her book, which suddenly seemed far better.

Celia Mardham did not look at Lord Levedale when he entered the drawing room with the other gentlemen after dinner, though it took an effort of will. She was feeling beleaguered, having endured a trying conversation with Miss Darwen, who was telling her about the exhibition she had seen at the Royal Academy, or rather, those personages whom she had seen also viewing the paintings. The notables were all people Celia felt she would never meet, and the others were people of whom she had never heard. Listening was a chore. She had also the beginnings of a headache, in part from Miss Darwen's droning, but she told herself that the other part was definitely not because Lord Levedale had been sat next to Marianne at dinner and had flirted with her throughout. There was no doubt about it, and it both confused her and made her feel very low. All she wanted to do now was go slowly upstairs to her bed.

He came towards her, smiling, but in response she looked reproachful. He felt guilty.

'Miss Mardham, you look fagged to death. I hope I can bring you good news before you retire.'

'Good news, my lord?'

'I have been thinking, about today, and . . . being spontaneous. How would it be if you could drive yourself to the Dower House, whenever you so desired?'

'Drive myself?'

'Yes. If the vehicle were suitable, not something high and with a considerable step, and you learnt to drive, you could have some independence.' She looked interested, but a little wary of being pleased. 'I have spoken with Lord Mardham, and he and your mama have given permission for me to teach you to drive, if you will accept learning from me, and in a little pony cart.'

Her heart gave a jolt. It would be a form of independence, and he was offering to teach her. The only question was, in view of his pursuit of Marianne, why was he doing so?

'I . . . Would it not be an imposition, sir?'

'It would not. You know it would not.' The way he looked at her made her head spin rather than throb. 'And your father has said we, he, would be happy to order you a low phaeton from Gloucester, and you could have a pair of small ponies to go between the shafts, and for your birthday, which I gather is quite soon.'

'At the end of the month,' murmured Celia, in a daze.

'Will you? Will you agree?' He sounded eager, and she nodded.

Miss Darwen, too involved on the far side of the room in telling Lady Corfemullen how to get wine stains out of muslin, disliked the look, and the way in which Celia looked back. On top of the way he had entertained The Ninny throughout dinner, it quite ruined her evening.

CHAPTER NINE

The next day was Sunday, and so the pony cart could not have the additional step put in place by the blacksmith, but Lord Levedale was assured that it would be taken into the smithy first thing on the Monday morning. Miss Darwen, who clearly felt that she had not been assiduous enough in her attentions, dogged Lord Levedale to the point where he thought the only answer might be to throw a stick and yell at her to fetch it. She prevented him talking with Marianne Burton by nigh on commanding her to play the piano to entertain everyone, and Miss Burton was too overawed to refuse. She then gave a running commentary upon the performance in a stage whisper, which was highly disconcerting to both the pianist and the audience. Mr Wombwell, who had volunteered to turn the pages for Miss Burton, spent a considerable time restoring that lady to equanimity. He appreciated Lord Levedale's approaches of The Ninny, or, as he called her, The Money Pot, as little as did Miss Darwen. His methods were, however, rather more subtle. Marianne, bearing her sire's warning in mind, received his compliments with pretty grace, and enjoyed them, but did not take them as seriously as he thought.

When Lord Levedale was placed next to Miss Mardham at dinner, Miss Darwen was sat immediately opposite, and her conversation was so wayward that both he and Miss Mardham were mesmerised into listening. Sir Marcus, to Miss Darwen's left, gave up and applied himself to his food, but Lord Deben, struggling manfully to keep up with her and be gentlemanly, barely ate a thing. She began by warning of the dangers of eating too many ices, because they 'froze the digestive tract', and in one sentence then passed on to religious tracts and how they proved that educating the masses and teaching them to read was the first step to the guillotine. When Lord Deben tentatively suggested that a high rate of literacy was not reported to have existed among the sans-culottes, she gave him a withering look, and said that one could not believe everything that came out of France now that it was led by 'That Monster Napoleon'. Unable to think of an answer to this, Lord Deben looked desperately across the table to Miss Clandon for some form of moral support. Her look suggested he had made a good point, and he felt a lot better, but he was now way behind in the conversation, because Miss Darwen was talking about French spies. Lord Levedale could not hold back from asking, across the table, if she had ever met a French spy.

'I do not know, my lord. How could I do so, since they are spies, and by nature dissimulate? I can say that the young man who served me at the perfumiers I honoured with my custom in Bond Street short-changed me by a shilling, and he had a French accent.' She said this as if it were proof positive that he must also be sending copies of troop movements and government documents to Paris.

Celia Mardham swallowed a sugared plum, whole, and her eyes watered. Her father seemed to find Miss Darwen a constant source of entertainment, and gave clear signs of hanging upon her every word. Lady Mardham, in contrast, would have far preferred that she be afflicted by a putrid sore throat which robbed her of her voice and would necessitate her returning immediately to her parental home.

Sir Marcus only heard of the driving lessons when Lord Mardham and Lord Levedale had departed for Gloucester on the Monday morning, and he became quite agitated, walking up and down, muttering 'It will not do, it really will not do'. He then went in search of Celia, whom he found sat with Miss Clandon upon a stone bench by the terrace door, where they were hiding, most reprehensibly, knowing that it left Marianne to suffer from Miss Darwen. They were discussing 'The Affliction' and how her presence was ruining the party. At the sight of Sir Marcus' face, Celia gave a sigh.

He bowed, and made a stilted compliment about the two young ladies forming a composition not unlike a classical marble statue. Sir Marcus requested a few minutes with Miss Mardham upon a serious matter, and Sarah looked at Celia, who frowned, but nodded. Sarah wondered for a moment if the man was going to make a declaration, but if he was, then his expression was far from adoring. She made an excuse that she wanted to gather some greenery for the arrangement of flowers in the dining room, and walked along the path that turned with the angle of the house. It was there that she came, most unexpectedly, upon Lord Deben. He did not look happy.

'My lord? Is something the matter?'

He looked at her, and the look reminded her of her father's spaniel, who had a gaze of entreaty that would melt a heart of stone. Her heart was most definitely not of stone.

'I did not come here to be lectured by . . . a gorgon, or is it a harpy? My Greek mythology is rusty.'

He was obviously rather ruffled, and Sarah spoke soothingly.

'Of course you did not, sir, and it is very wrong of

Miss Darwen to do so.' No other person fitted any of the words in his description. 'She is but this Season's debutante and you are a man of the world . . . I mean . . .' Sarah faltered, which was unusual, for when she did speak, she was normally quietly sure of herself.

'I know what you mean, Miss Clandon.' He did. For all that he found females incomprehensible, he knew just what she meant. 'But to remonstrate with her, even if I could formulate the right sentences, would be bad form.'

'And you are always the gentleman, my lord.' The compliment was heartfelt, and he coloured and disclaimed in a mumble. When he dared look at her their eyes met, and he was struck yet again by a feeling of peaceful contentment edged with excitement.

Sarah, not knowing how best to soothe Lord Deben's shredded nerves, and indeed self-esteem, tried diverting his mind from his mistreatment, and regaled him with Sir Marcus's cumbersome compliment.

'It made me feel as if I were semi-clad and had the tip of my nose missing, which was not at all nice.'

'Good Lord, I should say not!' exclaimed Lord Deben, rather forcefully, since his mind was filled with the thought of Miss Clandon 'semi-clad', though nasally complete, and it overwhelmed him. As a distraction, it worked totally, but not as she had intended.

She was somewhat startled by his vehemence, and then his cheeks turned red, and for no reason that she understood, she blushed also.

Lord Deben wished there was a seat. He felt he ought to sit down, if not lie down. He felt hot, and a bit dizzy, and was trying not to focus on the images created in his brain whilst they crowded one upon the other; Miss Clandon, loosely draped in diaphanous fabrics, and holding aloft an urn, which was what he associated with Greek females; Miss Clandon, similarly draped, and sat, in a curvaceous way, upon a rock with some chain about her ankle. He gulped.

'Andromeda.'

'I beg your pardon, sir?'

'Or was it Aphrodite? No, a goddess could magic a chain away.' He was talking to himself, but Sarah worked out his train of thought, and the pink cheeks became scarlet.

'My lord!' She was caught between horror and amusement. It did not occur to her that he had deliberately conjured up thoughts of her *en déshabillé*, and in some ways it was funny, had it not been so personal.

His eyes widened. He saw that she saw what he was thinking.

'I am most terribly sorry, Miss Clandon,' he gabbled. 'Unintentional . . . would not insult . . . banish immediately . . .' Well, he would try, though they were the sort of thoughts that made for a fellow drifting into a reverie with a rapt look on his face. He sincerely hoped that she had not imagined the

144

same degree of 'semi-clad' that he had done, and told himself that neither Andromeda nor Aphrodite were customarily depicted 'disporting themselves'. He was only half correct, but it made him feel a little better.

They stood there, embarrassed and yet vaguely elated by being able to be united by thoughts without effort. Her bosom rose and fell rather more quickly than usual, he noticed, whilst concentrating on not noticing it. There was silence between them. Miss Clandon was the first to make a recovery.

'I acquit you of any intent, my lord, I promise. Perhaps it would be best if we returned indoors, and ordered refreshment. I will do so via Miss Mardham, who may be hoping for her own means of escape.'

Miss Mardham was most definitely wishing that she might escape. Sir Marcus did not, thankfully, sit down beside her, but stood before her and decried both her recklessness, and even more so that of Lord Levedale, whom he castigated as 'thoughtless in the extreme'.

'When I heard, Miss Mardham, I cannot convey to you in terms strong enough, since they would be unthinkable in front of a lady, how appalled I was. My dear young lady, you must have been captured by your own imagination, but it is impossible. You cannot do such a dangerous thing as drive yourself.'

'You think I would prove incompetent, Sir Marcus?' Her flash of anger was barely concealed, but he was not actually listening to her.

'In your condition, with your . . . problem . . . it would be to risk your life upon every journey.'

'We are talking about driving a pair of ponies and a low-slung vehicle that would be most unlikely to overturn, and I would not be driving at pace. The risk is very small. I might as well fear to step outside the house lest I trip.'

'And for that reason you ought never to do so without someone upon whom to lean for support. You are inclined to be too brave, Miss Mardham, too daring. It must be a temptation, I allow that, for you do not wish to see your life as inhibited, but—'

'I very well aware of my life being "inhibited", sir, I assure you, and whether I "wish" to acknowledge it or not changes matters not one jot.'

'Then I beg that you will see sense over this ridiculous idea of driving.'

'It is not for you, Sir Marcus, to beg or otherwise. My father, who is a man of sense, has found no reason to forbid either my learning to drive, or thereafter driving myself, with a groom. If he is content—'

'He has been seduced by Lord Levedale's enthusiasm for the plan. Lord Levedale can have no understanding of what it is to live with someone who is infirm, the extreme fragility . . .'

'I am not a china ornament,' Celia interjected, but Sir Marcus was too lost in his own argument.

'. . . that renders treacherous the actions that normal persons find simple. He has developed this ludicrous idea merely to show himself in the light of—'

'Enough, sir.' Celia stood, grabbing the back of the bench to steady herself, and pushing away the hand that he thrust towards her. 'I am not in a fatal decline; not so weak that every single action must be undertaken with someone on hand to guide me. You have no right to interfere, nor judge the actions of my father, Lord Levedale, or indeed, those I choose myself.' Her voice shook a little.

Sir Marcus looked as though he had just awoken to the idea that she was not simply going to agree with him, as a man and therefore wiser, and meekly give up the idea. He blinked in bafflement, and then attempted to extricate himself from the situation by a series of jumbled self-exculpatory phrases. Of these, Celia made out 'only trying to see that you come to no harm', 'no disrespect to Lord Mardham', and 'once you have calmed yourself'. This last had the reverse effect, since it was putting the 'blame' for not agreeing with him upon her female weakness and inclination to hysteria.

Sarah Clandon saw the situation in a glance, and hurried forward, suggesting that Sir Marcus withdraw.

Thinking that she meant Celia was about to dissolve into some distempered freak, he obeyed upon the instant, leaving Celia tight-lipped and fuming.

'I am sorry, Cousin Celia. I ought not to have abandoned you, but he looked as if what he had to say was serious but private.'

'What he had to say,' murmured Celia, through gritted teeth, 'was impertinent in the extreme. How dare he tell me how to live my life; how dare he treat me as though I were his sick wife reincarnated. Oh Sarah, he makes me so very, very angry.' With which she sat back down upon the bench, and wept with frustration.

In blissful ignorance of the awkwardness at Meysey, Lord Levedale drove Lord Mardham to Gloucester, where he intended to visit Courts, the coachmakers. Lord Levedale was well aware that it was also the opportunity for Lord Mardham to discover whether he was right in letting him teach his daughter to handle the reins, but had no concerns. He knew himself to be a decent whip, competent and tidy, without being ridiculously daring.

Their conversation ranged over a selection of topics, mostly quite general, and at no time was Miss Mardham's name mentioned by either until they reached the premises of Messrs I & J Court in Northgate Street. Mr Joseph Court came out of the workshops to greet them as soon as they had crossed the threshold. Lord Mardham had been a good customer over the years, and was one of Mr Court's more illustrious patrons. His lordship explained the commission, and Lord Levedale, slightly to Lord Mardham's surprise, drew a folded sheet from his pocket, on which he had drawn a sketch of his idea.

'My mother had a similar vehicle, and I thought that with some minor adjustments to the step . . .' Lord Mardham stepped back and let Lord Levedale and Mr Court discuss the finer points of the phaeton.

'As your lordship says, this would be very stable, nice low centre of gravity, and since speed is not an issue, there are no problems which we might think to encounter. It's glad I am that you have an understanding, my lord. Many's the time a young gentleman has come to us, fired with ideas, but which would not work when put together.'

'The thing is, Court, how soon could you have the thing "put together"?' interjected Lord Mardham. 'You see, Miss Mardham's birthday comes at the end of the month and it would be nice to have it near that time.'

Mr Court tapped a finger to his lips, and frowned.

'Well, my lord, I would usually say a good six weeks, depending upon the finish. The painting takes a tidy time, especially if there are decorative details.'

'I think Miss Mardham would prefer something of simple elegance, since it is for local use, not to trot about the countryside showing off. How about if it was one colour, a decent blue, and darker coach lines, with no curlicues or extravagancies?' suggested Lord Levedale.

'That would take off a good few days, my lord, because of the hardening of the paint required. If your lordships would be so good as to wait here a minute, I will have a look at what we have in progress.'

Mr Court withdrew into the workshops, from whence the sound of plane and saw emanated. He returned within a few minutes.

'I have had a good look at the books, my lords, and we have a repair that is of no urgency,' by which he meant that the client was a yeoman farmer whose gig might be put back a fortnight without anyone wondering at it, 'and I took receipt of a nice pair of wheels just the size you would need for the larger pair in this case but yesterday, in preparation for another commission due in October. If we treated this as our priority, I reckon as we could have the vehicle ready for October the fourth, a Friday that is. Would that be acceptable, my lords?' He looked from one to the other.

Lord Levedale expected to have left Meysey before then, but he knew that it would have been unreasonable to think it might be built in the twinkling of an eye. Lord Mardham looked pleased.

'Indeed it would, for her birthday falls upon the twenty-seventh, and that is pretty dashed close. A pair of twelve twos, would you say, to fit between the shafts?'

'Aye, my lord. Twelve-two to thirteen hands, no more. A nice little pair of ponies would have no troubles with just the lady and a groom up behind, and not doing long distances.'

'Best we look out for a pair next week in Cirencester

and then, if there is nothing that takes our fancy, we can try the sales here or in Cheltenham.' Lord Mardham was thinking out loud. Lord Levedale was pleased to be included in the 'we'. It was his idea, after all, and he was central to the whole plan. They concluded their business with Mr Court, discussing the cost with every appearance that it was something of indifference to each, though it was not. It was Lord Levedale's turn to take a step back during this part of the process, and he manifested a great interest in the book of designs that the firm had built up over the years to show prospective clients who were not quite sure what they wanted.

With the shaking of hands, matters were concluded, and the noble lords, feeling very pleased with their morning, repaired to take luncheon at The Old Bell, which lay conveniently close, and where they had stabled Lord Levedale's curricle and pair.

'Are you a good judge of horseflesh, Levedale?' enquired Lord Mardham, as he surveyed his lamb collops.

'I think myself a reasonable judge, sir. Having said which, from choice I take my groom with me, because Jeb Knook can spot a "wrong'un" as he calls them, from fifty paces. He also seems able to form an opinion of temperament in the time it takes to trot a beast up and down, and I am not at all certain about that myself.'

'Well, a wise man knows his limitations,' remarked

Lord Mardham, sagely. 'We will take him with us to Cirencester. It is not a large sale, and quite a few of the animals are for farm work, but Bathurst has had some very tidy carriage horses from it, and I have told Richard time and again that the chestnut he bought at Tattersall's for a hefty sum was no better than a riding horse I bought five years ago at the local sale for half the cost.'

'London prices, my lord. I am not a Town man, at heart. I rather like rural society. There is an honesty to it, and junketing about at parties making small-talk to people one barely knows is all very well for a Season, to see how it is done, but palls pretty soon. My father would disagree with me on that, but then we disagree on a number of things.' There was a touch of bitterness in Lord Levedale's tone that was not lost on Lord Mardham. Since Lord Mardham did not think particularly highly of the Earl of Curborough, this did Lord Levedale no great harm in his eyes.

'I am a social fellow, but agree, it is better to be social at home, or with one's friends, not making how-de-dos to all manner of people one "ought to know" and could not care a fig about.'

It occurred to Lord Mardham that a man who had no great love of London and prancing about at balls might be just the man for Celia, if he could see past her infirmity. The tragedy of it was, he could not see that any young man was actually going to do so. Thinking of his daughter made him confiding.

'You know I think this will do Celia the world of good, having something to be excited about,' Lord Mardham mused. 'Life has been rather grim for her these last eighteen months, and she has put a very brave face upon it, poor girl. There was she, all ready to go up to Town and be a success, and then . . .' He sighed. 'One can never tell what lies around the next corner of life.'

Lord Levedale nodded, but was thinking that around the next corner lay the possibility of him finding himself married, which was rapidly becoming a more attractive prospect, but to Miss Marianne Burton, which was not attractive to him in the slightest.

CHAPTER TEN

Celia was a little early for her first driving lesson. It might be in a humble pony cart but it was a promise of independence, and in addition, time with Lord Levedale. Since they were not going to leave the estate, and he had her father's permission, there would not be a groom in the pony cart, which would have made things very cramped. She came out, leaning on her stick, and went to the pony's head to speak soft words to it and make friends. She missed horses, and getting to the stables was almost impossible, whilst chatting to the animals that pulled her mama's barouche would have resulted in being taken to task for acting like a stable boy. The pony was old and placid, and appeared imperturbable.

Lord Levedale emerged from the house to see

Miss Mardham rubbing the pony's velvety nose and whispering blandishments in its ear. He smiled to himself. She turned at the sound of his tread upon the gravel.

'Now, do not tell me this is Thunderer, or Flyer, my lord.'

'To be honest, Miss Mardham, I did not ask his name, but he ought to suit our purposes very well. I will ascertain before our next lesson. If you prove as apt a pupil as I confidently expect, I will go with your father to the next sales at Cirencester, if not Gloucester, and we will find you a pair of nice little sweet goers, even in all paces, and of polite temperament, whom you may name yourself.'

'If it proves to be the case, I think Paragon and Perfection might be in order, sir.'

'Perfectly good names, both, ma'am.' He smiled at her. It was a very natural thing to do, and she smiled back. 'And now, Miss Mardham, if you would take your place in this formidable chariot, we will commence your first lesson.' He swept his arm in a theatrical gesture, and Celia hobbled round to the rear of the little cart and climbed in. The additional step, which she remarked upon as being very convenient, made it a lot easier for her, but Lord Levedale's hands hovered close, in case of need. She turned before seating herself.

'Which side, my lord?'

'Oh, I will have you handling the reins almost from the outset, Miss Mardham, so take your place as the driver. I can manage from the "wrong" side for a short while, and after all, this is not quite how you will drive your phaeton and pair.'

She settled herself and arranged her skirts neatly about her, and then Lord Levedale climbed in. It was not the sort of vehicle in which he had ever travelled before, and sitting sideways on to the pony would feel a little odd, but the principles of driving remained the same. He looked at Miss Mardham and her patent eagerness. With his long legs and her inability to bend the knee of her bad leg sufficiently to tuck her foot right back, their knees were so close they could sense each other.

'The prospect of a phaeton and pair is terribly exciting, sir, though I am sure I should not admit to it.'

'Why not? I was as proud as punch when I got my first turn-out.' He made no suggestion that her excitement had anything to do with her restrictions. He took the reins, recommending that she observe for a few minutes. She did so, and they were silent, only the steady trot of the pony's hooves disturbing the peace. The silence became unnatural, and Celia felt the need to converse.

'I have to say, my lord, that I am aware of two very lowering thoughts.'

'You are, Miss Mardham? And what might they be?'

'That you are doing this out of pity, and that you are also, having discovered the advantages when we visited the Dower House, doing it to avoid "The Darwen".' Celia dropped her voice melodramatically.

'Ah, upon the latter point you have me.' He grinned. 'I admit that it occurred to me that even she would draw the line at offering to act as groom. She is so very . . . dogged.'

'In more ways than one,' agreed Celia, recalling the lady's comment at breakfast, which had again drawn attention to Celia's disability.

'Which leads one, very reprehensibly, to wonder which breed.' He comprehended so easily, and his smile was infectious.

'Something with a nasty bite, and a tendency to snap. The sort I would assume is sent down rat holes, sir.'

'Infelicitous, Miss Mardham, since she appears to be chasing me. Ergo, I am a rat.'

'Oh dear me. I apologise, my lord. You are most definitely not rattine.' She bit her lip to stifle the giggle.

'Thank you.' He bowed his head in mock acknowledgment of the compliment. 'And where did you acquire your Latin?'

'I am no bluestocking, I assure you, sir. It was merely that I learnt animal names from my brother when he studied it. I was at the curious stage. I promise that I could not decline a fifth declension noun if you offered me a diamond necklace.'

'Yet you know a fifth declension noun exists. That ought to be worthy of a pearl pin at the least.' Their eyes met, and both held laughter. 'Have you ever wondered why learning is considered a bad thing for the fair sex, Miss Mardham?'

'Well, it might be that if we were to be taught in the manner of boys, we might excel them. I doubt we would be as easily distracted. I think some of it is silly. If it is acceptable for a girl to learn Italian, why not Latin?'

'I think some of the subject matter is not best suited to young ladies.'

'You think we could not cope with the description of battles, my lord?' She cast him a questioning look, and he realised it was entirely genuine.

'You put me to the blush, ma'am. The Romans had, er, different morals, shall we say, and certain subjects were written about quite openly.'

It was Celia whose cheeks actually changed colour.

'I am sorry. I did not mean to . . .' She paused, but then rallied. 'And if such things are inappropriate for young ladies, why should they not also be so for youths?'

'A fair point. Now, having agreed upon Miss Darwen, discussed education, and being on a suitable stretch of driveway, I think, Miss Mardham, it is time that I did as I promised, and taught you how to handle the ribbons.' He thereby avoided answering her first point.

It occurred to her that for all the excitement she had felt at the prospect of learning to drive, she had completely forgotten about it in the last few minutes. Lord Levedale brought the pony to a halt, and began to explain the basics of handling the reins, and controlling a horse without being upon its back. Being seated opposite each other in the little pony cart, and with him assisting her, it was impossible for their knees not to touch, especially since Lord Levedale was so long-limbed. Indeed, the height of the seat meant that his knees stuck up rather obviously, and made him feel frog-like. He made a valiant attempt to deny the frisson that being in such close proximity to Miss Mardham created, and failed.

'Now, you should have no problem feeling the pony's mouth. You are a horsewoman, so will understand the connection and keeping him up to the bit.' He was adjusting her hold upon the reins, and even though both parties were gloved, it took all his concentration not to dwell upon the delicacy of her fingers. His throat felt dry.

'I am a horsewoman no longer, Lord Levedale.' Celia gave a twisted smile, and her voice held regret.

'You no longer ride, ma'am, but that is not the same thing at all. If you have an understanding and love of the animal, you are a horsewoman still. I saw you with this fellow when you came outside. It was noticeable that you went first to him, and introduced yourself, checked him over. You did not simply come to the step and get in. No, Miss Mardham, you are a horsewoman still.'

She looked at him, and there was a film of tears in her eyes. Everyone noticed what she could not do. This man was asserting what she could do, ability she retained.

'If you knew . . .' she whispered.

'I do not know, but I can in part imagine. You said that you feared I was teaching you to drive out of pity. "Pity" is not the right word. I feel for your restricted lifestyle, and wish to offer you any assistance that might make it possible for you to do more.' There was nothing light-hearted about his tone.

'You do not simply seek to do things for me and accentuate my feebleness. That is a kindness in itself, sir.'

'You are not feeble.' A spark of anger flared against her seeing herself as being some form of charity case. 'You suffered an injury, a potentially fatal injury, and you survived. Does that not prove you are far from feeble? You do not give in to the disability fate has imposed upon you, but challenge it in the way you live day to day. It would be easy enough for you to have a servant assist you down the stairs each morning and sit in a chair all day, having everything brought to you, but you do not "play the invalid" Miss Mardham. You are frustrated, because you fight. I have never met a woman with such strength. It is your leg that is weak, not You.' He spoke with an intensity that took her breath away.

They stared at each other, and then stepped back from the emotional brink.

'My apologies. I spoke heatedly, Miss Mardham.'

'None are needed, sir. What you said was a great compliment.' She contrasted it with the way Sir Marcus wanted to treat her in the completely opposite fashion. 'Now, turning. How is that best accomplished?'

Teaching the very fundamentals of driving, and with a docile pony that knew exactly how to respond, did not take up all of Lord Levedale's mind. This was a good thing, since the rest of it was in some turmoil.

The lesson lasted for a little over an hour, with the promise of another the next day. He judged an hour to be long enough to assimilate the skills of the lesson, and not so long that he might give in to the urge to woo Celia Mardham.

What he did not realise was that she already felt as though something very special existed between them. She had no experience of flirtation, and whilst she saw his behaviour towards Marianne Burton in that light, what they experienced – the light banter, the mutual understanding – was not, in her mind, at all similar.

She arrived back at the house most confused, and not about the act of driving. They had been on such good and easy terms, frank and open with each other, comprehending each other so easily, that she felt a true bond between them. He was the most charming man she had ever met, and yet he was not 'charming' her. When she was with him she felt light-hearted, and light-headed too. Was he intoxicating? She would have smiled at that, but the other side of it all was that she found his manner with Marianne upset her. She could not see it as genuine, felt it was some strange game, and yet he persisted, as much as he might with Miss Darwen forever at his heels. She could not ask him why he behaved like this. Was his natural familiarity with her a brotherly sympathy? Was it because he was a kind man who saw her plight and sought to alleviate it, which was in part what he had admitted? Lord Deben was a kind and thoughtful man, but he had not offered to teach her to drive. Was it madness to feel as she did about Lord Levedale?

Her head was full of questions, and very few answers. When Lady Mardham waylaid her, keen to hear what had happened, she was disappointed to see the frown upon Celia's brow.

'Did something go awry, Celia dear? You look displeased.' She could not believe Lord Levedale had misbehaved, but one never knew with men.

'Oh no, Mama. Everything went very well. It is just . . . I am unsure of things.'

'Of course, my love, you will take time to master it all.' Lady Mardham misunderstood, but Celia was happier that she did so. 'I think it very adventurous of you to make the attempt.'

Celia did not want to say that thus far, controlling the pony had been very easy. Part of her wanted as many lessons as possible, and not to improve her skill with whip and reins. For one whole hour she had Lord Levedale to herself. They could speak as they wished, and oh, the thrill that had run through her when his hands had held hers to correct her hold upon the reins. It must end in disappointment, but it was too magical to lose even a minute of it.

Lord Levedale, had she but known it, was in as muddled a state. What worried him was that although he had many questions, he did possess some of the answers. He had told himself that he had offered to teach Miss Mardham to drive, was putting his efforts into giving her this independence, because he could offer her nothing else. If he was to save Silvertons he must be successful with Miss Burton, who thus far seemed quietly receptive to his approaches, though Wombwell was making strenuous efforts to supplant him. In a bizarre way, the less he wanted to marry Miss Burton, the stronger were his efforts to achieve the goal. It was as though the more he saw the path to his own happiness, the more he stepped aside from it, because it would be selfish, and trod purposefully upon the path of duty. That Miss Burton might find life as a 'duty' wife less than entrancing had occurred to him, but he had told himself he was just making excuses.

Actually being alone with Miss Mardham was going to complicate things enormously, and it was all his own fault. He had told himself that he would control his feelings easily enough, since they had but a week's knowledge of each other, even though that was after he had driven her to the dowager's and enjoyed every second of the outing. It was then that he had formulated the driving plan, when aware of the 'danger'. He was an idiot. The pleasure of the interlude to old Lady Mardham was as nothing to the lesson. This last hour had been emotionally intense. He had never felt so very aware of another person's physical being, never wanted every excuse for the slightest of touches nor tingled when they occurred. He felt so drawn to her, more relaxed than with anyone he had ever met, and simultaneously tense with an excitement which made it hard to concentrate on anything but how beautiful she was, in body and character. There had even been moments when she had looked at him and he had struggled not to take that sweet face between his hands and kiss her.

'Damnation,' he muttered, as he tossed his gloves onto the table in his chamber.

It was an expletive that might well have been repeated by Mr Wombwell, and Sir Marcus Cotgrave. Miss Darwen would not swear, of course, but was equally annoyed. All three had watched Lord Levedale set the little pony trotting off with uncharitable thoughts, and all three were mystified as to why he was 'making up' to two young ladies at the same time.

Mr Wombwell was the most resentful. Having discovered that The Money Pot was worth enough to see him clear of his debts, he had resumed his pursuit, which had led to much hand-wringing by his parent. He could not tell her his reasons for overlooking the girl's plebeian ancestry and so she 'bleated' at him whenever they were alone. Having only dropped the flirtation for a couple of days, it was most irritating that in that short time Levedale had joined the lists vying for The Money Pot's hand. After all, the man lived in deepest Devon and was interested in farming, so what possible need had he for money? He was also distracting The Money Pot. There was no other possible reason why she should be accepting his own experienced advances without any sign of becoming lovelorn. Mr Wombwell knew he could be pretty irresistible, and by now would have expected a girl as innocent and inexperienced as Miss Burton to be watching him whenever she thought he was not looking, her eyes filled with yearning, his name being murmured into her pillow at night. The process had such an inevitability to it that it was almost boring, and he was seriously considering giving up ingénues. The chit evinced no sign that she was desperate for him, and the only reason must be that part of her was taken up with Levedale, who was making a play for an heiress he did not need, damn him.

On top of which, most inexplicably the man now appeared to be chasing after the Mardham chit. There was no other explanation for his offering to teach her to drive in that ridiculous rustic cart. What sort of deep game was Levedale playing? Well, with luck the hobbledehoy would form a passion for him, and Mardham, if he had any sense, would soon be muttering about 'man of honour' and 'doing the decent', since there was no other way he would ever get the girl off his hands. That would hoist Levedale by his own petard, and leave the path clear for himself with The Money Pot.

Sir Marcus Cotgrave viewed the driving lessons as a threat, for Levedale was young and personable, which might turn a girl's head, but he also saw them as wilfulness on Miss Mardham's part, and very dangerous. He believed, totally, in what he had said to her. All ladies were delicate, although having encountered Miss Darwen he would now concede there were tough exceptions. Miss Mardham was so much more fragile than other young women. He knew how to care for such fragility, and was both taken aback and disappointed that she had not immediately recognised this. He had come to Meysey intending to convey his abilities to treat her as if made of eggshell, and have her place her future into his safeguarding with a grateful, pretty smile. Thus far she seemed to be regarding his thoughtfulness as insulting. These driving lessons would not make his wooing any easier, even assuming she did not end up dead in a ditch, and why Levedale should have thought up the idea, when he was patently chasing the Burton girl, was a mystery.

Miss Darwen was perhaps the most mystified of the trio. She had conceded, reluctantly, that The Ninny was pretty enough to attract a man, until he realised that she was simply a beautiful, empty shell. She was therefore working hard to keep Lord Levedale from his pursuit of the girl, for his own good as much as her own advantage. The Cripple ought not to be a rival at all, and keeping her in her place had been a matter of pleasure, not necessity, especially since Miss Mardham clearly refused to acknowledge her inferiority. Now she would have to rethink her strategy. What Miss Darwen could not in any way comprehend was why Lord Levedale, an otherwise sensible and seemingly honourable man, appeared to be going out of his way to rouse tender emotions in the breasts of two women at once, one of whom being a girl no man would select as a partner in life. This madcap idea of driving lessons took up his time to no purpose. That he might be doing so from any feeling of altruism did not occur to her, since she had never entertained an altruistic thought in her entire life. It was obvious to her that he had the best option already before him, and she was ready to accept his offer and direct him straight to her papa as soon as he made his declaration. Men were such fools.

CHAPTER ELEVEN

Marianne Burton set pen to paper to write once more to her papa. She had promised to be a frequent correspondent and it was now a week since her last letter. In part this was because her time had been taken up as a good guest, and in part because she was unsure what to say that might not worry her parent, or leave him as perplexed as she was herself. However, a promise was a promise, and so she would write.

Dearest Papa,

This leaves me in the best of health and I hope reaches you in the same. I have been quite occupied here at Meysey though you would say it was time spent in frippery things. I often sit

with Celia and her cousin who is the one I told
you was poor and plain. She is actually a nice
girl called Sarah who is very good at Spillikins
because she has a very steady hand and only fails
when Lord Deben smiles at her.

Or when Miss Darwen cheats, thought Marianne, as on the previous evening, when she had 'accidentally' nudged the table just as Sarah Clandon made her move upon a stick that would have won her the game, and the pile of sticks moved to make any successful extraction impossible.

Miss Darwen whom I said was a bit superior because
of her London experience and too much jewellery
has not proved very nice. She says very cutting things
about poor Celia which is unfair not least because
poor Celia cannot easily get up and walk away as I
said to Celia herself.

Marianne did not like to say that Miss Darwen said cutting things about herself also, because it would upset Papa, and she knew that she was not very good at countering the barbs. Instead, she smiled sweetly, and pretended that she had not heard. She made no pretence of being clever in terms of knowledge, but she was not stupid, and it was obvious that Miss Darwen's words and actions set up the backs of the other members of the party. Lord Levedale had remarked that he thought her own manner of ignoring the insults reflected very well upon her, which was nice.

This was where the letter became difficult.

Mr Wombwell is very attentive but I have remembered your warnings about him, dearest Papa and do not take his flowery compliments to heart. He is most amusing but not in any way kind. Lord Levedale is much the nicer and very polite. He does not set as much store upon how he looks but is more the true gentleman I am sure.

In fact he paid court to her as much as Mr Wombwell, and, she thought, with as little interest of heart. Yet he did not seem to want her to fall in love with him. It was most peculiar. With Mr Wombwell it was some rather unpleasant game, but with Lord Levedale . . . she was unable to think of an answer.

The weather today was quite overcast but Lord Levedale still gave Celia a lesson with the pony and cart which is a bit old-fashioned and is very kind. Lord Mardham says that he will buy Celia two little ponies and a nice low phaeton so that she can drive herself to see her grandmama who lives in the Dower House.

Mr Mardham has taken the gentlemen out this afternoon to shoot Sir Marcus Cotgrave though did not accompany them saying that his shoulder was too stiff. The weather for tomorrow is supposed to be better because an old man in the village knows about such things and said so to Lord Mardham. We are going to have an archery contest which will be splendid fun. I hope I do not hit anyone but it would be nice to hit the target.

I am having a lovely time but of course miss you very much.

Your loving and obedient daughter

Marianne

She was enjoying herself, but a part of her wondered why, when one of the other ladies mocked her, one gentleman was trying to ensnare her for sport, and another was paying court to her seemingly against his natural inclinations. In fact it was because most of the other members of the party were about her own age, and at home with Papa there was not the opportunity to giggle with another over the extravagances of a fashion plate, or discuss novels, or watch the 'dance' of the way people related to each other. She was also learning a lot. Mr Wombwell and Miss Darwen were, for example, remarkably similar, in that they were blinkered to the feelings of anyone else. Marianne had never encountered anyone quite as selfish. It isolated them, and they either did not notice or did not care. The one dressed very well, whilst the other only thought that she did, and they would have been horrified to have been seen as alike, but they were. As an only child, Marianne had not had to share, or think of others as those with siblings must do, but her governess had been swift to reprimand her for selfishness, and now she saw how wise Miss Rye had been.

Rather more lowering was discovering that being beautiful was no guarantee for finding love. Sarah Clandon was not beautiful, but Marianne was fairly sure that Lord Deben was decidedly smitten with her, and she had done nothing except be herself, and like him in return. Perhaps, thought Marianne, as she sealed the letter, Cupid's arrows had struck them. She laughed to herself, and hoped that more tangible arrows did not strike anyone on the morrow.

Celia's daily driving lesson had not started well. She was certainly mastering the essential skills, and Lord Levedale had sought out a gateway so that she might learn to negotiate a narrow opening with ease. It could not be said that Celia was in a mood to receive instruction, however, and her agitation was sensed by old Pom the pony, who was unusually fractious. When Lord Levedale held open the gate the cart positively shot through, and so close that he had to step back smartly to avoid being crushed. He gave Celia a very considering look as she pulled up.

'Perhaps you ought only to drive when you are not out of temper, Miss Mardham.'

'I am not out of temper,' she said, with a scowl.

'Pom thinks you are, and so do I. Do you want to try the gate again, or wait until later?'

'I will try again, my lord.' She pursed her lips, turned about, and made another attempt, which was better in that he was not so likely to be run over, but lacked finesse. She came to a halt, and he shut the gate and climbed back into the cart to sit facing her.

'You are not my usual pupil this morning. What is it that has set you on edge?'

'Nothing.'

'You are a very poor liar, Miss Mardham, which is, of course a compliment.'

'Then you ought to keep it for Marianne.' The response was out so swiftly. She gasped at her own waspishness, and he frowned. She closed her eyes for a moment, and then said, in a very small voice, 'I am sorry, my lord, that was unforgivable.'

'Not unforgivable.' He wished he could explain everything, but it would sound all wrong.

She thought his silence was because, whilst he might forgive her, he was disappointed in her.

'I hate myself sometimes, you know.' She was staring straight ahead, between Pom's ears.

'Why?'

'Because I am not me.' She sighed. 'I know that makes no sense, but it is too difficult to put into words.'

'Try.' He took the reins from her grasp, and as his hand touched hers it lingered for a moment.

'It is not just my leg that is deformed, you see. The accident has deformed "me", the way I feel, the way I lose my temper. I was, I think, an even-tempered person, much more likely to smile or laugh than be angry and sharp-tongued. I am afraid that one day I will forget how I was.' She took a deep breath, and swallowed the lump in her

173

throat. 'It is not everyone else's fault that I cannot do things, although I do wish they would not keep reminding me. Sometimes I get angry with them for that and sometimes I get angry with myself for feeling angry. How foolish is that!'

'Not foolish at all, Miss Mardham.' He thought it rather heart-breaking.

'I am becoming so bitter and twisted, like my limb, that I will end up as unpleasant as Miss Darwen,' she said, sadly.

'You will never be in the slightest way like Miss Darwen,' he said, with vehemence. 'You berate yourself for the anger that stems from your frustration. She would never do so, in your place. There is nothing generous about her, just self-opinionated self-worth. Now, tell me why your anger has come to the surface this morning.'

'Because she proposed the archery competition, and I would so much like to join in.' Celia bit her lip, and there was a slight catch in her voice. 'I want to be part of life, not just observe it.'

Lord Levedale struggled with himself. Each lesson it was harder to hold back from her; every day he wanted her the more, but this was greater than mere desire. He wanted to hold her in his arms and reassure her, promise her that everything would be all right, as though he could perform some miracle, which he could not. She felt not only that her physical disability made her unlovable, but that she was unworthy of love because of her anger, which stemmed from frustration, and her fighting her limitations, not a meanness of spirit. He could not tell her just how worthy of love she was, that he was already falling deeply in love with her. The best he could do would be to solve her problem for the morrow.

'Why can you not do so? You can stand.'

'I could not balance, drawing the bow. I would be lopsided, or unsteady upon the dreaded patten. Have you ever drawn a bow, sir?'

'I confess that it is something I have not done, so if I am asked to join in, please stand well behind me.' There was a flash of a smile and then he was serious once more. 'But could you not join the competition sat upon a chair, one without arms like a dining chair?'

She pondered this.

'I suppose so. But Miss Darwen would say that was cheating and . . .'

He halted the pony cart and looked squarely at her.

'This is nothing to do with her, just you. Forget she exists. If you wish to join in, do so, and to be honest, nobody else would think you gained any advantage.'

'Miss—'

'If you mention her name again, Miss Mardham, I am driving you straight home, is that clear?' he spoke severely, but his eyes did not chastise.

'Yes, sir.'

'Good. And for your information I could not give a fig for what she thinks, and I doubt anybody else does either.'

'No, sir.'

'And I am not a schoolmaster.'

'No sir.' At last there was a trace of a smile upon her lips.

'So no more, "yes, sir", and "no, sir".'

'No . . . my lord.'

'Good girl. I mean . . .' She was looking at him in such a way he dare not say anything more. He must think of Silvertons, of those long-dead ancestors, anything but how much he cared about her.

'I think I could manage the gate properly, now,' she said, softly.

Upon their return from driving, Lord Levedale retreated to his bedchamber, ostensibly to change into garb suitable for shooting. In fact he did so without any thought as to what he was putting on, and it was a good job that his valet had the dressing of him. Welney thought his master particularly preoccupied, and not happily so. It distressed him, because he considered Lord Levedale a good employer and generally an open and cheerful person. He therefore even forbore exclaiming when his lordship ran his hand through his locks in an act expressive of his mental perturbation.

'There we are, my lord. And I hope as you bag a good number of birds.'

Lord Levedale thanked him, rather abstractedly, and went down to join the hunters. Welney shook his head and tutted.

Mr Richard Mardham was in a very good mood, and laughing with Lord Pocklington. Lord Deben was seemingly studying the wall, with a rapt look on his face, and Mr Wombwell, whom Mr Mardham could not avoid inviting upon the shooting expedition, was inspecting his nails.

'Ah, there you are, Levedale.' Mr Mardham looked up the stairs as he heard the tread.

'I am sorry. Have I delayed you?'

'Not at all, my dear chap.' It was not quite true, but the fellow was being jolly decent, teaching Celia to drive, and that was the cause of the delay. 'We should get a good bag today, and before you start upon "partridge cake" and such, let me tell you Cook is expecting enough birds to do for a fine dinner on Tuesday. They will have hung nicely by then.'

'Partridge pudding,' murmured Lord Deben, and Mr Mardham wondered whether his friend had been thinking of food whilst contemplating the wallpaper.

'Quite possibly, Debs.'

With which he led the gentlemen to the gunroom to select the guns of their choice.

It could not be said that Lord Levedale accounted for many of the birds, not that he proved a poor shot but rather he did not raise his gun very often, and thus quite a few Gloucestershire partridges lived to fly another day. Lord Pocklington, by contrast, kept his loader and the gundog very busy. When they eventually returned, with enough of a bag to keep Cook dressing birds for half a day, everyone agreed it had been an excellent day's sport.

Miss Darwen was in buoyant spirits. She considered herself rather a good toxophilite, among the many other things at which she excelled, and had no doubt that she would shine among the other ladies. The Ninny had already admitted that she had never held a bow in her life, except one made of ribbon, which Miss Darwen thought a very weak joke, but had caused an uncommon degree of amusement among certain of the other guests. The Poor Relation was the quiet sort who was probably fearful of nasty, sharp arrows, and The Cripple was patently unable to participate. It was unlikely that the older ladies would take part, and if she were to lose to any of the gentlemen that would be perfectly acceptable because . . . they were men. She could look coy and ladylike and murmur about how much stronger they were. If she beat them she could be 'Diana the Huntress'. All in all, it promised to be a very good day, and suggesting it had been inspired. It did not occur to her that it would be far better to win in a closely fought contest with archers of comparable skill. All that mattered was that she won and was the centre of attention. Had one enquired of several members of the party, they would have preferred her to be the centre of attention by being the target.

She was seated next to Lord Levedale at dinner, which enabled her to tell him all about her past successes at the butts in inexhaustible detail, but even she became aware that whilst being polite, he was only half attending to her. This was disappointing, but at least he had been equally quiet before the meal, and had not engaged any of the ladies in conversation other than his hostess.

He had been discussing Celia's aptitude as a whip, making much of how sensible and safe a driver he expected her to be, and praising Lady Mardham for her wisdom in agreeing to her learning. He had realised early in his visit that her ladyship liked to think that everything was going well because she had arranged it so.

Lady Mardham did not know what to make of Lord Levedale. In her more hopeful moments she thought his attention to Miss Burton was a feint to distract from his gentle wooing of Celia, but, she asked herself, why would he think that necessary? Or was he doing so to keep Mr Wombwell from breaking the girl's inexperienced heart? She could not fathom it at all. The driving lessons were, at the least, a good sign, and if anything would show poor Celia in a good light, it would be to do with horses, even now. Her lord had reported that the viscount had put a lot of thought into the design of the phaeton, and was eager to be involved with the purchase of a pair to go between the shafts. That, she told herself, was not the act of a man who was disinterested. His manner this evening was almost melancholy, and she wondered what had occasioned his lack of spirits. Had she even had an inkling that it was because he found himself falling ever more deeply for her daughter she would have been ecstatic, until she got to wondering why that made him miserable.

The truth of the matter was that Lord Levedale was in an impossible position of his own making, as he knew full well. If only, he thought, he had followed his instincts from the start. Instead he had brushed them aside in an effort to do the right thing, and thus done the wrong thing, utterly. He was pretty sure that Miss Mardham liked him, though he would not go so far as to say that she was in love with him. After all, she was without experience, and her feelings might be acute, but just calf love that would fade as quickly as it had appeared. Deep down he did not think that the case, but he was not himself so well versed in love that he could judge for certain. If her feelings were genuinely engaged, then had he been honest with himself he might now be contemplating requesting an interview with Lord Mardham that had nothing to do with buying horses. Two weeks was a very short time in which to have come to this momentous decision, an almost laughably short time in fact, but he would be requesting permission to pay his addresses in form, not whisk Celia Mardham down the aisle within the week by means of a special licence.

However, he had refused to believe his own feelings, and had resolutely set his sights upon Miss Burton. That young lady did not, thankfully, appear bowled over by him, but might rightly think herself slighted if he abandoned her now. Celia Mardham was hurt by his pursuit of her friend, as her outburst today had proved, and the last thing in the world he wanted to do was cause her unhappiness. In the beginning he had told himself that marrying a beautiful girl with money that would save the family pile was perfectly in order, even if he did not love her, since he was not in love with anyone else. Now he was in love with somebody else. Was his happiness worth setting at nought for the sake of his profligate sire, and the ancestors in the family vault? More importantly, was Celia Mardham's? If he was not sure of the answer to the first question, he was perfectly clear about the answer to the second. After all, he had promised his spendthrift parent that he would see if he and Miss Burton would suit, and no more. Well, they would not. If he put aside family duty – and it was easier to say than do – then before he made his feelings obvious to Miss Mardham he had to disengage from Miss Burton in such a way that it seemed a natural and gradual step, not some random breach. Women were complicated beings and he wished for a moment that they were more like men. Then he could have simply gone to the one and then the other and explained he had made a perfectly honest mistake. Had they been men, though, he would not be in this situation at all. He would sleep on it.

In fact he lay awake much of the night, and when he dozed, his dreams were tangled.

CHAPTER TWELVE

'The old man in the village' was perfectly correct. The next day dawned with every sign of being a perfect September day. Dew spangled the cobwebs on the shrubbery, and a cock pheasant stalked boldly across the lawn. When the maid opened Celia's curtains, Celia sighed. She wished it was raining. For all Lord Levedale's advice, she foresaw embarrassment and being patronised. If she did not shoot well, there would plaudits for having 'done ever so well, considering'. 'Considering' was one of those words she had come to hate.

She came down to breakfast a little before Sarah, who had become even more quiet over the last couple of days, and appeared preoccupied. Lords Deben and Levedale were in the breakfast parlour, where their natural male preference for few words over the repast lay trampled in the dust by Miss Darwen's unstoppable conversation. They both cast Celia looks of desperation, but she could not think of any way in which she might help them. She advanced into the room. Miss Darwen was in the act of pouring herself a third cup of coffee.

The idea hit Celia like a bolt of lightning. It was reprehensible in the extreme, but it might save the gentlemen. She contrived to stumble a little as she passed Miss Darwen's chair, and grabbed the back of of it, pulling it so that Miss Darwen was pouring coffee not into her cup but onto the table and thence onto her skirt. She exclaimed, and rose quickly, shaking her skirts to avoid the hot liquid penetrating her petticoats, and with a furious reprimand to Celia upon being so clumsy. She nearly toppled Celia properly as she did so, and Lord Deben, who was the nearer of the gentlemen, leapt up to prevent her falling.

'I am quite all right, thank you, my lord,' declared Celia, and there was the tiniest hint of a smile in her eyes. Lord Levedale noted it, and knew what she had done.

'You are alright? It is I who have suffered, and yours is the fault! I will have to change my gown, and, oh, it is soaking into my . . . person.' Miss Darwen was outraged. 'How could you be so clumsy, even you?' She threw down her napkin with which she had been dabbing at the brown stain, and almost ran from the room.

'You are a wicked young woman, Miss Mardham,' murmured Lord Levedale, with a slow smile.

'It was the only thing I could think of that would

rescue you and Lord Deben, my lord.' Celia was all wide-eyed innocence.

'"Rescue"?' Lord Deben caught on. 'Oh, I should dashed well say you have, Miss Mardham. And put yourself at risk to boot. A heroine is what I would call you. That . . . woman, had been going on and on and on from the moment she walked in. Quite put a fellow off his breakfast.'

'You see, sir? Lord Deben appreciates me.' She was looking at Lord Levedale, and dimpled.

He laughed, and the smile lengthened, and sparkled in his eyes, but his words were gently chastising.

'All very well, Miss Mardham, but you did put yourself at risk, and for what? If you had fallen, you might have been hurt.'

'Life is full of "ifs", sir,' she lifted her chin, and challenged him, 'and "if" we never risked anything we might as well be put in the family vault anyway.'

'Bravely said, Miss Mardham,' applauded Lord Deben.

'Some things are worth a risk, I will agree, but all you did was save two bachelors from a ruined breakfast.'

'All? Well, in my case I was nearly ready to jump out of the window.' Lord Deben sought to lighten the seriousness.

'But we are on the ground floor, and you would have merely landed in the flower bed, three feet from the window ledge, my lord.' Celia giggled.

'Might have landed in a spiky plant, rose bush, that

sort of thing. So you definitely saved me, ma'am.' He grinned.

'And the only "award" we can make you is to offer you a cup of coffee. May I pour one for you, Miss Mardham?' Lord Levedale's eyes had not left her.

'You may, sir, as long as you do not spill it.'

It was nearly eleven o'clock when the two straw butts were dragged into position, and the targets secured to them with hazel thatching pins. Miss Darwen, who had been forced to change her raiment even down to her corsetry, was in no mood to 'take prisoners', as Lord Pocklington remarked with a shudder. Her lips were tightly compressed, which Lord Deben said was at least one advantage, though, he added, the looks she gave Miss Mardham made the arrows look like 'blunts'.

Chairs were brought out so that Lord and Lady Mardham, and those others not competing, might watch in the manner of some mediaeval competition. A chair was also brought out for Celia, and Lord Levedale saw that it had no arms to it. She glanced at him, and her look warned him to keep the secret.

'We ought to draw lots to see who is matched? There are eight of us so . . .' Miss Darwen was already taking charge. Somehow it seemed less irritating to let her get on with it.

'Nine,' announced Celia.

'You? You cannot take part,' Miss Darwen snorted.

'I can. I will do so from a chair.'

'Well, that gives you an advantage.'

'In what way, Miss Darwen?' Lord Levedale had opened his mouth to speak, but it was Lord Deben who voiced the question first.

'Well, it is . . . obvious.'

'Not to me. Explain.' Lord Deben, who had been most certainly terrified of Miss Darwen for a fortnight, appeared to have overcome his dread of her quite suddenly. Lord Levedale wondered if the coffee incident had been the catalyst. Sarah Clandon's eyes widened, and she smiled.

'Er . . . she will have a more stable position from which to draw the bow and loose her arrows.'

'But the chair is limiting in the drawing of the bow,' interjected Lord Levedale, keen to show that Deben was not alone.

'And besides,' Miss Darwen ignored him, 'it makes the numbers uneven. We cannot have nine.'

'Oh, for Goodness' sake, I will make the tenth,' declared Mr Wombwell, already bored with the proceedings.

'Thank you, Mr Wombwell.' Celia nodded her thanks.

'Anything to oblige, Miss Mardham, and to get things moving.'

As a hint, it failed. Miss Darwen had to make out tickets with the names of the contestants, and have Lord Mardham draw them from a basket.

'Mr Mardham shoots against Sir Marcus, Lord Deben against Lord Pocklington, Lord Levedale against Miss

Clandon, Mr Wombwell against Miss Mardham, and I take on Miss Burton.' Miss Darwen's smirk made it clear she might as well have a walkover.

In this instance, she was right. Miss Burton, who had to be assisted to nock her arrows, and who could not draw her bow to its capacity, dropped short of the target three times, missed once, hit it twice near the edge, and managed to get one arrow into Miss Darwen's target. Her final shot was, however, close to the bull, and she was delighted.

'Back to ribbons for me, I think,' she gurgled, and made a pretty curtsey to Lord and Lady Mardham. It was agreed by everyone except Miss Darwen, that she had entered into the spirit of the event, and tried hard.

The gentlemen removed their coats so as not to constrict their movement, or indeed, split the seams.

Lord Deben rather unexpectedly beat the sports-mad Lord Pocklington, who took his defeat in good part. He clapped his friend warmly upon the back, and suggested, with a grin, that as Deben was the shorter, he had a lower centre of gravity and was thus obviously a better design for an archer.

Mr Wombwell lost to Miss Mardham, and was not helped by his mama sitting with her hands over her eyes, fingers barely parted, and gasping every time he loosed an arrow. Lord Deben whispered to Miss Clandon that the last person he was likely to hit was himself, so her maternal nerves were pointless. By the same token, however, it did not help Miss Mardham that Sir Marcus sighed heavily every time she nocked her arrow.

Richard Mardham was a far better shot than Sir Marcus, but that gentleman was still suffering from the shock of Miss Mardham taking part. He was quite glad to step down because he could then sit by Celia and, with a mixture of entreaty and command, try and make her see that to have proved her point was foolish but noble, and that to 'risk permanent injury' by taking part in later rounds was 'unthinkable'.

To this, Celia, white-lipped with anger, answered that unless the chair was likely to collapse beneath her there was no likelihood of injury, and that she had every intention of remaining in the competition until defeated by a better archer.

Lord Levedale had watched the other participants, and although he had never handled a bow before, he made a fair attempt, with one shot falling wide and short, but all the others at least hitting the butt, and three of those in the inner, and one in the bull. Miss Clandon scored very highly, to Lord Deben's delight, and Miss Darwen's surprised annoyance. Lord Levedale made the error, however, of trying a little too hard with his draw, and extending his left arm so that it slightly everted, and the bowstring caught him smartly down the inner part of the arm. He winced.

'That will mark me as the novice idiot,' he murmured, and rubbed his arm.

'Is it bruising, my lord?' enquired Celia, with concern.

He rolled up the sleeve to the elbow, revealing a pale

forearm already disfiguring with a dark purple bruise.

'Oh dear. I ought to have warned you about that. It is an easy mistake to make.'

'Indeed you ought, Miss Mardham.'

She beckoned a servant, and sent them away to bring witch hazel and a cloth. When they returned she bade Lord Levedale present the forearm and bathed the bruise with the witch hazel.

'It will help the bruise come out, my lord.'

'It appears to be doing that pretty well without assistance, ma'am.' He was watching her dabbing tenderly at his arm, and was very aware of her touch. It made the discomfort worthwhile.

'You must keep this bottle and apply the tincture before retiring, and as far up the arm as the bruising occurs, sir.'

'Yes, Doctor.'

'There. That will suffice for the present. You may roll down your sleeve.' Celia thought that sounding calm and medical would prevent him noticing that her fingers trembled very slightly. It did not.

It was only now that Miss Darwen realised that the field of ten had become five.

'An ideal opportunity for you to retire, Miss Mardham,' whispered Sir Marcus, close to her left ear. She shook her head, and he sighed.

'We can either each take three arrows and compete against the others in turn, or one person gets a bye.' Miss Darwen disliked the latter idea, and was relieved when the more complicated plan was adopted. She did end up 'confused', as she claimed, declaring, with a simper, that she had won, and Miss Clandon was shown at the bottom of the table, when in fact of all the archers, it was Miss Clandon who had not lost a round.

'You must have your board upside down, Miss Darwen.' Lord Deben did not sound as if he believed that at all. He was a such a good-natured fellow that to hear him with an edge to his voice was most disconcerting. 'I think you will find that in fact, Miss Clandon is the champion.' He glanced at Sarah Clandon, and his look held admiration, and more.

'I am not sure . . . perhaps . . . oh yes, an easy mistake.' Miss Darwen could have taken up her bow and committed an act of violence, although she was not quite sure whether she wished first to shoot Lord Deben or Miss Clandon.

'Well,' Lord Mardham rose, and extended his hand to Sarah, 'we ought to have a prize.'

'As long as it is not this bottle of witch hazel,' murmured Lord Levedale, and winked at Miss Mardham.

Lord Deben stepped forward with a rose, held cautiously, and presented it to Lord Mardham with a bow, in the manner of a herald.

'The prize, my liege.'

'Excellent. Then here is your prize, Miss Clandon, as the best archer in the Meysey tournament.' He presented it with as much of a flourish as Lord Deben. Sarah blushed, and mumbled something about 'luck'.

'Oh yes. That last shot against Mr Mardham was a fluke, to be sure.' Miss Darwen sounded as sour as she looked. She was ignored.

Lord Mardham might hand her the rose, but Sarah had eyes only for the gentleman who had thought to pick it for her. Lady Mardham frowned, and suggested that they now all adjourn indoors and make ready for a light luncheon 'to celebrate'. Lord Mardham then had the idea that Sarah should, as victor, or rather victrix, take the seat of the lady of the house at the head of the table. His lady, he declared, would happily vacate the place on this occasion. Whether happy about it or not, Lady Mardham did as he wished, and a highly embarrassed Sarah took 'the seat of honour'. Perhaps embarrassment was the reason for her lack of appetite, or at least that was what Lady Mardham hoped.

As soon as the meal was ended, Sarah took her 'prize' upstairs to put in a glass of water, although she had every intention of pressing it upon the morrow. Then, whilst the others went back into the garden, Celia with Sir Marcus hovering about her to her great agitation, she sought the privacy of the book room and attempted to write a letter. There she sat with steepled fingers, gazing at a Meissen group upon the mantelshelf. It depicted a shepherdess, lamb and crook in her hands, and with a lovelorn shepherd at her feet. The pragmatic Sarah disliked the piece, because the shepherdess was dressed in a gown decked in knots of ribbon and wore an ornate hat, and the shepherd was in a blue coat with gold buttons, and very white stockings that would have been suitable garb for a ball, thirty years past. It did, however, have relevance to her cogitations.

Sarah was unsure what to do. Had her mama been on hand it would have been so much easier, but although she attempted to write to her understanding parent, everything Sarah wrote came out in a jumble and was cast into the hearth. Lord Deben was not, she conceded, as intelligent as Lord Levedale, as handsome as Mr Wombwell, or as athletic as Lord Pocklington. He was, however, worth more than the combination of all three in her very humble opinion. There was a kindness to him that lit him from within, and when he smiled at her, Sarah felt warmed by the light of it.

She had told herself, repeatedly, that his thoughtfulness was exhibited to all the young ladies, and that her own predisposition towards him was making her feel that there was some indeterminate but wonderful connection that was lacking in his relations with Cousin Celia, and Marianne. He had undoubtedly been bowled over by Marianne's beauty upon first meeting her, but Sarah did not blame him for that in the least. What man could not fail to be struck by such a staggeringly attractive young woman? And yet . . . she smiled to herself at the recollection of how, when the other young men had been vying to attract the attentions of Marianne Burton, Lord Deben had held back, had made sure that she and Cousin Celia were not left as mere bystanders. He treated her cousin as he would a sister. Was she fanciful to think that he did not treat her in quite the same manner? There were times when their eyes met, and then her insides performed strange revolutions, in a nice way. The last few days she was sure he had been watching her, and today . . . He had thought of the rose, he had stood up to Miss Darwen to make sure that she, Sarah Clandon, was acknowledged as the winner, and he appeared more delighted than if he had won the competition himself. There was even the tiniest suggestion that he had sent one of his own arrows a little astray in the final round, knowing that if he won they would be equal, and would need to shoot again. Was it fanciful to think he did not want to beat her, or make her think he let her win?

'Perhaps I am imagining it. I must be imagining it.' Sarah chided herself, and put away pen and paper with a sigh.

Lady Mardham entered the room to collect a list which she just knew she had left in the drawer of the escritoire, just as she had previously known it must be by the clock in the green saloon, and before that within the pages of the book that she was endeavouring to enjoy because her friends did so.

'Sarah dear, whatever are you doing here? I had thought you would be upon the terrace with the other young people. Have you a headache?'

'No, no, ma'am, I assure you I have not. It is just . . .' Sarah did what she thought best, and confided in Lady

Mardham, since she must stand in loco parentis during her visit.

Lady Mardham listened in horror as her recent suspicions were confirmed. Lord Deben had not figured at all in her plans for Celia, but that he should show any inclination towards Cousin Cora's dab of a daughter was unthinkable. How would it look if Sarah Clandon emerged from this sojourn with her relations with the likelihood of an offer, whilst Celia's hand remained unsought? It was too, too shaming.

'Are you sure, my dear? You are, after all, inexperienced, innocent. You might easily misconstrue mere polite attentions for something . . . something else.'

'Yes, ma'am. That is why I am so confused. I am persuaded there is more, but realise that I am ignorant of so much. Do I let him see that I am not indifferent to him, or . . .'

'You must not put yourself forward, my dear child. That would be ruinous. Might I suggest you continue as you have thus far, and let me see for myself how he behaves. I stand as your dear mama would, in her absence, and would not wish you to overstep the mark, however innocently.'

'I will willingly be guided by you, dear ma'am.' Sarah smiled shyly, glad that the burden was at least shared.

'Then go and put on your spencer and join the others, there's a good girl. I will think upon this.'

The last phrase was heartfelt. As Sarah went away, Lady Mardham sat down and tried to calm her disordered nerves. If what the girl said had any basis in fact . . . no, she must be imagining it. She had no experience of men, could not tell . . . and yet . . .

Taking a deep breath, Lady Mardham got up and took the obvious course. She went in search of her husband.

'You will just have to write to Deben's father and tell him about the calamity about to befall. Tell him to warn Deben off, call him home or something.' Lady Mardham wafted her hands about in a vague gesture.

Lord Mardham's eyebrows rose in consternation.

'Write to Eskdale and tell him to . . . No, I most certainly will not. Good grief, can you imagine what he would think? After all, we invited the girl to stay with us. How can we then say she is beneath Deben's touch? Besides, Clandon might be a younger son, but his birth is good, and Deben cannot be in need of a rich wife. He is also, by the by, of age, so Eskdale could not stop him marrying whomsoever he wishes.' He paused, and said, gently, 'It strikes me that whilst no great match, it would be perfectly acceptable, my dear.'

'Perfectly acceptable to Cora Clandon,' snorted Lady Mardham. 'Absolutely! Can you not see how she must gloat over that . . . that Nothing of a daughter . . . catching the heir to an earldom, when our poor, poor Celia remains upon the shelf.'

'Never saw your cousin as the gloating sort. She might fall upon your neck with gratitude, but gloat? No, she would not do so.'

'So you will do nothing?'

'I will do nothing, other than give the chit my heartiest congratulations if the the thing comes off.' Lord Mardham did not shout or bluster, but his wife knew when he would not be moved upon a subject.

'And see me, and our poor dear Celia, the laughing stock of the county,' Lady Mardham sniffed, turned on her heel, and stalked out.

She considered writing to Lady Eskdale herself, but some of what her lord had said made painful sense. Lady Eskdale, with whom she was not upon more than nodding terms, might well wonder why the Clandon girl had been invited to Meysey at all. She could not be told it was to provide Celia with company without rivalry.

The problem remained uppermost in Lady Mardham's mind all through dinner, where she took especial notice of Lord Deben's manner towards both Sarah and the other young ladies. He was sat next to Celia this evening, and was unfailingly polite and entertaining, but Lady Mardham noted with disquiet that when he had cause to look across the table his eyes dwelt a little too long upon The Poor Relation.

When she retired for the night, she instructed her maid to plump up her pillows, so that she might 'have a thinking night'. Lady Mardham was convinced that her very best plans and ideas always came to her propped up in bed. She ignored the fact that it had been one such nocturnal cogitation which decided her upon having the morning room repapered in lilac and fuchsia stripes. The result had not been happy, and had involved a positive explosion of ire from her lord, and the removal of every very expensive sheet of it just in time for the arrival of the matching curtains.

Lady Mardham was not an unfeeling or unpleasant woman, but she was one with very strict priorities. At the top of her list came herself, followed by her son, her daughter, and then her husband. Whilst her conscience pricked her over the course of action she was about to take, she solaced herself with thought that it was best for Celia, and of course for herself, and that she would not have had to take the step had her spouse not been peculiarly unhelpful.

CHAPTER THIRTEEN

Although she usually broke her fast in the comfort of her bed, Lady Mardham presented herself for breakfast, much to the amazement of the senior footman, who almost dropped a chafing dish of mushrooms. Mr Richard Mardham choked over his coffee, and had to be patted firmly upon the back by Lord Pocklington.

Lady Mardham cast him a mildly reproving look, and graciously partook of tea, toast, and a coddled egg. Her presence had a damping effect upon the conversation of the gentlemen, who had addressed their appetites in suitable silence, but thereafter had been arguing good-naturedly over the likeliest spots to provide good sport with a twelve bore. Her ladyship appeared impervious to the change in atmosphere, however, and sat in regal state, embarrassing her son further by chastising him for attempting to drink his coffee when it was patently too hot.

He cast the other men a look of apology. At least they all possessed, or had possessed, mothers, and would understand that mothers always treated one as if still in short coats. He would rather scald his mouth than linger in the breakfast parlour with his parent. Shortly thereafter he rose, and made his excuses, which signalled the others that breakfast was over.

Lady Mardham sat quietly to await the young ladies. She wanted to speak with Sarah before she encountered Lord Deben, and this guaranteed it. In fact Sarah entered before any of the others, for she did not feel very sociable just at present. She stopped upon the threshold, seeing Lady Mardham, and made a small 'oh' sound as she gave a little curtsey and bade her hostess good morning. She was aware of an agitated feeling in her stomach.

'Good morning, my dear. A fine morning, is it not? I am so glad you are up betimes, for I wished to have some private word with you, upon the subject we discussed yesterday.'

Sarah wondered why Lady Mardham was not more open, since they were alone.

'Yes, ma'am.' Sarah came and sat, which at least prevented her knees from knocking.

'Now, I paid particular attention to Lord Deben's manner last evening, as I said I would. You were so very right to consult me, my dear child, before opening yourself to an awkwardness.'

Sarah's heart sank.

'I see, ma'am.'

'I do not blame you in the slightest, for you have nobody with whose manner you might compare Lord Deben's, other than the gentlemen here at present. He is the most considerate of others, which is very taking, and I can quite see that his ability to make one feel the only focus of his thoughts when he converses with one could lead to . . . a misapprehension. However, I observed him talking to poor Celia, and to Mrs Wombwell, and he was attentive, in the nicest of ways, to each. What you must do, my dear, is keep a hold upon your natural inclination in his direction, lest you place yourself in a difficult situation, and expose the both of you to acute embarrassment. I do not, of course, say that you should refuse to converse with him. In so small a gathering that would be both rude and obvious. You must simply behave circumspectly, and whatever you do, do not wear your youthful heart upon your sleeve.'

'Thank you, ma'am. I did not see, could not see, things in the wider context as you do. I am sadly ignorant.' Sarah could suddenly not face food. 'If you will excuse me, Lady Mardham.'

She got up, gave a tight smile, and withdrew. Only when she had closed the door behind her did she take a deep breath to hold in her tears, and rush up the stairs to the privacy of her bedchamber.

Lady Mardham regarded a half-eaten slice of toast accusingly, and sighed. It was for the best, but there was a twinge of guilt.

Sir Marcus Cotgrave had spent a troubled night. Miss Mardham's wilfulness troubled him greatly, and a small voice in his head warned him that although suitably youthful, she possessed a steeliness of character that would not make her the sort of wife he wanted, one who would defer to him in all things, be guided by him in all things. Despite this, her physical deformity, which was so unsightly, made him feel the need to protect her all the more. She was not capable of looking after herself, and her 'outbursts of independence' must be the result of her not being given the security of constant supervision and care. Yes, that was it. He must not be put off from his intention, which would make him happy, and keep her safe. Just thinking of the things she had undertaken since his arrival made his blood run cold. She had attempted to walk, outside, and over treacherously riven flagstones, without human support; she was risking life and limb each time she went out for those terrible driving lessons, and to cap it all, she had tried to join in an activity as if she were in some way a normal young woman. Her self-delusion was dangerous, but increased his pity for her. Given firm but gentle control, once taught to depend, he could make her safe, and she would come to dote upon him in gratitude.

This more rosy, and entirely fictitious, picture enabled him to finally fall asleep.

The morning began bright, but there were leaden clouds to the west, and the air was oppressive. A thunderstorm might be in the offing later. Sir Marcus rehearsed his declaration three times before his mirror, and then went to enjoy a late breakfast, ready to propose as soon as he could find Miss Mardham alone.

For a lady who could not move about with any ease, she proved remarkably elusive, and he eventually found her, unexpectedly, in the library, actually reaching up upon one tiptoe to select a volume.

'Miss Mardham!'

His sudden exclamation nearly made her fall over from shock.

'Goodness, Sir Marcus, how you surp—' Celia got no further. Sir Marcus had trod swiftly across the room, taken the book from her hand, and laid it upon a table.

'You must not. You cannot. Dear Miss Mardham, you appear dangerously unaware of the risks you run.' He dropped to one knee, with a slight grimace. 'I offer myself to you as guide, devoted always to your welfare, conscious always of your limitations. I will keep you from harm, teach you to accept the life that lies before you, enfold you in a love that protects.'

Celia was appalled, not only by the act of his proposal but by the picture he drew of what he could 'offer' her.

'I beg you will get up, Sir Marcus,' she managed, in a constricted voice.

'When you have said yes,' he declared.

'Then I fear you will miss dinner, sir.' He was genuine, which was in some ways the most frightening aspect of all, and to refuse him baldly smacked of being ungracious, but he had proved amazingly impervious to hints.

He blinked, not understanding. It occurred to her that Lord Levedale would have comprehended her in a heartbeat. Imagining Lord Levedale upon one knee brought colour back into her white cheeks.

'Give me your answer first, my dear.'

'My answer, Sir Marcus, is no, and I am not, and will never be your "dear". We should not suit, sir, I assure you. I am conscious of . . .'

'No. You are not conscious of so many things, my child. You do not see, from the ignorance of youth, the dangers and pitfalls about you. You have to marry me.'

'I most certainly do not.' She was now not so much stunned as flustered. 'What you offer me is a cage, a box as close as a coffin. I cannot and will not live my life that way. It is far better to take "risks" as you see them, than exist like that. Please, I beg of you, get up, and we will forget this unfortunate interchange ever took place. I wish you well, Sir Marcus, and life for you would not be well if I shared it with you.' She gripped her stick with both hands, not so much to steady herself as keep her hands from trembling

He looked at her in disbelief. She was refusing him. Even as this sunk in, the small voice in his head heaved a sigh of relief. Slowly, he got up, and dusted the knee of his trousers.

'I think you are mistaken,' he said gravely, but with a crack in his certainty. 'However, an offer is an offer, just that, not a demand.' This, from the man who had just said that she 'had' to marry him. 'I am sorry, sorry that you do not see a future with me, and sorry that I have unsettled you by my protestations.'

'You will be thankful later, Sir Marcus.' Celia controlled herself, and sounded calm again.

His response was a twisted smile and a bow, and then he withdrew. Celia sat heavily upon the nearest chair. She had just received a proposal of marriage, and rejected it. It was without doubt the right decision, but it was a momentous event nonetheless. It took her some minutes for her heartbeat to slow, and for her to feel able to face the world impassively.

Celia had no wish to reveal to her mama that she had refused Sir Marcus. She could imagine the peal that would be rung over her for her short-sightedness. Having created the situation whereby she might receive an offer, it would sound churlish to say that she had turned one down. Any offer should be grasped and clutched to her bosom, she had no doubt, and the 'excuse' that the man drove her to distraction would cut no ice.

In fact, Lady Mardham knew. She encountered Sir Marcus shortly after his declaration, and he revealed, without actually saying he had asked, and been rejected, that he had been 'hoping for too much in a certain direction'. It had put Lady Mardham on the spot, because she could neither console him with the thought that 'there were other fish in the sea', having waved her daughter as a 'fish', nor tell him, being a polite hostess, that he had ruined his own chances. She was honest enough to admit that was the case. Whenever she had seen him with Celia his attentiveness had been suffocating, and his attitude one of 'I know best in all things'. It was not surprising poor Celia had turned him down, in the circumstances. Lady Mardham was actually more annoyed with him than her daughter.

It was a nasty shock for Celia when her mama encountered her in the hall, and almost dragged her into the Small Saloon, opening the conversation with the phrase 'I understand, my poor child.'

'Mama?'

'Sir Marcus. I blame him, yes, I do. Had he set about it like a man of sense . . . but there. No point in crying over spilt milk. What is done is done, and, looking at it calmly, he has proved himself unsuitable.'

Celia now understood, but her brain reeled. She wondered if Sir Marcus had gone to her mama and complained about her refusal. She would not put it past him.

'We have to be positive, however,' continued Mama. 'There is still a chance that you will get the inheritance, and I quite see that he is much more likely to appeal to a young girl. He has pretty manners, and is prepossessing, in a lanky sort of way. You will just have to do all you can, my dear.'

'"He", Mama?' Celia knew, but feigned ignorance. It might be safer.

'Levedale, of course. What other reason might he have to teach you to drive and go to all the trouble with the carriage and ponies, if he was not interested, at the very least?'

'He is a thoughtful gentleman,' offered Celia, by means of an explanation of his behaviour.

'He is a man. A "thoughtful gentleman" is one who warns one of the puddle as one descends from a carriage, not one who gives up hours of his time to sit with his knees about his ears in a vehicle I am almost ashamed we own, even for the use of the staff.'

Looked at in this way, Lord Levedale's actions did seem more particular, but Mama was obviously forgetting Marianne.

'Would you have me catch him in a net, like one of the trout they brought back?'

'I have often thought,' mused Lady Mardham, 'that it would actually be so much easier if one could.'

Celia laughed, just a little hysterically, because Mama was not speaking entirely in jest.

'Then I had best go and dress for my lesson, Mama, and conceal the landing net beneath my pelisse.'

Celia tried to look as if her morning had been nothing out of the ordinary when Lord Levedale gave her his arm as they walked out of the door. The little pony cart, with Pom between the shafts, stood in front of the house, awaiting their pleasure.

'May we go and visit my grandmother at the Dower House this morning, sir? If we take the lanes there and come back across the park it will be a decent run.' Celia thought she might just manage not to reveal her jumbled thoughts if part of the lesson time was taken up at the Dower House.

'Miss Mardham, behold merely the tutor, not the navigator. You know the locality and I do not.' Lord Levedale smiled, and assisted her up into the pony cart. 'Although I did say to your father that we would be within the bounds of the park, for propriety's sake, and we are thus breaking the rules.'

'The lanes of which I speak are most unfrequented, and if by chance we encounter a flock of sheep and a shepherd, well, we brazen it out.'

'Behold me brazen, ma'am, and I bow to your knowledge of little-used thoroughfares.' He was grinning. He had no reason to feel in improved spirits, but somehow he did.

'How very trusting of you, my lord.' She laughed, and the groom at the pony's head looked up, not having heard her do so for so very long. 'I was glad to see at your first encounter that you refused to be overawed by my grandmama. She is very autocratic, but in fact dislikes what she terms "human rugs", those who let others "walk all over them".'

'I shall be very brave once more, ma'am, however frightening your relative might be. Behold, I do not shake at all, look.' He held out his gloved hands, and then made them tremble very theatrically. 'Oh dear, there goes my heroic status.'

'My lord, fear not. I think teaching me to drive, and risking me toppling you into a ditch, is heroic enough.'

'At no stage have you threatened to do so, though there was that incident with the gateway. I would have to say that, overall, a more able pupil one could not wish to find. It is only a pity that circumstance means you really ought not to drive a high perch phaeton, for you would manage a pair very well, and look splendid tooling it about the countryside.'

'This is more practical, and . . . how I look is no longer of any consequence.' The smile became lopsided, as she requested the groom to stand away from the pony's head and she told Pom to 'walk on'.

For a few minutes there was silence. Miss Mardham concentrated upon her driving, and his lordship simply did not know what he might say. Telling her that he thought her the most beautiful of creatures, however true, could easily be taken as cruel falsehood, or presuming too much.

The clouds were building in the west, and by the afternoon it would be stultifying, but at the moment there was just breeze enough to play with the wide brim of Miss Mardham's fetching straw hat and the scrap of veiling that kept any glare from her eyes.

He stole glances at her profile as often as he might without discovery. Her lips were slightly parted, her brows drawn together a little in concentration as she negotiated a bend and passed a farm cart. When she forgot her infirmity her whole being changed, and he could see the young woman that would have been, that still could be, if only she had the confidence that came from being cherished and loved. He loved her, he was certain of it, and perhaps it was that certainty which cheered him this morning. He loved her, wanted to cherish her, but everything was in a damned muddle.

He had made his mind up with regards to the family estates, and had determined to write to his father, but that was only a part of the problem. He still had to sort out matters with Miss Burton, and had no idea how to begin. He had also realised that his own financial situation, whilst sound, was not one where he was wallowing in capital. He had not had an allowance from his parent in several years, Lord Curborough having decided that he could live off the portion left to him at his mama's demise and the small property in Devon, and so his sire's indebtedness had not affected him in that way. He could live off his income, for his tastes were not extravagant, but it had struck him that going before Lord Mardham and offering for his daughter's hand with little more than five thousand a year would not make his suit instantly appealing. The idea that receiving any offer for Celia's hand might be greeted with boundless relief did not occur to him.

The rhythmic sound of shod hooves trotting along at a smart pace, filled Celia with a disproportionate degree of delight. She felt free, and the presence of Lord Levedale at her side, so close that sometimes as they turned a corner they came into contact, lifted her spirits even higher. Sir Marcus was forgotten.

'I fear Grandmama will decry this as a mediocre vehicle, but I could not be more pleased with it, you know.'

'It would be the better for a new livery, but it is neat enough, Miss Mardham, I assure you, on a temporary basis.'

'Yes, but Grandmama only ever goes out and about in a large old carriage with a team of four, regardless of the length of her journey. She will sniff at having a single pony.'

'I think she will be very impressed that you drive, Miss Mardham, and see that it is well suited to its purpose, and also safe. She would not want you driving something liable to topple over at the slightest inequality in the road.'

'You really mean at the slightest error on the part of the driver,' commented Miss Mardham, at that moment catching the thong of her whip in excellent manner.

He laughed, and made his denial.

The Dower House was some four miles from Meysey by road, and approached by a short curving driveway that revealed the house quite suddenly. The pony cart drew up before the front of the house. Lord Levedale got down and, quite without thinking, offered up his hands to take Miss Mardham by the waist and lift her down. She blushed, and wavered for a moment, before setting her hands lightly on his shoulders and permitting him to do so. He then took her stick from its restraint and handed it to her, whilst also offering his arm as though he were a beau offering to take her for a walk in the park.

The Dowager Lady Mardham was not an openly demonstrative person, but she was not unfeeling. She had not made a scene when she had found her husband was being unfaithful to her with a Bath courtesan, even as she was carrying his heir, and had been publicly tolerant of his behaviour thereafter; she was fond of her son, though never unwilling to tell him where he fell short, and she was deeply attached to her grandchildren, especially Celia. The child had frequently stayed with her during the school holidays when her parents were, in old Lady Mardham's words, 'gallivanting'. Not even her ladyship's long-serving maid knew how many tears had been shed when Celia, for whom she had the highest hopes, had suffered her life-threatening accident. Grandmama would not show pity, and some might have thought her comments bracing, but she always looked straight at her granddaughter, never fussed about her, and treated her like a normal girl.

When Chorley announced Celia and Lord Levedale, her ladyship, who had been nodding over some embroidery that was straining her eyes, looked up and gave that straight look.

The change in Celia took her quite by surprise. She had watched her bright and bubbly granddaughter become introverted and serious, but here was a girl much more like her old self. It did not take a woman as astute as Lady Mardham to see the reason. She had wondered, the first time they had come to see her, and now there was little doubt at all. The elderly lady surveyed Lord Levedale with her hawklike eyes, and saw his lips twitch. So he knew he was under scrutiny, did he? Impudent rascal.

'I have driven all the way here, Grandmama, and not cast Lord Levedale into a single ditch.' Celia sounded confident again.

'Driven? Yourself?'

'Yes, Grandmama. Lord Levedale has been teaching me, and Papa has ordered a low phaeton, from Gloucester and specially designed, for my birthday.'

'Has he, indeed. And you are going to tell me that my son, your father, who could not draw a daisy without it looking like an oak tree, spent hours upon this "design"?'

'No, no, Grandmama. Lord Levedale has designed it.'

'Really?' Lady Mardham stared at the viscount. 'So, young man, having designed a phaeton, you have been junketing about the countryside teaching my granddaughter how to drive. Why?'

The old woman was certainly direct. Lord Levedale did not as much as blink, but gave her stare for stare.

'Because, ma'am, many of the freedoms of movement we take for granted have been tragically lost to her, and it is a way in which she can reclaim her rightful independence.'

'Hmmm, sounds very noble. Are you very noble?'

'I hope, ma'am, that I am a decent sort of fellow. I claim no great nobility of character, however, for that would mark me as puffed up in my own esteem, and it would also imply that teaching Miss Mardham has been some form of chore, which it has not.'

It was Lady Mardham's turn to hide a smile.

'Grandmama, if you come to the window you can see the pony cart in which I drove here.' Celia thought exposing Lord Levedale to too much interrogation was a poor recompense for his kindness.

'Pony cart? What sort of vehicle is that for a young lady? More suited to a feckless curate.' Grandmama was not impressed.

'It is a safe sort of vehicle, and one into which Miss Mardham may climb without excessive difficulty, since it is one provided with two mounting steps,' Lord Levedale interjected before Miss Mardham could respond, and threw her a smiling glance. It was very brief, but Lady Mardham saw all that it contained. It confirmed her suspicions and delighted her, for, like everyone else, she had assumed Celia stood no chance of receiving an offer, and however poor her eyesight had

213

become, she could still tell a man in love. She walked, slowly, but very erect, to the window, where she could see Pom being made a fuss of by the stable lad.

'Good Heavens! You were on a public road in that contraption?' Her eyes widened.

'We did but pass a farm cart, ma'am, and no doubt the farmer thought we were locals on the way to . . . somewhere.' Lord Levedale made it sound unimportant.

'Tell me, Lord Levedale, have you seen many "locals" in driving coats with four capes?' Her ladyship raised a sceptical eyebrow.

'Er, no, ma'am, I have not.' He had the grace to smile, wryly. 'You have me there.'

'Of course I do. The quicker this fancy vehicle is purchased, and decent cattle to pull it, the better. Look at that pony.'

They looked at Pom, for whom they had developed a soft spot, since to each he meant the time they had alone together.

'He is a nice pony, Grandmama.'

'He is fat.'

'Not as fat as he was before the lessons, Lady Mardham.'

'Stop trying to be clever, young man.' The old lady turned to Celia. 'So what are you going to do when you can take yourself about the shire at whim, miss?'

'I am coming to visit you, most frequently, Grandmama.'

'Hmmm, do not come over meek as a nun's hen to

me, Celia. What is the real reason for these lessons.'

'To enable me to be free; to be able to move without a hobble, and still be in control; to be with horses again; to get out in the fresh air and . . . everything.'

'Comprehensive, I grant you.' Lady Mardham's voice softened. 'You have coped very well, child. You deserve some happiness.'

Lord Levedale wondered if the sagacious old lady was talking about driving at all, but she did not look at him, or indicate it by as much as the movement of a muscle. Lady Mardham was far too clever for that.

Celia, still imagining trotting about in the fresh air, took the statement at face value.

'I have never been one who thought that happiness was dealt out on the basis of deserving it. That is a good thing, since I would otherwise have wondered what heinous crimes I had inadvertently committed to deserve my fate. There are bad people who live long and seemingly happy lives being bad, and good people whose lives are a succession of disasters. The vicar may have an explanation for it, but I simply accept that it is so.'

'Which is rather a lot of philosophy for a casual visit,' remarked Lord Levedale, and once again their eyes met, and held.

Grandmama decided that if Celia was going to 'visit frequently' it would not long be from the other side of the park.

* * *

Upon the return journey Celia was rather quieter, though being within the park she had no reason to be concentrating harder upon her driving.

'A penny for them, Miss Mardham.' Lord Levedale looked at her. It was a pleasant thing to do.

'Oh, I was just thinking what a strange day it was, sir.'

'And we have not as yet gone much past noon. This implies either that you have found driving to be strange or . . . I am prying, and I ought not to do so. My apologies.'

'It is not the driving, my lord. Just that something particular happened . . . earlier.'

'He made you an offer, did he?' Lord Levedale sounded quite calm. Had she accepted, this morning would have felt quite different.

Celia was so surprised that she dropped her hands, and Pom obediently, but with some reluctance, broke into a canter.

'Look to your horse, Miss Mardham,' recommended Lord Levedale, evenly.

'But how could you know?' Celia brought Pom back to the trot.

'My dear Miss Mardham, I make no claim whatsoever to understand the fair sex, but I am quite able to "read" my own gender. Cotgrave has been working up to it from the moment he arrived.' He paused, and then continued. 'I cannot think why he believed you would suit each other.'

'Nor can I, my lord.' Celia responded with some vehemence, but then sighed. 'He meant well, I am sure, but I would far rather end my days a spinster than Lady Cotgrave. I would be . . . suffocated.'

If only . . . in other circumstances he could have told her, here and now, that he would not 'suffocate' her, but help her to do more, be more. He would encourage her, not, as he knew Cotgrave would have done, swaddle her with restrictions. He had overhead Sir Marcus at the archery competition, and wondered what sort of chump he must be to see that he was actually driving Miss Mardham to do the opposite of what he wanted by telling her what she must do.

Instead he could only smile, and suggest that she did not resign herself to a life of knotting fringes just yet.

CHAPTER FOURTEEN

Sir Marcus bore his rejection with a degree of calm disappointment. Celia Mardham was sufficiently similar to his much lamented wife that he had thought he might one day blend the two in his mind, despite Miss Mardham's obvious disability. It appealed to him to be the guardian of injured femininity, and he saw it as an important role, but in the end he accepted that the young lady disliked his care and attention. He missed his wife, but more than that he missed a woman in his life, a woman to 'be there' for him, run his house so that his housekeeper and cook did not bother him from week to week, a woman with whom he might find comfort and a little pleasure in the connubial couch. He liked pretty women, but he would prefer a young wife of average looks to an older one with looks but experience. He wanted no woman who might compare him with another man.

Having come to Meysey with the intention of securing a bride, he now found himself faced with returning to his empty house with no prospect of a new wife, or looking at another choice. Miss Darwen frightened him, and Miss Burton was clearly far too beautiful to look at a man old enough to be her father. Miss Mardham ought to have seen sense and realised that in her state she could not look to attract a young suitor, but she refused to admit this as surely as she refused to accept the limitations of her disability.

There was another option for him. Miss Clandon was uninspiring, but not ugly, she was quiet but not lacking in intelligence, and appeared pragmatic rather than romantic. He knew she had no prospects, and thus must be inclined to accept an offer from a gentleman who could offer her the elegancies of life, a house to oversee, and companionship. He resolved therefore, not to opine over what he might not have, but rather make a push for what still lay within his grasp.

Sarah had enough to deal with without Sir Marcus Cotgrave. She had cried, but then resolved to be a sensible girl. After all, she did not want to embarrass Lord Deben, for whom she retained the most tender feelings. It was her own silly fault, she told herself, for letting her own emotions sway her reading of his. Lady Mardham had saved her from making a terrible faux pas that would have seen Lord Deben lose any respect for her. She would remain friendly, but not give in to doing as she had in the past week, and looking at him frequently, or smiling to encourage him to sit with her, or letting herself imagine what it would be like to be sat very close to him, just the two of them, at liberty to talk of anything they wished.

At luncheon she toyed with the food upon her plate, still having little appetite, and sat on the same side of the table as he did, so that she might not inadvertently give in to gazing at him. She was still acutely aware of his presence.

For his part, Lord Deben thought Miss Clandon a little pale, and wondered if the excitement of the previous day had meant she had not slept well. Perhaps she had the headache? When she got up from the table, he looked at her, and she could not help but look at him. His spaniel eyes questioned, looked worried, and Sarah wanted nothing more than to burst into tears. Marianne however, wondered if she might come and turn the pages of her music for her, since she wanted to improve the pieces upon which Miss Darwen had commented adversely earlier in the visit. At least, thought Sarah, she would just be with Marianne Burton.

In this she was wrong, for after barely ten minutes Sir Marcus Cotgrave sidled into the music room as inconspicuously as he could, which therefore drew attention to him even more, and sat upon a rather hard chair to listen. Marianne frowned. She did not enjoy playing for others very much, and most certainly not when going over the parts where she was most inclined to go wrong.

'I wish he would go away,' she muttered after a while, as Sarah turned a page.

'Would it help if I took him away?' whispered Sarah.

'Please,' breathed Marianne.

Sarah stepped back from the piano, and smiled at Sir Marcus. He did not see that her smile was rather sad.

'I wonder, Sir Marcus, if you might oblige me in a small matter?'

'Dear lady, behold me at your entire disposal.' He did not quite sweep her a bow with a flourish, but she felt he might as well have done so. She then had to think swiftly, because she had no real idea what service he might perform for her.

'I find that . . . that there is a herbaceous shrub in the garden which I am sure that my mama would like to have in her own borders, but I am uncertain as to its name. You must be much more knowledgable, and if you do not know it yourself, then you will know in which horticultural volume I should seek it.'

The whole thing sounded very false to her, and Marianne had to cough to hide her giggle, but to Sir Marcus it was as manna from Heaven. Here was a young woman who saw, and accepted, male superiority.

'I shall do my poor best, Miss Clandon, but you are

perfectly correct. I will be able to find it in a book for you should its name not come immediately to mind.'

'Thank you. Perhaps we ought to go outside now, for there is most likely a storm brewing.'

'And young ladies are afraid of thunder, ah yes.' He offered his arm, which she accepted, inwardly cringing, 'But do you know, the thunder is of no consequence? It is the lightning which can cause catastrophic harm, to buildings or indeed persons.'

As they left the room, Marianne heard him saying that he had once seen a cow that had been struck by lightning. She returned to her sonatina with relief.

They were just about to step outside, and Sir Marcus was wondering whether Miss Clandon ought to put a cloak about her, 'just in case', when Lord Deben and Mr Mardham emerged from the billiards room. Lord Deben looked at Miss Clandon. She was still pale, still looked vaguely unhappy, but she was going outside with Sir Marcus?

Richard Mardham, who was aware that as the son of the house he was in part a host not just to his friends, was guiltily aware that he had rather ignored Sir Marcus, and so asked him if there was anything he might care to do after his 'walk'. While he did so, Lord Deben took the opportunity to speak, in a low tone, to Miss Clandon.

'Is there any way in which I might be of assistance, ma'am? Forgive me, but you do not seem quite yourself today.'

She looked rather lost, he thought.

'No, no, my lord. It is very kind of you, very kind, but Sir Marcus has offered . . . The name of a plant . . . I am quite well, I promise you.' Her words were disjointed.

She was a quiet girl, and he liked that calmness she possessed, but the young woman before him was not calm at all. In fact she looked as if on the point of panic. A thought struck him.

'Are you afraid of thunderstorms, Miss Clandon? It is a very common thing, I assure you, and the thundery oppression can give those of the strongest constitution a nasty headache. You ought perhaps to lie down, when you come in from the garden, if that is the problem.'

'Are you ready, Miss Clandon?' Sir Marcus turned to her.

'Yes, Sir Marcus.' She gave Lord Deben one glance, though she knew she should not do so, and he thought his heart might break then and there.

Lord Deben was on the other side of the table during dinner, and Sarah Clandon was next to Sir Marcus, who realised that the house party would not go on forever, and so was making up for lost time. Having seen that she appreciated the male propensity for being correct, he regaled her with a succession of stories in which he had been right in the face of opposition. She listened, attentively as he saw it, but it was just the veneer of politeness.

Lord Deben had learnt to read Miss Clandon, and he saw beneath the politeness. There was desolation, and when by chance she looked across the table and saw him looking at her, she averted her eyes and bit her lip. Had he offended her in some way? He could not imagine how that might be. She had been the happiest of beings yesterday when she won the competition and he had found her the rose. When she had looked at him he had been bowled over by the confiding nature of her smile that seemed just for him. He would have sworn that she knew he cared for her, and his feelings were reciprocated. So why, today, was she near to tears, and like a person drowning in despondency? Why did she avert her gaze?

Lord Deben was happy when those about him were happy. He strove always to keep them so, because his simple philosophy was that it was the most valuable thing in life. Thus, when they were unhappy, Lord Deben fell into despondency himself. Nothing had quite prepared him for how important it was to keep Miss Clandon happy, and so now he was almost distraught.

Miss Darwen, on the other hand, could have crowed. How were the mighty fallen! Only yesterday The Poor Relation had usurped her place, the victory that ought to have been hers. Today she was, for whatever reason, cast down, reduced to listening to the boring Sir Marcus, and Miss Darwen was as pleased as if she had arranged the misery herself. This made up, in a very small way, for the feeling she had that somehow she was losing control of the situation at Meysey. Yesterday had been a particular disappointment, but not the most important.

Flirtation or no flirtation, Miss Darwen was coming to the conclusion that Lord Levedale was not serious about The Ninny. She had done well in that direction, but had thus 'divided her forces' and not paid enough attention to his relations with The Cripple. She had worked upon the logical premise that he was simply taking pity on the girl, but this had been a mistake. Yesterday he had spoken up in support of Miss Mardham, and against herself, and although he returned from the driving lessons on occasion with a thoughtful look, on others he seemed dangerously happy. These lessons were conducted without so much as a groom, which was scandalous, but meant that perhaps The Cripple, whilst seated, was luring him into mistaking pity for attraction. She might have an ugly gait and a stick, but Miss Mardham was cleverer than she had thought, and highlighting her disability had not of itself done more than annoy her. Miss Darwen decided that she must act more forcefully, and also settle the score over the spilt coffee. She would think up A Plan.

It was at this point in the evening, just as the ladies withdrew, that the storm broke. Heavy drops of rain hammered the windows and rattled the glass, and out of nowhere came a flash so bright that even as she blinked, the light was visible on the inside of her eyelids, followed within moments by a loud crack of thunder. Her hand went to her cheek, and she let out a squeak. Miss Darwen was afraid of thunderstorms.

Lady Corfemullen put her hands over her ears, and shut her eyes. Marianne Burton sat with her fists clenched in her lap, resolutely trying not to cry out, and Celia, seated on a sofa next to Sarah, gripped her hand.

'I have no particular liking for storms, but am generally sanguine about them,' she whispered. 'That crack was unpleasantly close, however. It quite hurt my ears.'

The door opened. Lord Mardham led the gentlemen into the drawing room.

'We thought that in the circumstances, you ladies might prefer our presence rather earlier, so . . .' His words were cut short by a massive flash, a thunderclap that reverberated, and an enormous crash that made the room shake. Lady Corfemullen passed out, and slipped to the floor.

For a moment afterwards everyone was transfixed. Then Miss Darwen started laughing hysterically, Lady Mardham and Lord Corfemullen went to Lady Corfemullen's aid, and Mr Wombwell, looking out into the darkness, exclaimed 'Good God!'

A very sculptural pine tree just to the side of the

driveway had been struck, and cloven in two. The smaller part remained standing as a needle shape pointing skyward, but the greater part of the trunk had burst apart and fallen, the branches aflame, to land upon the gravel. The top of the canopy, however, had crashed onto the roof of the billiards room, which formed part of the single storey west wing.

Copthorne burst into the room in a most un-butler like manner, his face pale.

'My lord, a tree—'

'We know, Copthorne.'

'If fire catches in the roof, my lord—'

'Yes, yes, have the staff fill buckets.'

'Do you have a pump, my lord?' enquired Lord Levedale.

'No.'

'What about some form of grappling hook?'

'I have no idea.'

'A grappling hook could be used to pull the top of the tree from the roof and prevent the spread of the fire, and it would be an easy matter to put out the flames in the boughs if on the ground. Failing that we need a ladder so that water can be thrown onto the roof and keep it wet.'

'Yes, yes of course.'

'Gentlemen?' Levedale looked about the room. 'Our presence is required outside. Ladies, remain within doors. Copthorne, find rope, a hook, ladders, that sort of thing.' He glanced fleetingly at Celia, and then almost pushed the butler from the room. The other men followed.

Lady Mardham continued to fan Lady Corfemullen, Miss Darwen carried on laughing, and the other ladies crowded to the narrow window on the left side, from which they could see the stricken tree even through the rain running down the panes. Meysey was the sort of house that had grown over the centuries, with additions according to wealth and vogue. The core dated from the mid-seventeenth century, having been built by the Sir Rufus Mardham who disapproved of dancing. A century later a Mardham who thoroughly approved of entertainment had added two single storey wings, stepped fractionally forward of the central portion and each with a narrow window that looked across to its mirror image, and remodelled the front with a portico and large sash windows, so that its origins were concealed. On one side was the music room and a new withdrawing room, and on the other a library, reducing the previous one to a book room, and a billiard room. It was onto this end that the tree had toppled.

'We will burn in our beds!' declared Mrs Wombwell, histrionically.

'I hardly think any of us are contemplating going to bed, ma'am,' responded Celia, a little acerbically, and trying to make out the figures in front of the house. If something could be done swiftly, the fire might not spread to the building, and confine itself to the branches. Mrs Wombwell then began to sob, and wring her hands at the risk facing her beloved son. Celia doubted he would do any more than organise servants with buckets, lest his clothes become dirty, and was far more concerned for her brother, and for Lord Levedale. It soon became clear that a ladder was being placed against the library wall, and two figures climbed up onto the shallow angle of the roof. Both were in shirtsleeves. Another man positioned himself upon the rungs to hand up buckets. One then proceeded to douse the roof and nearest flames while the other appeared to be trying to pull branches with a rake.

The scene became infernal, with a backdrop of forked lightning and crashing thunder, and the foreground, red-lit by fire, full of people.

'Who is it on the roof?' queried Sarah, straining her eyes.

'I am not sure, but I doubt not my brother will be one. Is it . . . no, there is Pocklington at the base of the ladder, and I think Lord Deben is the man part way up. 'Ooh!'

At that moment the branches on the roof moved, sending up sparks, and there was a warning cry to watch out below. Everyone who could, fell back. The men with the ladder pulled it away, and then Celia watched as the pair upon the roof hauled at a rope. The angle of the fallen tree was changing, but they were perforce, pulling the danger towards them. Sarah gave a sharp cry as the top of the tree slid precipitately down the roof, and Celia gripped her stick very tightly. The men on the roof moved as fast as they could to the side, but one slipped in doing so, and slid off. The drop was no more than ten feet for a man of average height, but the tree followed him down, and for a moment he was lost to view.

'Who is it? Are they alright?' gasped Marianne.

'I do not know. Look, someone has gone to help them.' A figure dashed forward, an arm protecting their face from the heat, and pulled the injured man away from the flames, even as every available bucket of water was cast upon the fire.

'Come, let us go into the hall. Sarah, you know where the housekeeper's room is. I know there are salves and bandages kept there. Be quick.' Celia could not be quick but she knew what was needed. Sarah dashed away, and Marianne and Celia went into the hall. As Celia entered, the front door was pushed open and Deben and Pocklington supported Richard Mardham into the hall. They were all of them streaked black with soot and sodden with rain, and there was blood on Mr Mardham's face. Celia caught her breath but did not exclaim.

'Do not be too distressed, ladies. We look worse than we are,' managed Lord Deben. 'Mardham has hurt his ankle, but otherwise it is just rain, soot and a few burns.'

'Can you help him up to his chamber, gentlemen?'

asked Celia. 'It would be better to disturb the leg only the once.'

'Yes, indeed, ma'am. Come along, my dear chap.' Lord Pocklington adjusted his arm about her brother's shoulder, and the trio made their way, with some grimacing on Richard Mardham's part, to the stairs.

Sarah returned with a box as Celia followed on.

'There is Carron oil in the box, which will be useful,' noted Sarah. 'How wise to keep some ready in case of accidents in the kitchen.'

Celia nodded.

'My brother has hurt his ankle, Sarah. I think the other injuries are superficial. At least I hope so. Marianne, could you fetch up a dish of water, and then stay in the hall. If there are other burns and scrapes, send them upstairs.'

Marianne nodded, and disappeared.

Celia wished she could move faster. Sarah was already laying out bandages when she entered the room. In some ways it was fortunate that the gentlemen had been formally dressed for dinner, since removing a shoe and cutting off a stocking were far easier than removing a boot.

'How is it, Richard?'

'Hurts like the devil, my dear, but I'll live. Ow!' He exclaimed as she touched the swelling ankle.

'Can you move your toes?'

'Oh yes, but do not ask me to move the foot, I beg.'

'I shall not. We will send for Dr Stour, though

hopefully it is twisted rather than broken. Now, what injuries may be attended by "amateurs"?'

He held up his hand, which had redness along one edge from little finger to blackened wrist bands.

'I tried to protect myself. Thankfully, I was so wet, and Deben here got me away before the flames found much of me.'

'That was very brave of Lord Deben. Now, this will sting.' She was correct, and he hissed as she applied a lint pad soaked in the liniment to the injury.

Meanwhile, Marianne had brought up a dish of water, and clean cloths, and Sarah attended to the other two gentlemen. Lord Pocklington had singed eyebrows and a blister on his forehead. Lord Deben had abrasions from branches, and a burn to his hand. She administered to them impartially, focusing upon the wounds, but her heart beat the faster when she took Lord Deben's hand tenderly in her own. She dare not look him in the eye.

'It was a very brave thing you did, sir,' she murmured.

'Same as anyone would have done,' he said, watching her, and winced.

'Who was on the roof with you, Richard?' Celia was pretty sure that she already knew the answer.

'Levedale. He was the one who got a rope with something heavy to catch round a branch and tangle so we could haul it. It was damnably hot up there, I can tell you. He was a little quicker than I was getting out of the way, and then my foot slipped on a wet tile. We saved the roof though, Celia.' He sounded rightly proud, and she smiled at him.

There came a knock at the door, and several more 'walking wounded' entered. The stable boy had never been above stairs in the 'big house', and looked overawed on top of being singed. Sarah sent the two lords downstairs to pour themselves each a stiff brandy, and looked to the next casualty.

It was about twenty minutes later when, having made her brother as comfortable as possible, and placed a cold compress upon his ankle, Celia came down the stairs. Marianne was still sat, dutifully, upon a chair against the hall wall, and looked pale. The worst of the storm had passed over, and the rumble of thunder was in the far distance by now. The front door was opened once more, and Lord Mardham, his other male guests, and the majority of the household servants, trooped back inside, in various states of disarray. All were soaking wet, which Lord Mardham declared, trying to be cheerful, had undoubtedly saved worse damage occurring.

'Although I have no doubt there would have been a great deal of harm to the east wing if Richard and Levedale had not gone up there and tackled the tree.' He turned, looking for Lord Levedale to shake by the hand. Celia saw him for the first time. His face was streaked with black and with blood from a cut, his shirt grey tinged, ragged to one sleeve, and clinging to his torso. When Lord Mardham grasped his right hand he winced. He looked up towards the stairs, and saw Celia. He smiled, but then Marianne was in front of him, her lip trembling.

'Oh, my lord, is it not dreadful,' she managed, and collapsed in tears upon his chest. He was wet, sore, and filthy, and the last thing he needed was a weeping female casting herself upon him. He put one arm about her, cautiously, and spoke reassuringly. Celia made her way across the hall.

'You are hurt also, my lord.' She sounded calm, though part of her would have happily replaced Marianne and cried over him.

'Minor wounds, Miss Mardham.'

'Sarah is bringing down the lint and salves. Marianne, could you fetch more water and bring it to the drawing room?'

Marianne sniffed, and nodded as she lifted her head, apologising to Lord Levedale as she did so. He smiled a weary smile. He did not really want to think.

'Come, sir.' Celia hobbled into the drawing room. Lady Corfemullen was seated upon a sofa, pallid and with smelling salts in her hand. Miss Darwen was now silent, but sitting very rigidly, and one cheek was red. Lady Mardham, dealing with an unconscious woman and worrying about her husband and home, had eventually given up trying to calm the girl with words and resorted to the very practical answer of slapping her across the face. The manic laugh had been replaced by sobs, but these too had passed and now Miss Darwen sat like a statue. Mrs Wombwell cast herself upon the bosom of her son as if he had just led a forlorn hope. Lord Deben and Lord Pocklington were at the far end of the room, with glasses in their hands. Lady Mardham looked to her husband.

'It could have been a lot worse, my dear.'

'I have sent for Dr Stour, Papa, to look at Richard's ankle. I do not think he has broken a bone, but I am not properly able to judge.'

'Good girl.'

'Oh, my poor boy! I shall go up to him immediately,' cried Lady Mardham.

'Then take him a glass of brandy too, Mama,' suggested Celia, practically. She turned back to Lord Levedale. 'Now, my lord. Make yourself as comfortable as you can upon a chair and let me attend to you.'

He did as he was bid and sat, slightly slumped, in a chair. Marianne came in with a dish of water, concentrating on not spilling it, and set it at his elbow on a small table. The height made things difficult for Celia, and so she perched upon the arm of the chair, in far too close proximity for normal propriety, and commanded him to look up at her. The look upon her face eased all his hurts.

'You are a disreputable sight, sir,' she chided, but soothingly.

'Mmm.'

One hand lifted his chin, and she studied his face more closely.

'I shall remove the soot and dirt so that I can see the source of the cut more easily. Cuts upon the face always bleed profusely, even when small.'

'Mmm.' He let her wash away the grime, and though he wanted to gaze at her, his eyes half closed as he gave himself up to the delicacy of her touch. Once or twice he winced, but he said nothing and nor did she, and they forgot everybody else in the room.

'Ah, the cut is upon the cheek, just below the cheekbone. I imagine it was the lash of some twig. Keep still.' She cleaned the cut and very gently wiped salve upon it, then leant a little back to survey her handiwork.

'Yes, that is an improvement. Now, is your hand the only other injury, my lord?'

'Yes.' He held up his right hand, and the palm and base of the fingers were red, with a linear blister showing.

'These are thankfully not deep, sir. They will be most uncomfortable for a day or so, but there should be no lasting harm.' She placed a lint pad, liberally soaked with the Carron oil, upon the palm, and bound the hand with a bandage. 'The other gentlemen have broached the brandy. Would you care to join them?'

'Thank you, yes, but I am not so wounded I may not pour my own glass.'

'You may hold it, my lord, but if you are right-handed, and in a wearied state, I would not vouch for you not spilling brandy on Mama's fine carpet. I shall pour and you will hold.'

She stood, and made her way across the room. He followed. Miss Darwen, long ignored, was now sufficiently recovered to be aware of what was going on about her. She saw The Cripple hobble across the room, and Lord Levedale follow her. He then took a brandy glass and she the decanter, and poured him a generous measure. They looked at each other. Miss Darwen hissed. She really would have to do something, and if The Plan did not achieve her goal, then it would simply have to be revenge.

CHAPTER FIFTEEN

Lord Levedale awoke to a throbbing hand, and the realisation that his half-written letter to his sire would remain in that state for several days. The generous quantity of brandy, and his exertions, had meant that sleep had claimed him swiftly upon being helped to bed by Welney, who had fussed over him whilst also apologising for his own begrimed appearance. The valet had been rather proud of 'his' gentleman, but at times very fearful for his safety, and put a very tired Lord Levedale to bed with the tenderness of a nursemaid.

Summoned from the nether regions of the house by the bell, Welney appeared, fully prepared to shave Lord Levedale's chin, since his lordship's own use of a razor would be out of the question for a day or so, but when he saw the redness upon his cheeks and the cut, he shook his head.

'I fear, my lord, that just for today it would be better for you to remain unshaven, terrible as it is for me to say it. I am sure you will be forgiven, in the circumstances. By tomorrow I would be hopeful that I could shave you without doing damage to the skin. It is, might I say, a little puffy.'

'Do I look totally disreputable, Welney?'

'Shall we say, my lord, a little piratical.'

'Pass me the hand mirror then, and I will see the damage.' Welney did so. 'I see what you mean. Not a sight for the ladies.'

Privately, Welney thought that the ladies might find Lord Levedale's appearance rather dashing, since it was consequent to courageous deeds and not any slovenliness of person, and would not persist.

In addition to his rough face and sore hand, Lord Levedale found that a wide variety of muscles were complaining of ill usage, and he was eased into his coat with some grimaces, and even a groan. He went down to breakfast slowly, and did not notice the additional swiftness of the footman who was by the breakfast parlour door, and who opened it for him with a certain relish. This morning was for 'heroes'. He found the others who might be so named, and a couple less deserving, gathered over their gammon and eggs. Despite his aches, he laughed.

'What a sight we present, gentlemen. You would

have thought we had to repel a siege last night.'

'Morning, Levedale. In a way did we not do so?' Lord Pocklington had a black eye to add to his red cheeks, and had been ribbing Lord Deben about it, since he was convinced the viscount had kicked him as he descended the ladder with more speed than grace to avoid the falling tree. 'Besieged by the forces of nature, we were, but we emerged battered but undefeated.'

'Talking of feet,' remarked Lord Deben, 'has anyone heard how Mardham does?'

There was no answer. Sir Marcus, who had been well to the rear of anything approaching danger, privately thought the young men were treating the whole thing far too lightly. The house might have burnt to the ground had the wind been greater, the rain less. He failed to understand that they knew this as well as he did, and knew that there had been some risk to themselves. Their reaction was to make a jest of it all, a reaction which Sarah's military brother would have recognised in an instant.

Lord Mardham's entrance provided the information they sought. Mr Richard Mardham had sprained the ligament in his ankle, and it was tightly strapped. He had been told to put no weight upon it for a week and then the doctor would assess it once more.

'There goes our shooting,' sighed Lord Pocklington.

'Not at all, Pocklington. My son would far rather you stayed about to entertain him of an evening, and had some sport in the day. He only regrets that he cannot play the host as he would wish.' Lord Mardham was very proud of his heir this morning. The boy had proved his courage, and also how much Meysey meant to him. It did his father's heart good to know that. If he had asked that his friends be allowed to shoot every partridge on the estate, Lord Mardham would have agreed. He looked at Lord Levedale.

'Are you feeling too beaten about to go to the sales in Cirencester, Levedale.'

'Oh Lord! Of course, the sales are today. I had forgotten. Well, I cannot drive myself, not with this hand, and I look the devil, but if you are prepared to be seen with me, my lord, I would come with you. Looking at horseflesh might take my mind off my burns and bruises.'

'Excellent. I will send to the stables to order the carriage for, shall we say in an hour? And have your groom make ready to come with us.'

'Then I must let Miss Mardham know that there is no lesson this morning.' Lord Levedale was not sure whether this might not be a good thing. Last night she had been wonderfully calm and sensible, and yet her every touch had been a caress, and he told himself that he was not imagining it. She had no doubt been gentle with all her patients, but surely he was the only one to have felt there was magic in her fingers. If he were alone with her this morning he could not guarantee remaining gentlemanly.

He ate his breakfast, putting up with the indignity of

requesting his gammon to be cut up for him, and went upstairs to prepare to go out. As he passed Richard Mardham's bedchamber he halted and knocked. A strong voice bade him enter, and he went in, to find Miss Mardham sitting upon the edge of her brother's bed. She made to get up, but he implored her not to move on his account.

'I am come to see how you do, Mardham. We had quite a battle, we two, up on that roof. Just wanted to say, I could not have had a better fellow at my side.'

Richard Mardham demurred, but was clearly pleased.

'I could not do less, Levedale. After all, in part this is my house and I'll be da . . . dashed if I would see it burn to a cinder.'

'How does the ankle?'

'I will be laid up with it for a week without it bearing my weight, at the least. Celia says I must not grumble.'

'Well, and you ought not, Richard. You are very fortunate that you did not break the bone, which would have meant far longer laid up, fortunate also that Lord Deben pulled you away before you were badly burnt.' Celia thought that he had come off very lightly.

'By the by, Miss Mardham, despite my disreputable appearance, I am going with your father to the sales in Cirencester this morning, so I am afraid our lesson must be abandoned.'

'Or take place this afternoon, sir, if you are back betimes.'

'I am agreeable, ma'am, but can make no promises.' He only wished, in an entirely different context, that he might do so.

Whilst generally preferring to drive himself, Lord Levedale was today grateful for the well-sprung and cushioned comfort of Lord Mardham's carriage. Jeb Knook was upon a sturdy cob, following behind, and the journey into Cirencester was not long and upon a decent road. The fortnightly livestock sales were well attended, and included a decent number of driving and riding horses. Being interested in farming, Lord Levedale was perfectly content to look over the sheep and pigs as well as the carriage horses. He let his groom run his eye over the pens before the animals were trotted out for inspection, and confided to Lord Mardham that Jeb Knook was like having a spy in the enemy camp.

'He finds things out, just by leaning over a rail and chatting as though no more interested than someone passing the time of day. Yet many is the time I have been warned off because, for all that the horse may look good and be advertised as sound in wind and limb, Jeb has found out from the seller's man that it is a wind sucker, or crib biter, or simply lazy. He will come back and give us the pick of the sale, and let us choose after that.'

So Jeb Knook wandered about the yard, the innocent everyman, and looked and listened. He returned in under an hour, and touched his cap to Lord Mardham and nodded at his own master.

'There are three pairs of ponies you might take a look at, my lords. The others are not for Miss Mardham. The flashy chestnuts are matched for colour, but do not 'get on' and cause trouble between the shafts, the thirteen hand bays tend to pull, and the smaller pair are unevenly paced, as you will see when you look at their action. If I was you, I would consider Lots 52, 68 and 77. Pick of the bunch is 52, but if they go too high . . . Nice pair of Welsh geldings, eight and ten, know their work and eager to please. The man with 'em says the owner is hoping for a hundred and twenty guineas for the pair, and that would be a fair price to my mind.'

'Thank you, Jeb.' Lord Levedale pressed a coin in his groom's hand and told him to go and wash the dust from his throat but be back to them in time for the likely ponies to appear in the sale ring. Then he and Lord Mardham wandered as casually as possible past the pens where the selected lots were enclosed.

'I think Miss Mardham would be delighted with any of the three, but agree with Knook that the grey Welsh geldings have the edge. Whilst it is of no real importance, their being grey will look particularly good with the blue livery, and ladies like a thing to look "pretty",' murmured Lord Levedale.

'I am with you on that, and if they go beyond a hundred and forty, we will try for the bays with no white markings rather than the ones with the crooked blaze and the star.'

They watched as the early lots came and went, and Jeb Knook came up quietly and stood just behind them looking down into the ring.

'Lot 52, gentlemen, as nice a pair as you could wish to find, well matched and good temperaments. Who'll start me at sixty guineas?' The auctioneer glanced about the ring and picked up the first bidder. Two men vied for the ponies up to ninety five guineas and then one fell out, and Lord Mardham gave the nod. The figure still rose, but by one hundred and twenty the opposition was dithering.'

'One more will have him, my lord,' whispered Knook, behind Lord Mardham, and so it proved.

'Not a bad price,' declared Lord Mardham, very pleased, as they threaded their way back through the yeoman farmers and horse dealers.

'The man you was up against was a dealer, my lord, I am willing to wager. No doubt he had an eye to sending them to a bigger sale at Oxford or maybe up to London come the spring, and making double.'

This made Lord Mardham feel even better. He offered to buy luncheon, but Lord Levedale said that he did not really look fit for the public, and so they returned straight to Meysey in very good spirits, even if Lord Levedale's hand was aching. Lord Mardham took the opportunity to thank the viscount for his efforts the previous evening, which left Lord Levedale feeling embarrassed. It did, however, encourage him to think that if he presented himself as a suitor for Miss Mardham's hand, his actions, which had been instinctive, would count for something to offset his modest wealth.

Celia was watching from the drawing room window in some eagerness, and wondering if her father and Lord Levedale had been successful. She was also able to watch as the fallen trunk of the stricken tree was sawn into lengths and dragged away by one of the farm horses. She was rather sad to see it go, for it had been part of her view from the house all her life, and the jagged remnant pointed accusingly at the sky from whence had come its doom. A ladder was once again giving access to the billiards room roof, and two workmen were replacing damaged tiles.

Eventually she saw the carriage coming along the curving drive. She went to the drawing room door and waited as they entered the house.

'Well?'

'A good sale, Miss Mardham. Excellent selection of Old Spot and Tamworth gilts, I thought, did not you, my lord?' Lord Levedale looked at Lord Mardham, who picked up the theme.

'Indeed, and that Devon bull would have won prizes.'

'But what about my ponies?' Celia almost shouted.

'Your ponies?' Her father managed to look as

though he had not looked at a pony all morning.

'You remember, my lord, the two really quiet old ones.' Levedale's lips twitched.

'Quiet? Old? You are roasting me, Say you are, Papa?' Celia's face was a picture. Her father laughed.

'Of course we are, my dear. Levedale's groom is bringing them over this afternoon, and as tidy a little pair as you would wish.'

'May I see them, or must they remain a surprise until my birthday?' She looked from her father to Lord Levedale and back again.

'What do you say, Levedale?'

'If Miss Mardham would care to stop at the stables during our drive this afternoon, sir . . .'

'Oh yes! Please say I can, Papa?' She was clearly excited, and it seemed very unfair to hide the ponies away for a week just to tease her.

He nodded his assent, and she came and gave him a hug, and kissed his cheek, calling him 'the best of papas'. He liked that.

Lord Levedale could only watch and wish she would hug him and kiss his cheek too, if she could find a bit that was not red and sore.

Luncheon was an odd affair. Lord Mardham was in a very good mood, Celia was excited, and Lord Levedale quiet but contented. By contrast, Sarah Clandon, much to Lord Deben's concern, still looked wan as she listened to Sir Marcus, and Miss Darwen was so suspiciously silent that Lord Pocklington remarked afterwards that it was unnerving. It was as though, after a couple of weeks in close proximity, and gradually blending, the party had suffered a lightning strike like the pine tree, and shattered into parts.

At half past two, the pony cart was in front of the house. Celia admitted to Lord Levedale that she felt a bit guilty when Pom looked pleased to see them.

'It is like when one outgrows one's first pony. It feels wicked to say "Thank you, that will be all. I have learnt all I can from you and now I want something more exciting."'

'Well, I am sure when you have your phaeton you can drive round to the stables and give him an apple occasionally. Just do not confuse him with your grandmother, because offering her an apple on your palm would not go down well.'

Celia giggled, but was then more serious.

'Talking of palms, my lord, how is yours?' He was not wearing a glove on his right hand, since it would not fit over the bandage without it pressing painfully tightly.

'Sore, truth to tell.'

'Oh, I am so sorry.' Her face fell.

'Why so? You did not make it sore, and in fact you have made it much better.' He smiled at her. Today felt a good day, a day when he could forget the ancestors, see letting Marianne Burton down gently as the work of but a few minutes, and rejoice that things he was

248

doing were making this wonderful girl happy. She smiled back as she climbed carefully into the back of the cart. They sat opposite each other, deliciously close, each thinking how much closer they had sat last night. Pom looked round as if to ask why they were not yet setting off, and Celia sighed.

'Pom does not approve.'

'Of what, Miss Mardham?' It was a daring question, a little too daring, for Celia blushed, and shook her head. She set Pom off at a steady trot.

'You do not need me any more, Miss Mardham,' he said softly, as she negotiated a bend, and she turned her head swiftly, her expression panicky.

'But I do, sir. I do. I am not nearly good enough to drive without you.'

'Alas, ma'am, I am like that first pony.' His smile was awry.

'No, no you are not.'

'You wait. When you have seen your new pair, and when you have your spanking new phaeton, you will want to drive alone, with just the groom.'

She shook her head, and there were tears in her voice.

'No. Please do not speak of it. I won't, I cannot.'

'Forgive me. I have ruined your afternoon, clumsy fool that I am.'

She could not tell him how much more being with him meant to her even than the independence he was giving her. Deep down she knew what he said was true, and that also their time left together was very limited. Perhaps in another week he would be going. She felt as if when he did she would stop breathing. Last night, when Marianne had cast herself upon his chest, he did not look as a lover should look, or at least how Celia thought one should look. If he did not offer for Marianne then perhaps he might be persuaded to come and visit again.

'Miss Mardham?'

'I am sorry, sir?' He had said something, and she had not heard a word.

'I asked if you would like to do another circuit of the park before going to the stables.'

'Oh, I see. Yes. Please let us go around once more.'

So Pom trotted obediently around the park, and Lord Levedale did not see the specially planted trees, nor the berries in the blackberry thicket. He just watched her profile, and loved her.

When Celia set the pony heading back to the stables, his pace picked up a little.

'Oh dear, my lord. I fear poor Pom thinks we are going 'home' and that will be the end of his labours.'

'Well, he has only to take us back to the house, so it is not asking much of him.'

They passed under the archway into the stable yard, and Lord Levedale commended her on the way she negotiated it. Celia blushed. A groom came out to hold Pom by the bridle, and Lord Levedale climbed down, offering his hand without thinking, and making a sharp intake of breath when she took it.

'Oh my goodness! Are you alright, my lord?'

'My fault,' he managed, through gritted teeth.

'No, no, not at all, It was foolish of me not to think . . . I should remove the bandage and check it?' She sounded unsure and very contrite.

'Not now. Come, for we have your ponies to see – and name.'

Harrop came out and touched his cap to Miss Mardham, smiling broadly, both knowing that she had a treat in store, and because it was good to see her back in the stable yard. She avoided looking at the loose box where her hunter used to be.

'Now, Miss Celia, you come and see these two little beauties.'

He led the way, slowing his own pace, into the main part of the stable, where the ponies were in adjacent stalls.

'They'll settle in easy, being together,' he said, cheerily.

'Oh,' breathed Celia. 'Oh, they are beautiful, and so . . . sweet.' She put her hand out so that the first pony could snuffle at her hand.

Lord Levedale repressed a grin. Trust a female to think of 'sweet'.

'Knook says as they move well, my lord,' commented Harrop, looking at him, as though he too was finding 'sweet' hard to take.

'Good. They are eight and ten years old, geldings of course, and their names are up to you, Miss Mardham.'

'But did I not say Paragon and Perfection?'

'That was before you saw them, Miss Mardham, and perhaps such names need to be deserved. Will you wait until you have tried them out?'

'If you wish, my lord, but I am sure I shall not change my mind. Shall I, Paragon?' She leant down to drop a tiny kiss on the velvet nose. The pony blew through its nostrils, and she laughed. 'See. He agrees.'

Harrop shook his head, smiling tolerantly. He had helped her onto her first pony, watched her fall in love with all things equine, and here, a year and a half after what had happened to her, she was back in the stables. It was a quarter of an hour before Celia could tear herself away, promising to bring apples on her next visit. Pom, waiting patiently, was rewarded with a pat and the same promise, and then they set off back to the house, with the stable lad standing on the rear step.

'Thank you, my lord,' she said softly, as she got Pom to trot on.

'You should thank your father, not me.'

'But it was your idea, and I have no doubt you were instrumental in choosing them.'

'Ah, now that is untrue also, since it was Jeb Knook, my groom, who selected them. I merely approved.'

'I still thank you, and all I can do is to offer to put more salve upon your poor hand when we are indoors.'

'That would be more than enough thanks, ma'am,' he said, gravely, but when they stepped over the threshold all thoughts of dressings were forgotten.

Lady Mardham was having one of her spasms, and the house was in uproar.

'What on earth is going on? Mama, what is the matter?' Celia paled.

'You probably know only too well, Miss Mardham.' The voice was icy, and belonged to Miss Darwen, standing in the doorway of the yellow saloon. 'My ruby pendant has been stolen.'

CHAPTER SIXTEEN

Celia looked at Miss Darwen blankly, and then, slowly, the import of what she said sank in.

'Oh dear, oh dear,' bemoaned Lady Mardham, whilst clutching her *sal volatile*.

'It has been stolen, I tell you.' Miss Darwen's voice took on its most strident and discordant tone.

'It would seem unlikely, my dear,' Lady Mardham offered, nervously. 'Any intruder would be noticed as a stranger about the house.'

'And what's more, why was only that taken if there was a burglar?' chimed in Richard Mardham, from the head of the stairs. He had heard his mother in 'one of her takings' and hopped, dressing-gown clad, to find out what was going on. He was now affronted at the thought of his familial home being infiltrated by a light-fingered thief.

'Go back to bed, Richard,' recommended his sister, but he ignored her and began to make his way very gingerly down the stairs.

Celia hobbled towards the yellow saloon, with Lord Levedale in her wake. Miss Darwen drew aside, lips compressed and her expression unpleasant. Celia entered the room to see Lord Deben on his knees, searching under a sofa, and Sarah Clandon checking behind the clock. Lord Pocklington was standing, furrow-browed, clearly trying to recall something. The other members of the party were sat, self-consciously, about the room.

'I do not care if anything else has been taken or not. My ruby pendant is missing.'

'Raven,' blurted out Lord Deben, and everyone turned to look at him. He stood up, colouring. 'What I mean is, a bird stole it. Ravens like shiny things, or is that crows? Or jays? Or magpies? Well, anyway, some member of the crow family is noted for taking shiny objects. One got in, spied the trinket on your dressing chest and flew off with it.'

'They steal eggs, do ravens,' commented Lord Pocklington. 'My gamekeeper has awful problems with them. Was the thing ovoid?'

'No, and . . . I have never heard anything so ridiculous,' snorted Miss Darwen. 'I have not had my window open.'

'Ah, but a maid might have opened it, to freshen the room, er, to remove the odour of soot, or such, after she cleaned the grate.' Lord Deben was persistent, and Sarah Clandon, despite all, smiled to herself.

'This is fanciful.' Miss Darwen glared at him.

'No more so than thinking your chamber has been burgled.' Richard Mardham had arrived at the doorway, and leant against it, glaring at Miss Darwen with thinly disguised dislike.

'You must admit, Miss Darwen, it seems odd that only this one item was removed.' Lord Corfemullen was the embodiment of calm reason.

'No, my lord, because the thief stole the item specifically. I have worn the pendant several times and it has been admired.' She looked to Celia Mardham, and her eyes were hard.

'If you are suggesting . . .' Celia controlled herself with some difficulty, 'I only said something nice about it to be polite. In truth I found it garish.'

'You say that now, but . . . I want every servant's room searched, and every bedchamber.'

'You may want that, Miss Darwen, but I will be da . . . dashed if our retainers are to be treated in that manner.' Richard Mardham looked to his sire.

'We have never had any petty pilfering, beyond a couple of eggs from the chicken coop, young lady. It is inconceivable that any of our servants have stolen anything.' Lord Mardham finally intervened.

'So you will do nothing, my lord?' Miss Darwen looked most dissatisfied.

'I will have Copthorne alert the staff to the item

having been mislaid, and ask them to keep a lookout for it. There will be a logical answer to this, and it will not involve the constable.' Lord Mardham gazed steadily at Lavinia Darwen, and under that gaze she lowered her eyes.

'I hope so,' she mumbled, and sat, with just a trace of a flounce, upon the sofa beneath which Lord Deben had been hunting.

When a cup of tea was offered to her, she glared at Lady Mardham as though she might have her pendant hanging covertly about her neck. Lord Mardham remained impassive, but what he later commented to his wife was scathing. Lady Corfemullen launched into a long-winded narrative about a ring she had lost some years previously and had only discovered when a damaged floorboard had been lifted in her bedchamber.

'And there it was, as shiny as the day it disappeared, barring a few cobwebs, and with no sign of damage. I cannot think how it got there, for although the floorboard creaked, there was no wide gap along it at any point.'

For once, her husband did not mind if she went on at length. He even interjected a comment that enabled her to continue. Lady Mardham threw him a grateful look.

Lord Levedale had remained in the background, observing, and thinking. Something did not ring true. Miss Darwen was an odd female, but he would swear that any woman who had had a valuable piece of jewellery stolen would be upset, not just angry. There was absolutely no sign that Miss Darwen was shocked or had shed a tear. He had not thought beyond that, but it did not feel right.

When all that could be said about the missing jewel had been said, and tea had failed to make the situation any better, there was an uncomfortable silence. Richard Mardham was persuaded to go back upstairs, but his mama promised, as to a little boy, that he could come down to dinner if he was good. It made him grimace at Celia.

Lord Pocklington invited Lord Deben to play cards, Lord Corfemullen invited his lady wife for a stroll about the shrubbery, which made her blush, and Lord Mardham went to hide in the library. Sir Marcus began to converse with Sarah, which amounted to a lecture on the subject of servants, and the importance of employing those who were not related, lest they support each other in situations such as the current one. She listened in silence, which he took as hanging upon his every word, and was in fact her feeling how insulting Miss Darwen had been to Lord Deben, and how little he deserved such shabby treatment.

Miss Darwen stared very hard at Celia, her eyes almost boring into her. It was intended to intimidate, but Celia held firm. Miss Darwen might feign outrage, but Celia Mardham possessed the real thing. This awful young woman was making the most appalling accusation, and upon no possible evidence. Eventually,

Celia simply got up, and left the room.

She went upstairs feeling suddenly tired. Perhaps the events of the previous evening, and the excitement of today were catching up with her. She rang for Horley, and lay upon the bed for a few minutes.

Her maid looked at her and shook her head.

'I said as you ought to take things quiet today, Miss Celia.'

'I know, and you were right, Horley, but until the last hour it has been a very good day.'

'Would you be wishful to wear the blue tonight, miss. I got that mark out of it where the teacup dripped the other evening.'

'Yes, why not, and the pearls please.'

Matilda Horley went to the dressing chest and opened her mistress's jewel box. She took a deep breath.

'Well I never!'

'What is it?' Celia sat up a little too quickly, and felt a bit dizzy. Her eyes refocussed. 'Oh!'

Horley had a ruby pendant dangling from finger and thumb like a mouse caught by the tail.

'Something is mightily wrong, Miss Celia.'

'But it cannot be there. I do not understand.'

'It was not there after luncheon, when you changed to go driving, that is for sure, because you wanted the figure-of-eight pin for your neckcloth, and I took it from the box. This here gewgaw was right on the top when I opened the casket, and it was not there then, I would swear upon the Good Book itself.'

'So it was put there. Oh Horley, how awful. She, Miss Darwen, specifically said she wanted all the bedrooms searched, and she kept making it clear she thought I had it.'

'That would be because she knew, in a way, miss, that you did. Nasty thing to do.' Horley shook her head.

'But what do we do? I mean, if I take it to her she will say I have given it back because she raised the alarm, and still say that I stole it.'

'Ridiculous, that is, Miss Celia. As if you would!'

Celia frowned. It would be far better if the whole episode had never happened. She took a breath.

'Go to Lord Levedale's room, Horley, and see if he is there.'

'Me? Go to a gentleman's bedchamber?'

'Yes, for this is an emergency. Tell him I need his help most urgently.'

'You're never inviting him in here, Miss!'

'Oh, be sensible, Horley. You will be here also.'

Much discomposed, the maid scuttled off, hoping that nobody as much as saw her knock upon the door of his room. She was fortunate in that he had come up early to change, knowing that tying his neckcloth would take longer than usual with a largely disabled hand. Welney came to the door.

'Mr Welney,' whispered the maid, blushing. 'Is his lordship within? I have a very urgent request from Miss Celia.'

Welney's features remained schooled into impassivity

as he relayed the message to Lord Levedale. His lordship, who had just been very cautiously shaved, because he said he would rather put up with the discomfort than look any more ragged, wiped the vestiges of soap swiftly from his cheek, pulled on his shirt, and came to the door, cravatless and attempting to do up his wristbands. Welney sighed, and reached to do them for him.

'I am at Miss Mardham's service.'

He followed Horley to Celia's room, and looked in both directions before entering, conscious of the impropriety. Celia was sat by the window. A distinctive ruby pendant lay in front of the jewel box.

'Horley found it in my box, and it was not there when I went out driving with you, my lord.' Celia's voice was vehement.

'I do not doubt it, Miss Mardham. Do not think for one moment that I even considered it got there other than by the hand of she who "lost" it.'

Celia felt a wave of relief sweep over her, and it showed upon her face.

'But what do I, we, do now? If I take it to her and say, "It has been found" she will insinuate that I have merely become too scared of discovery and returned it, and she will still besmirch my good name.'

'None here would believe her, Miss Mardham.'

'Not even with a whisper of doubt, sir?'

'Not even a whisper.' He looked at her, trusting him to find the best resolution to her problem, and thought it not an imposition but a privilege. 'We have two possibilities, as I see it. Either we ensure she and her maid are not in her room, and replace the pendant, which, incidentally, is quite revolting, in her own chamber, or I "find it" somewhere where she might have dropped it. She will have to accept it as truth, for she cannot easily accuse me of wanting it, and she will know also that it was really found here. She cannot declare it, which will frustrate her.'

'Leaving it with her is safer, yes?'

'Not really, Miss Mardham, because she can continue to pretend it is missing. If I perform a conjuring act before dinner, in front of everyone . . .'

'Yes, I see, but it makes things difficult for you, sir. You have to . . . lie.' Celia looked so innocent he could have hugged her.

'Think of it this way, ma'am. The truth is that one of your guests secreted this item among your belongings to cast doubt upon your honesty. One can only guess the reason.'

'Yes, why should she do it?'

'Because, forgive me sounding vain, she has been throwing herself at my head this past two weeks, and sees your having driving lessons as a block to her success.'

Celia blushed.

'Oh, but . . .' She was going to ask why she had not placed the pendant rather among Marianne's jewels, but then realised the reason. 'And she could not do so with Marianne, because Marianne has much better pieces and everyone knows she can have everything she wants.' Just for a moment, Celia was not thinking of worldly goods, and her voice was sad rather than bitter.

Lord Levedale thought it rather that Miss Darwen could not face being less admired than a girl she would dismiss as 'substandard', but did not reveal the thought.

'We are countering a lie, a dangerous one, with a lie that will be known to the liar, but in all other ways appear a consoling truth, for there will have been no theft, no problem. All we need to decide now is where it might have been dropped, and yet not found this morning by the maids.'

'But surely, my lord, if she had dropped it in innocence, she, or her maid, would have noticed when she came to disrobe?'

'A fair point, Miss Mardham, but did she not wear it last evening, with an assortment of jangling bangles?'

'Yes.'

'Then there is the answer. She was hysterical, remember. When she calmed down she would not have been thinking clearly, and the maid would have been distracted by the alarm and excitement.'

'I did not sleep a wink before two of the clock, Miss Celia, I was that upset', added the maid.

'That settles it. She lost it when she was coming upstairs. Perhaps she had been fingering it nervously, which unhooked the clasp.' Lord Levedale was warming to his theme. 'Yes, that was it, and so where did it slip to the floor?'

'My lord, there is one of them big plant stands, a "jardineer", next to her chamber door. The stand is not quite solid to the floor. If it fell, and slipped out of view there, I doubt the maid would brush under the stand every day, not unless she thought Mrs Howsell was a-watching her.'

'Well done.' Lord Levedale smiled, and Horley blushed for the second time in ten minutes. He pocketed the pendant. 'Now, if you will be so good as to check that the, er, coast is clear . . .'

The maid bobbed a curtsey and went to peer out of the door. He glanced at Celia, and then could not resist it. He winked.

Lord Levedale went down to dinner feeling rather pleased with himself. What he was about to do would certainly put Miss Darwen off him for life, and he was doing it to assist Miss Mardham. He entered the room to find everyone but Sir Marcus Cotgrave already present. It was a pity, but delaying revealing his 'discovery' would be suspicious. There was also the very unexpected presence of the Dowager Lady Mardham, not so much seated as enthroned near to the fire, and clearly assessing the company for signs of weakness. Hoping she would not be a complication, he took a breath, and beamed at the assembly.

'I have to say I feel like the wizard in a children's fable, but . . . Miss Darwen, I have wonderful news for you.' He pulled the pendant from his pocket, and let it dangle, catching the light, from his little finger.

'Where did you find it?' gasped Miss Darwen, in an almost accusatory manner.

'And why did you not put it straight back?' murmured the dowager, gazing at it through her lorgnettes with undisguised revulsion.

Lord Levedale kept his composure.

'It was concealed under the foot of a jardinière, next to your chamber, Miss Darwen. You see, I thought about it while changing for dinner. It could not have been stolen. Ergo, it was lost. Now, you wore this last night, as I recall, and last night was very . . . distracting for you. In fact I am sure you handled the pendant just as you are touching the necklace at your throat right now. If you observe, the clasp has been slightly deformed, no doubt by pulling upon the chain.' He had forced the clasp with his nail scissors, which he thought a good added touch. 'When you went upstairs you were too upset to notice the pendant slip off, and it lay where it was not obvious. I retraced the steps you must have taken to your chamber, and the plant stand was the only object that hid anything at floor level.'

'I say, what an amazingly clever thought, Levedale,' declared Lord Pocklington. 'You ought to give lectures to those Bow Street Runner fellows.'

Levedale smiled, but was looking at Miss Darwen, who had turned a slightly sickly shade.

'So here is your property, restored to you, undamaged.' He stepped forward and dropped it into her hand. She thanked him, without enthusiasm, and without looking him in the eye. 'And I think perhaps you also owe Miss Mardham an apology, for having implied she might be involved in its loss.'

She looked at him then, her eyes narrowed. He knew all, she could tell, and in that moment she hated him.

'Of course,' she said, dully. 'But it was a natural assumption to make.'

'Only to someone, ma'am, of your nature.' His words were said very quietly, but they stung.

Old Lady Mardham pursed her lips, but her eyes glittered with a smile. As for Lord Deben, he had not smiled in nearly two days. He smiled now.

Lavinia Darwen's plan had been, she thought, quite elegant. Since Celia rarely came up to her room once downstairs, and was always very easy to hear from the clumping sound of her stick, it would be easy to place the pendant in her trinket box. She, the victim, would then raise a hue and cry and demand that rooms were searched. The pendant would be found and Celia be dumbfounded as to how it got in her room, denying all knowledge. She would say, quite sensibly, that she was a most unlikely thief, being so slow and obvious, but that was the really clever part of The Plan. The accusation would be that she had got her maid to steal it, on her behalf. Since calling in the constable to arrest The Cripple was never going to happen, putting her maid under threat of transportation, or even death, would be far more real and upsetting. Lord Levedale would be disgusted at the deception and putting a servant under pressure to commit a possibly capital crime. There would be no need to actually call in the constable of course. The damage would be done without that.

However, somewhere along the line, it had all gone very wrong. The rooms had not been searched, through the 'weakness' of Lord Mardham. She would have had no compunction in searching the rooms of her guests in such a case. His annoying daughter must have found the pendant, and persuaded Levedale of her innocence by looking pitiful, she supposed. He had now clearly proved himself unworthy of her own attentions. It was at least a blessing she had found out now, before she had accepted him.

Even though the 'theft' had been solved, the afternoon's unpleasantness hung over the dinner table like a pall of heavy cloud. The conversation was in general desultory, although the Dowager Lady Mardham, seated at the end of the table so that she could watch everybody, cast lightning bolts of a scathing nature at whomsoever she chose. Sarah Clandon, seated next to Lord Deben, quizzed him gently upon his meagre knowledge of ornithology, in an attempt to drive the look of discontent from his pleasant features. Lord Deben did not enjoy being treated like an idiot by the likes of Miss Darwen. Engaging in friendly joshing banter with his friends was one thing, but her attitude had been genuinely dismissive, and it rankled, hours later.

'I see no reason why a gentleman ought to know about birds, other than being able to identify the ones he shoots,' interjected the dowager. 'My nephew Gerald once shot a peacock whilst staying at Woburn, and was never invited again. Foolish boy. It is not as though a peacock looks anything like a pheasant.' Her glance around the table challenged anyone to disagree with her.

Miss Darwen was in a first rate huff, and thus did the unthinkable: she took on the dowager. Lord Mardham, for all he was angered by her earlier behaviour, regarded her with awe.

'A female peacock, or to be exact, a peahen, might be mistaken for a pheasant at some distance.'

The dowager fixed her with an icy stare.

'Which is why I said he shot a peacock, miss, and a peacock would no more be mistaken for a pheasant, of either gender, than cheap trumpery be mistaken for a piece of decent jewellery.'

The younger Lady Mardham winced.

'My papa bought me my pendant, ma'am.' Miss Darwen did not reveal that he had done so to stop her making a scene in a Bath jeweller's shop.

'That only goes to show that men will do anything for a quiet life.' The dowager made a highly educated guess that was remarkably accurate. The despised pendant was not the sort of piece a man would buy, being far too fussy, but would appeal to an immature girl. Without waiting to see if Miss Darwen could make a response, her ladyship turned her attention upon Sir Marcus Cotgrave, who was seated on one side of her. Sir Marcus, who had arrived late, and heard of the pendant's discovery second-hand from Lord Corfemullen, had limited himself to recommending that the ladies all check the repair of their jewellery at frequent intervals. Upon finding himself sat next to the dowager, he was so intimidated that he had said not a word to her and focused upon working his way through several tartlets, the parsnip soup, a raised pie, a dish of salsify and a summer pudding. This marked him down in the dowager's view as 'a human rug', and she therefore proceeded to tread all over him.

'Tell me, Sir Marcus, has your cook died?'

'My cook, ma'am?' Sir Marcus blinked in consternation.

'Yes, your cook.'

'Er, no. When I left she was in perfect health, as far as I know, Lady Mardham.'

'Oh.' The dowager appeared perplexed, and Sir Marcus, unused to the ways of wily old ladies, walked straight into the waiting trap.

'Why did you think otherwise, ma'am?'

'Because, sir, you have paid almost undue attention to most of the dishes on this table, without paying attention to either myself or Miss Button to your left.' Marianne looked across at Celia, but very wisely, said nothing. 'Remaining silent at dinner is ungentlemanly. A gentleman's dinner table is a social place for conversation interspersed with eating. We are not the starving poor who have to grab what they can before anyone else takes it. I assumed you had been denied suitable sustenance before you came here.'

'Er . . .' Sir Marcus shrank in his seat, and the dowager delivered the *coup de grâce*.

'And if you as much as look at another helping of potted crab you will regret it all night. Nothing is more inclined to bring on colicky disorders than an excess of crustaceans.' She paused for one moment. 'But there. Who am I to tell you what to do?'

The dowager had not raised her voice, and yet everyone was attending to her. They remained silent, except for Miss Darwen, who tittered discordantly.

'I do not see what there is to amuse you, Miss Darwen. I rarely make jests, and should I be about to do so, I would inform you of it.' Old Lady Mardham looked down the table towards her son. 'I see your father's cellar still has wine worth drinking in it, Mardham.' She glanced at Lord Corfemullen, to her right. 'My late husband was, at the least, a good judge of vintage.'

'He and your papa would have got on famously,' Lavinia Darwen murmured, looking across the table at Marianne, who blushed.

The dowager, who had heard her daughter-in-law's 'confession' about Miss Burton's origin before the young lady had appeared for dinner, was not going to give Miss Darwen pleasure by asking why. She had made her own assessment of the 'Button' girl, and found her manners as good as her looks, but she was lacking in spark. Putting the worried Lady Mardham at ease, she had described her as prettily behaved, but the sort to bore a man of sense before the bride visits were completed. However, she added, 'she will do well, since men of sense are a rarity.'

'You know, I think he would, my dear,' The senior Lady Mardham gave Marianne one of her less intimidating smiles, and ignored Miss Darwen. 'Gentlemen need but a common interest to put them on the best of terms, and your papa is a man of discernment, as one can see from your pearls. I would have given my eye teeth for a string as fine when I was young, although we wore them longer.'

Marianne blushed furiously, but was not as red as Miss Darwen. In one fell swoop the ghastly old woman at the end of the table had elevated Sir Thomas Burton to being a gentleman, when he was but a jumped-up wine merchant, and had praised his daughter's jewels, clearly in contrast to her opinion of the ruby pendant. Miss Darwen thought she had also overheard the phrase 'tawdry bangles' before dinner, and she was the only lady wearing more than one bracelet. She opened her mouth, but could think of nothing to say, and thereafter sat in morose silence for the rest of the meal.

Lord Levedale was seated next to Celia, and was enjoying the dowager's masterly assertion of her superiority over everyone. It was a useful distraction, for he wanted to say so much to Celia that he dared say little. For her part she was intensely aware of him, and felt such a co-conspirator that an added bond existed between them. She felt an odd mixture of elation and disquiet. If he felt as she felt, he would have spoken by now, and for all his kindness, his laughter and his looks, he had not once spoken of his feelings about her. Time was also running out.

The ladies withdrew, with an admonition from old Lady Mardham for the gentlemen not to linger over their port, since she would be wanting the tea tray brought in early so that she might go home to her bed. She made it sound as if she was present at great personal cost to her health and well-being, though the truth of the matter was that she was enjoying herself immensely. She ignored her daughter-in-law's proffered arm to lean upon, and pointed her stick at the most prepossessing of the footmen, indicating that she would prefer his support. William did not know whether to feel proud or petrified. Once ensconced in the chair of her choice, she dismissed him with a smile, which he later admitted to be even more frightening. She then commanded Mrs Wombwell and Lady Corfemullen to sit by her.

Lady Corfemullen, being a relation, had known Lady Mardham since girlhood, and had long ago learnt that the best way to deal with her was to hold one's own but never pick a fight with her upon any topic. Mrs Wombwell clasped her hands together tightly, and perched so close to the edge of her chair that her knees trembled.

'Your son has a very good tailor, Mrs Wombwell.'

Maria Wombwell looked even more worried. This might be a compliment, or it might be a cutting remark indicating that it took a good tailor to make her beloved son look as he did.

'I believe he patronises Stultz, ma'am.'

'I don't need the man's name.' Old Lady Mardham sniffed. 'Is he dyspeptic?'

'His tailor, ma'am?'

'No, of course not his tailor. Him. Your son.'

'Oh. No, no, he is not of a dyspeptic nature, although prone to headaches, poor boy.'

'He looked dyspeptic throughout dinner. Either that, or he was sulking.' The dowager had no doubt which was true.

'He has had a very enervating few days, what with the thunderstorm and the fire.'

'From which he seems to have sustained no visible injury.' Lady Mardham had recommended to her grandson that he 'stop playing upon roofs', with a wry smile and a comment that it was good to see he had a care to his inheritance. She was proud of the boy, and had noted the healing abrasions upon the other young gentlemen. She admired physical courage in a man, and made no comment upon their temporarily impaired looks. Mr Wombwell's flawless complexion set him apart, and damned him.

'Thank the Almighty, no,' declared Mrs Wombwell, reverently, failing to notice her ladyship's less than admiring tone. 'I was so afraid for him.'

'Needlessly so, no doubt.'

Celia, knowing her grandmother so well, caught the inflexion, and choked, even as she was describing her new ponies to Sarah. Mrs Wombwell simply looked uncomprehending, and the dowager gave up poor sport.

CHAPTER SEVENTEEN

The next morning Lord Levedale felt he ought to at least try and finish the letter to his father, though it risked being illegible and would undoubtedly be painful. There was a noticeable change in the forming of the letters when he recommenced, and he grimaced frequently. He had read through as far as he had managed before his accident, and liked it as little as he had before, but they were the right words.

Sir,

I have endeavoured to find it within me to make Miss Burton an offer, but, despite the pressures upon the Family to find Funds in short order, I am not prepared to make either her or myself unhappy by an act of foolish obedience to Duty. She is, as you said, a young lady of beauty, and is neither vain nor coquettish, which is common among her sort, but there is no spark at all between us and both would very soon find themselves most miserable with the other.

I should also add that I am still, in part, hoping to fulfil your request, by setting up my nursery in the near future, but that is still dependent upon the young lady, and her parents, accepting my suit.

That was as far as he had got. What he had to do now was explain to a man who had never thought of duty to his name until he had dragged it down into the dust, why his own refusal to submit to it was laudable and not reprehensible.

'Damn it, why should I apologise to him?' muttered Lord Levedale, but the need remained.

It is not a requirement to be deeply in love with the woman for whom one offers. This I accept, but to offer for a woman when deeply, and I believe irrevocably, in love with another is morally wrong. My attachment to the Family estate is strong, but does not override every other feeling.

I realise that this will disappoint you, but suggest that you listen to Ruyton, do what you can to salvage some shreds of the family past from the sale room, and live quietly within your means, perhaps at the Slapton property.

At this he smiled, wryly, imagining his sire's outrage at the thought of living in a five-bedroomed house with stabling for a hack and four carriage horses, in what he had termed 'Dismal Devon'.

You have created this situation and then placed the burden of extricating us from it squarely upon my shoulders. If I have failed to achieve your aim, consider that it is not entirely my own fault.

I remain, Sir,

Your Obedient Servant

Levedale

That was as false as could be, but there, it was done. Now he could look to Miss Marianne Burton, and find the words to explain he had tried to like her enough to marry her, and had failed. He groaned, and this time it was not because of his hand. Those were not the words, for a start.

He went downstairs, flexing the bandaged right hand cautiously. Celia was just emerging from one of the smaller saloons and saw the action.

'Your hand gives you discomfort, my lord.' It was not a question.

'I have had to write, Miss Mardham, and it objected.'

'I am not at all surprised, sir. Might I remove the bandage and apply more of the Carron oil. It should not be allowed to dry out. I was remiss yesterday, in not asking to change the dressing, but we were, perforce, distracted.'

'You are in charge, Miss Mardham.'

'Then I shall send for my requirements, and be in the breakfast parlour in five minutes. Even the changing of a dressing to the hand is not really a public thing.'

'Thank you, ma'am. I will be there. How does your brother, by the way?'

'A poor patient, or rather most "impatient", my lord. The better part of a day in bed with the limb elevated has done much good to the injury, but not his temper. He was persuaded to take breakfast in his bed, but will be downstairs before long. He was never one to be cooped up.' She smiled. 'Now, I must order my salves. Do excuse me, sir.'

He bowed, and she went to send Joshua below stairs. He awaited her in the breakfast parlour, and turned a chair sideways to the table. Miss Mardham returned a few minutes later, followed by the footman, who remained in the room, clearly at her behest.

'Now, my lord, we will see if you have caused any damage by your too early use of the hand.' The liniment, lint and bandaging were set upon the table, and she sat before him and began to unwind the bandage from his hand.

'I think I might apply a fresh dressing each morning, sir,' she commented, as the palm was revealed. 'That is a little dry, but it is showing signs of healing. The redness is decreased for the most part on the fingers, and it is the palm itself where your writing has exacerbated the inflammation. Might I suggest that you refrain from commencing any major treatise for another week.'

'I can promise you that, Miss Mardham.' He was watching the top of her head, bent over the injury, thinking how much he would enjoy her ministering to him each day, though it was something which took no more than a few minutes. When the hand was bandaged once more, Celia stood up.

'If the weather worsens, sir, I fear Pom will remain in his stall for today. I am very conscious that the number of lessons remaining available must be limited, and, despite your comments yesterday, I still believe I need your supervision.'

He was equally conscious of time passing – and as regretful.

Mr Wombwell was under the distinct impression that Levedale's interest in The Money Pot was dwindling, and whilst he loathed the idea that his own charms were not sufficient to turn a rival into a non-starter, his situation was that he was quite prepared to increase the determination of his own pursuit to fill the void. He took advantage of Miss Burton being alone after breakfast, Miss Mardham and Miss Clandon having disappeared within the house. He had not, however, considered his mama. In total ignorance of why her son had resumed his charming of a young woman so clearly beneath him, she could only assume that by some odd bewitchment he found her irresistible. It was clearly her duty to protect him. She therefore followed in his wake, and came to sit with Miss Burton, and sought to enter into conversation with her. Her son's hints were not subtle, but they were ignored.

'I was wondering, Miss Burton, if you had plans for the autumn? After you leave here.' Mrs Wombwell spoke with a patently false degree of interest.

'I am returning to my papa, who has missed me these last few weeks, ma'am, and I do not think we have any immediate plans.'

'Ah yes, Sir Thomas. He must be a good judge of wine.'

'He is rather one who employs good judges of wine, ma'am.' Marianne caught the note in Mrs Wombwell's voice. She had heard it before.

'A general does not lead cavalry charges, does he, Miss Burton,' purred Mr Wombwell, standing up for Sir Thomas. His effort did not quite work.

'Does he not? I confess I know nothing about battles and soldiers. Miss Clandon might know.' She looked slightly unsure. 'Papa says that many people judge a wine upon the bottle, and do not really understand what lies within.' She said it innocently, but Mrs Wombwell wondered whether the chit was making some very subtle but scathing comment.

'Does that mean he ensures his bottles have the best labels?' tittered Mrs Wombwell.

'I think, ma'am, that he ensures that contents and label are suitably matched, but I have no knowledge of business, and of course Papa leaves all that to his employees. All he does these days is oversee the quarterly profits.'

The word 'profit' sounded well in Mr Wombwell's ears.

'It is right that you should stand apart from such things. Business is no part of a lady's life, Miss Burton.'

'Nor a gentleman's.' Mrs Wombwell was looking at her son.

'Papa says,' announced Miss Burton, as if he were the Oracle of Delphi, 'that if one looks at the most aristocratic gentlemen, their forebears found their way to prominence by fighting for the winning side, paying for the best hospitality, or turning the blindest of eyes. I am not sure to what, but that is what he says, and before every silver spoon existed, there was a wooden one.'

'Most philosophical,' murmured Mrs Wombwell, with a twisted smile.

'Indeed, I should like to meet your papa,' declared Mr Wombwell.

Marianne smiled. She was perfectly sure the feeling was not reciprocated.

* * *

Sarah Clandon wanted to go home. She also wanted to stay as long as Lord Deben remained at Meysey, and in neither situation could she be happy. A small voice in her head said that over the last few days, since she had obeyed the instructions of Lady Mardham and been more distant, Lord Deben had not been his normal self. In any other man she would have said his mood was thoroughly miserable, but perhaps that was because she herself was miserable, and viewed anything regarding him in an odd way. She was certainly seeing the path that Sir Marcus Cotgrave was taking, and it led straight to the altar. It made her all the more miserable because she knew that she ought, for very sensible reasons, let him reach the point of a declaration, and say yes. The thought filled her with gloom, but she had neither money nor looks, and no realistic chance of an offer based upon 'deeply felt affection'. Just at this moment she could not face the word 'love' in connection with anyone except Lord Deben. She could enumerate so many things that made her love him: he was kind, sweet natured, normally a happy person, and thoughtful; he was handsome, in her eyes, with those spaniel brown eyes, and well proportioned figure; and if he had been afraid of Miss Darwen, nobody could accuse him of physical cowardice having seen his brave act in rescuing Mr Mardham from among the flames of the burning tree. She had been so very proud of him the other night, it had taken all her strength not to tell him how very,

very greatly she admired him, all her strength to keep from kissing his grazed cheek.

Reality was not Lord Deben. Reality was Sir Marcus Cotgrave, and the mere thought of kissing that particular cheek made her shudder, but it was all there was. Mama would tell her to be practical.

Celia found Sarah, gazing out of the window. It was raining persistently now, which would mean no driving, but in a gently melancholic fashion that echoed Sarah's mood.

'I was looking for you, but you slipped away after breakfast.'

'I am sorry, Cousin, was there something you wished me to do?'

'Oh no, it is just . . . What is the matter? You have seemed so different these last few days.'

'Nothing. Or rather, nothing that anyone can help me resolve.'

'But can you not even tell me what it is, Sarah?' Celia sounded genuinely concerned, and Sarah took her hand.

'I can tell you, because we are friends.' She paused for a moment. 'I think Sir Marcus is going to make me an offer.'

'Oh no! How awful!'

'Not awful in some ways, I am afraid, and I have not the luxury of being able to afford to refuse him.'

'"Luxury"? I do not understand.' Celia was confused. 'You do not like him.' A frown creased her brow.

'No. I do not, but part of me thinks that whether I do so or not is . . . irrelevant.'

'But how could you marry a man you did not like, perhaps not even respect, Sarah?'

'By considering the alternatives.' Sarah sighed, and gripped Celia's hand. 'I know he has looked at me because you made it clear his suit was not welcome. I am, as always, a second choice. I do not think him a fool. He must realise that a young woman would not happily commit to a future at his side unless there were no alternative. In me he has found such a one. I have no prospects, Celia. Mama did not expect me to find a husband by coming to stay with you, but I am reasonably sure that she would greet any offer with huge relief.'

'Even from a man of similar age to your papa?'

'Yes.' Sarah bit her lip. 'You see you have at least the prospect of living with your parents and then, should your mama have cause to go to the Dower House, why, you would go too. You have that much security. There is Charles, my brother, who is in the army, but even purchasing his majority is currently likely to be beyond him, even with Papa's aid, and he is thus inclined to volunteer for dangerous tasks in the hope of a field commission. I worry about him a great deal. Even if, as I pray, he returns safely, and one day inherits Three Elms, there is little beyond two small farms to rent out for income. He will want a wife and children of his own, and I would be a real burden upon him, Celia.'

She sighed again. 'So you see, if Sir Marcus does make me an offer, I feel I am duty bound to consider it most carefully.'

Celia shook her head.

'It is all so unfair.'

'I must try and look upon the brighter side. Since he is so much the elder, I must have reasonable hope of outliving him and then living quietly and comfortably as a widow.'

'Oh Sarah!' Celia had a catch in her voice, half laugh and half tears. 'Listen to yourself. The best you can dream of is widowhood.'

'Not the best I can dream of, Celia.' She blushed, and whispered, 'I can dream of someone kind and thoughtful and . . . someone like Lord Deben. I know it is merely sweetness of temperament and true gentlemanliness, but he makes me feel as important as everyone else here.'

'Do not I do so?' Celia looked worried.

'Ah yes, but I meant, among the young men. Cousin Richard is . . . cousinly, Lord Pocklington is bemused because I do not like horses, or hounds, or dead birds, and Mr Wombwell treats me as if I were a speck of dust upon the sleeve of his coat to be brushed away and forgotten.' She did not mention Lord Levedale, because she thought it clear that he had eyes for Celia alone, Marianne notwithstanding. 'Lord Deben has always treated me as if I were an equal to you, or your mama, or . . . any other lady. It is his way, I know, and not specific to me, but . . .' She sighed.

'He is a very nice man,' agreed Celia.

'A very nice man,' echoed Sarah, with a sigh. 'However, one has to be sensible. I just wish being sensible were not so grim.'

Sir Marcus watched Miss Clandon during luncheon, so obviously that Lord Deben became quite annoyed and scowled down the table at him. He did not think that Miss Clandon liked being stared at in that way, and he most certainly thought it intrusive, especially as she was much as she had been on the day they had arrived. That day she had been trying to pretend she was not there at all, and he felt that after a while she had unfurled, like some little flower. If she had been a flower, her petals were starting to drop, and she looked worn. Some burden afflicted her, and Cotgrave, the insensitive swine, was taking advantage. For a while Lord Deben actually wondered if he might take Sir Marcus aside and warn him off, but then he thought how he had no right to do so. At the end of luncheon he therefore went to make a fourth at cards with Richard Mardham, Pocklington and Lord Corfemullen. Sarah watched him leave, and felt strangely abandoned. She retreated to the small saloon, but knew she would not be alone for long. Indeed, it was only a couple of minutes before Sir Marcus entered, and feigned delighted surprise.

Sarah watched him, with a depressing sense of inevitability, as he came towards her. He had a look upon his face, a confidence tempered by just that shade of doubt. After all, she thought, he had already been refused once during his stay. She tried to compose herself, and as he drew close he thought how very restful she looked.

'Miss Clandon, I find you unoccupied. You are so industrious a young lady I had thought to see book or needlework upon your . . .' He suddenly felt embarrassed at saying 'lap' or even 'knee', and amended his sentence, '. . . in your hand'.

'I was thinking, Sir Marcus.'

'That is fortuitous, since there is a matter I would raise with you, upon which I would ask you to think.'

This was it. Sarah's sad smile remained, and she nodded.

'Of course, Sir Marcus.'

'Miss Clandon, I am in the unfortunate situation of not still being married.'

Had it not been her to whom he was saying this, Sarah could have laughed. As a way of beginning a declaration it was . . . probably unique.

'My natural inclination is for the comforts and gentle contentment of marital union, the opportunity to care for a lady, to have those tasks in life most suited to the distaff taken from my unwilling shoulders. You have struck me as a most competent young lady, restful, understanding of the strengths that pertain to each gender. To be plain, I feel that I would be very happy if you would accept my offer of marriage.'

Sarah sat very still. She had but to say yes and her

future was secure. The trouble was that it felt secure in the manner of being a prison cell into which she must step. For a minute she could not breathe. She could not do it, not right now, not today. She could not, would not, for all that it was the obvious answer to her situation.

'I would ask you to give me a little time, Sir Marcus, before I give you my answer. I am of course honoured, but this is the most important decision of my life, and I would be rash in the extreme to make my choice without the greatest thought.' She smiled, and he did not see that it was a desolate smile. 'I think we both understand that this is not a match based upon the tender passions. We have not got to know each other well, but that is something that obviously comes with time. You do understand?'

'I understand, and commend your good sense, Miss Clandon. Indeed it is one of the things I admire in you, one of the many. I can only say that I think we will deal extremely together, and anticipate your answer with excitement.' He did not look excited. He lingered, and for a terrible moment Sarah thought he considered 'a little time' to mean minutes. In fact did he not quite know how to end the interview, and eventually cleared his throat, mumbled something unintelligible, and left the room.

Sarah could not bear to be with the others. She felt crushed, oppressed by good sense. She had no feelings for Sir Marcus Cotgrave. How could she have, when her poor heart was already given to another? Unreciprocated it might be, but her love was real and deep. To mope in spinsterhood for a man who had merely shown her kindness, and thereby be a burden upon her parents and then her brother, was not sensible. She must cast dreams aside, and face cold facts. Sir Marcus had made her an offer. She had put him off so that she might compose herself, but to do more would be foolhardy. The course open to her was not one she wished to take, and it seemed so cruel when a far better future had been glimpsed, imagined, and faded like a dream upon waking. She was profoundly miserable.

On impulse, she went upstairs, took up cloak and bonnet, and slipped back down and out into the soft September rain that fell in fine drops that permeated clothing almost by stealth.

CHAPTER EIGHTEEN

Some quarter of an hour later, Lord Deben, who had been wondering whether writing Miss Clandon a note would be too forward, entered the room where the other young ladies were sat bent over stitchery, and remarked upon her absence.

'I have not seen Cousin Sarah for some time, my lord. She was a little pallid after luncheon. Perhaps she is laid upon her bed.' Celia berated herself, silently, for not sending to find out if this were the case.

'I see. Thank you.' Lord Deben could scarcely go up and knock upon her door. He withdrew, and went along the passageway towards a small saloon where he might think without being disturbed, and it was then that he caught sight of a bedraggled figure sat upon the terrace. Without considering either coat or hat for himself, he went immediately to the door that gave access to the outside of the house upon the southern aspect.

She sat there, the rain soaking into her cloak, dripping off the poke of her oldest bonnet. Her face was cold and wet, tears and rain meeting, melding in her misery. So lost was she in her despondency that Sarah did not hear the footsteps.

'Miss Clandon. What on earth are you doing out in this?' He saw her cheeks. 'You have not had some bad news concerning your brother, I hope?'

She shook her head, but did not look at him. It took one worry from him, for had she been bereaved he was not sure how he could make her feel any better. She was very wet.

'You will be soaked to the skin and catch some fatal inflammation of the lungs.' Lord Deben was horrified. 'Really, dear girl, I had an aunt who looked as fit as a flea and shuffled off this mortal coil in ten days flat from such a condition.' He tried to sound light-hearted to conceal his concern.

'I do not think, sir, that at this moment such an eventuality sounds unwelcome.' Her voice was barely above a whisper.

Lord Deben discarded any pretence, and sat beside her on the wet bench, ignoring the cold wetness seeping into his breeches.

'Then consider me, for there could be nothing more unwelcome.' He reached out a hand, and laid it upon one of hers. 'Nothing.'

She turned her face to him, her eyes reddened and puffed, a loose strand of hair plastered down one white cheek. In that moment there was no doubt in him, only a deep certainty.

'I know it must seem foolish, after such a short acquaintance, but the thought of being without you . . .' He took a deep breath. 'I want you to be happy, and more than that, I want you to be happy with me. Is there anything I can do to . . .'

She said not a word, but he read her response in her eyes. His free hand went to her cheek, and he leant slowly towards her and kissed her, softly. She trembled, both from emotion and the cold, and his arms went about her.

'Come indoors and get dry and warm. I have much I wish to say to you, need to say, but not whilst we drown. Please?'

She nodded into his shoulder and they rose as one. He placed her hand upon his arm and led her indoors. The warmth within made her even more aware of how cold she felt, and she shuddered.

'Dry clothes, and . . .' Lord Deben felt the need for brandy, but doubted young ladies would share the inclination, '. . . tea. Hot, sweet tea. That's the thing. Upstairs with you.'

'But what about . . .'

'No more words until you have obeyed my commands, Miss Clandon.' He sounded firm, but smiled at her.

She lifted the sodden hem of her skirts and almost ran up the stairs. Lord Deben, decidedly wet about the nether regions, followed once she was out of view. He needed to think. He had not gone outside intending to make Miss Clandon a declaration. In his heart he knew it was what he wanted to do, but she had somehow withdrawn from him these last few days. He had gone from certainty to uncertainty, and his head had not quite worked out how he might propose to a young lady who might not want to hear what he had to say. There were considerations, problems even, but seeing her there, bedraggled and miserable, he had cast all else aside. Now he had to be sensible, for her sake as well as his own. He would have to go to her father, and persuade the colonel that in barely more than three weeks he had reached the momentous decision that he wanted to spend the rest of his life with his daughter. That might not be easy. He also needed to speak with the object of his affections without his teeth chattering, and ascertain that what he thought she meant was what she meant, because he meant what . . . Lord Deben laughed, much to the consternation of his valet.

'My lord?'

'Do I look mad to you, Stockley?'

'No, no, my lord,' averred the valet. 'Though to have gone out without a suitable coat in this weather was . . . reckless, if I may dare to say so.'

'Reckless indeed, Stockley, but you see, I was rescuing a damsel in distress.'

'Ah, I see, my lord.' Stockley saw rather more than his employer might have thought.

* * *

Half an hour later, and with his hair dry and his person as neat as a new pin, Lord Deben went in search of his host. He found him, rather inconveniently, enjoying a good burgundy and discussing the wheat harvest with Lord Corfemullen. That peer, with great insight, conjured up an entirely spurious reason to absent himself, seeing 'a young man burdened', as he later said to Lord Mardham.

Lord Mardham took up the decanter.

'Would you care for a glass, my boy?' Lord Mardham thought Deben looked as if he needed it.

'Er, no, or rather, yes. Thank you, sir.' It felt like one of those interviews Lord Deben could recall from school, minus the threat of the cane. He accepted the proffered glass but did not drink. 'Thing is, sir, I was hoping for . . . I mean . . .'

'Advice perhaps? *In loco patris*?'

'Exactly so, sir.' Deben looked relieved.

'Then sit down, my boy.'

Lord Deben sat, rather upright, and on the edge of his chair.

'I find myself in a sort of predicament, you see.'

'I rather thought that to be the case.'

'You did?' Deben wondered how his host could be so perspicacious. 'Well, I am at a bit of a loss as to how to proceed. You see . . .' He explained his situation to Lord Mardham, who listened with a suitably serious expression, even when it all became a bit muddled.

'In essence, then, you want to be absolutely clear that Miss Clandon reciprocates your affection before repairing to her sire, and wish to be closeted alone with her for that purpose, and you fear that he might not take your declaration of perpetual devotion to his daughter seriously, based upon the brevity of the acquaintanceship.'

'Yes, sir. In a nutshell.'

'Well, upon the first point, nobody expects you to make a declaration in public. Damned embarrassing if you did. I will speak to Lady Mardham, and she will arrange that you and Miss Clandon may have a private interview.' He did not say that he might have to throw a jug of water over his wife first, if she threatened hysterics at the news. 'As to the second point, I cannot guess Colonel Clandon's response, but you are not a here-and-there-ian type of young man, and I am sure he will judge you fairly. He might well suggest that you pay your addresses in form, and that no announcement be made for a month or two, but I should think he would be delighted, dear boy, quite delighted.' Lord Mardham did not add that he would be relieved also. 'There is no money, of course, but you do not look as if your pockets are to let, and the Clandons are a good family, with connections. Lady Eskdale may sigh a little, for mamas always seem to dream of "brilliant matches", but you have found yourself a thoroughly nice young woman, and I, for one, wish you well.' With which Lord Mardham held out his hand and shook Deben's with some vigour.

* * *

295

The jug of water was not required, not quite. Lady Mardham certainly made loud clucking noises, which reminded her spouse of a very angry hen, and asked, rhetorically, what she had done to deserve This Disaster, but agreed to letting Sarah speak privately with Lord Deben. She then went to find The Poor Relation and sent her to wait in the crimson saloon. Shortly thereafter, a footman was sent to request Lord Deben's attendance. It could not be said that he found his hostess as enthusiastic as his host, but after warning that he was most likely to break his mama's heart and health by the step he was about to take, and that 'desperate young women will accept any offer they receive', she sent him to the crimson saloon. She then went to write a letter to Cousin Cora, with the implication that it was entirely through her altruism and good offices that the match had prospered. Once she had told herself this a few times it was easy to believe it, and it made her feel a little better.

Lord Deben felt a little battered, but when he stepped into the room and Miss Clandon turned and smiled shyly at him, everything else was forgotten.

'I am sorry. I should not have gone outside, but I was feeling very low and . . . You were very kind.' A voice in her head told Sarah she must still grant Lord Deben the chance to escape, though her heart did not doubt, could not bear to doubt.

'I was very impertinent, kissing you as I did. It just . . . happened.'

'I understand.' Her heart missed a beat. Was he

escaping after all? 'You wish to forget it, and . . .'

'No. No, I want to remember it always, want to . . . repeat it.' He came close, close enough to take both her hands and kiss them. He looked at her, his smile awry. 'I have not got a way with words, not like Wombwell, and I am going to get this all wrong, but I have to make you believe that it is possible to fall in love, properly in love, in three weeks.'

'I do believe. Indeed, I know it to be true.' She blushed, a soft pink suffusing her cheeks.

'You do?' His hold upon her hands tightened.

'Yes. For it is what I have done also.'

He had prepared sentences, rather a lot of them, ready to persuade, entreat, beg, promise. He forgot them all. He swallowed convulsively, and managed three words.

'Marry me, please.'

Sarah could not master even the single affirmative, and simply nodded, her eyes very wide and now thankfully rather less red. He let go of her hands to pull her gently into his embrace, and hugged her. Mr Wombwell, had he seen this mode of seduction would have laughed derisively, but Mr Wombwell had never actually been in love. Lord Deben found hugging very much to his liking, for Miss Clandon was soft and yielding, and when he laid his cheek to hers her skin was peach-soft and there was a hint of some floral perfume in her hair.

'I must go to your father, and do this in form. I hope he will say yes,' he murmured, somewhere about her left ear.

'Papa has always said he wants my happiness, so he must say yes.' Sarah sighed. 'I never thought I would feel this happy, ever.'

The only possible response to this was a kiss, and this kiss was not cautious or consoling. It was a kiss that claimed, promised, and even demanded. Lord Deben was not possessed of more than average understanding, but the slightly bumbling air owed much to his desire to rub along well with his fellows and even more to a lack of purpose in his life. Now he had a purpose, a responsibility, and he embraced it as joyously as he did her body.

It would have been impossible for the putatively betrothed couple to have acted as if nothing had occurred. When they joined the other members of the party before dinner it took an effort of will for each to drag their eyes from the other. Lord Deben wanted everyone to be as happy as he was, though of course that must be impossible, and so he announced that he and Miss Clandon had 'come to an understanding' and that he would be seeking permission to pay his addresses as soon as possible.

The majority of his auditors were delighted by the news, and for a few minutes there was much hand-shaking and expressions of congratulation. Lady Mardham was, however, resigned, Sir Marcus Cotgrave disappointed, Mr Wombwell totally indifferent, and Miss Darwen shocked. She looked daggers at Sarah

Clandon. Lord Deben meant nothing to her, but she regarded the match as insulting. Miss Clandon was her junior by a year, was a Nobody who would never have made a London come out, and yet here she was, ensnaring a husband and the long-term prospect of being a countess.

Marianne Burton was all emotion, her eyes misted, clasping Sarah to her as if she were her best friend in the world, and exclaiming how wonderful and 'desperately romantic' it was. Celia was even more pleased, but less demonstrative. She leant to kiss her cousin's cheek and whispered that she must come to her room and tell all later. Lavinia Darwen shook Sarah's hand, and smiled acidly.

'You must consider yourself very fortunate.' Somehow the implication was not that Sarah was fortunate to have found love and a decent young man, but that she had found any man at all to offer for her. Sarah ignored the insult, being upon a cloud of happiness that the barb could not reach. Any further comment was prevented by Copthorne announcing that dinner was served.

The buoyant air continued through dinner, although Mr Wombwell, seated next to Miss Clandon, maintained his attitude that she was essentially invisible, and all but ignored her. Lord Deben was seated upon the other side of the table, however, and not so far away that glancing at him would mean leaning, and turning her head to an obvious degree. Sarah tried to ration herself, and failed.

When their eyes met there was the memory of that first evening, when he had tried to show that she was not insignificant by offering her various dishes. Then there had been kindness in his eyes, now there was warmth, and it was all he could do not to beam at her. She could not say what she ate, nor afterwards recall what Lord Levedale, seated to her right, said to her.

The ladies withdrew, leaving Lord Deben to a little light-hearted joshing from his friends. Lord Levedale was more of an observer, conscious of a sense of guilt because he felt jealous. Deben had fallen in love with a girl, she with him, and there seemed no obstacles that would prevent their very happy union. He was delighted for them both, but reflected that it was so much less complicated than the cobble in which he found himself. He was in love with Celia Mardham, desperately so, and he had indications that she was far from averse to him, but he had been paying his attentions to Marianne Burton for the better part of three weeks, and that young lady might feel justifiably hurt if he now made her friend an offer. He did not think Miss Burton was in hourly expectation of a declaration, nor that her heart would be broken, but it was an ungentlemanly thing to pay court to a young woman without any intentions in that direction, and it made him feel a cur. It was the behaviour of men like Wombwell, of men of his brother Laurence's set.

The ladies, with the gentlemen absent, were keen to hear all about the romance, although Sarah Clandon was reluctant to do more than express her feeling that she was the luckiest of young women.

'Fortunate indeed, for you will have rank and wealth, but let us be honest, Lord Deben is scarcely more than a fool.' Miss Darwen had been seething all through dinner, and her temper was now unleashed.

The other ladies looked shocked. Lady Mardham pursed her lips, and Lady Corfemullen shook her head, mentally vowing that if any daughter of hers were as ill-mannered she would have the governess take a slipper to her. Miss Clandon did not look shocked. Her eyes narrowed for a moment, but then she smiled serenely.

'I doubt Lord Deben is bookish, Miss Darwen, but in many ways he has a remarkable understanding, and has qualities you are clearly unable to recognise, not possessing them yourself. He is kind, generous of spirit, and seeks the happiness of those about him. I am supremely fortunate to be loved by such a man, a man who will undoubtedly make me extremely happy, as I hope to make him.'

Marianne Burton so forgot herself as to clap her hands together in approbation of this short speech. Miss Darwen turned puce, which was a most unbecoming shade, especially when combined with the necklace of garnets about her throat.

'You are saying . . . How dare you! You are Nobody, Nothing, a mere . . .'

'"Poor Relation"? I am, in terms of wealth. But you see, Miss Darwen, I am no longer poor because I have been given something of far greater value than wealth, though title and wealth comes in its wake. I have been given the love and affection of a man of heart and character. I am not altogether sure you would either recognise those qualities or think them important.' Sarah's smile lengthened, knowing the other ladies in the room would agree with her. 'So it is I who pity you, "poor" Miss Darwen, for all your London Season, and your air of superiority.'

Celia wondered if it were possible for a woman to explode through sheer chagrin. Lavinia Darwen drew herself up to her full height, by means of sticking up her chin defiantly, and thus lengthening her neck, announced that she had the headache, and requested permission to retire before the gentlemen joined them. Lady Mardham assented with relief.

'Oh bravo, Sarah,' giggled Celia, as the door closed behind Miss Darwen. 'That left her with nowhere to go but her bedchamber.'

'I am sorry, ma'am,' Sarah looked to Lady Mardham, 'but I could not bear her to insult Lord Deben.'

'I understand, my dear. In the circumstances, and you have had a very enervating day, it is entirely forgivable. I am only sorry I ever invited that wretched girl. I disliked her in the schoolroom, but assumed she had been improved for her Season. How wrong I was, to be sure.' Lady Mardham was still tutting quietly to herself when the gentlemen entered.

* * *

302

'So?' Celia dismissed her maid, sat upon the edge of her bed, and looked at her friend.

'Oh Celia, pinch me. I cannot truly believe this afternoon, this evening, are real.' Sarah heaved a great sigh, and, seeing Celia pat the bedcover, sat down beside her.

'I say again – So?'

'So I thought I would simply have to accept Sir Marcus, and be practical, but it made me so very low, Celia, that I went out and sat alone in the rain.'

'I am not sure getting wet would have helped, you know.'

'Ah, but in a way, it did. You see, Lord Deben espied me outside, and came to find out why, and to urge me to come within doors, and . . . And I discovered he had not just been "being polite", as your mama thought.'

'Mama?'

'Yes, you see I asked her advice, when I thought perhaps Lord Deben was being a little particular in his attentions. She said he was just a very polite and thoughtful young man, which is true, and that I must not seem to encourage him, because it would make things awkward for him, and I did not want that. So I tried not to look at him, or speak too much with him, and . . . he looked confused, and I felt miserable. Then Sir Marcus began to single me out and . . . but it is all over, and he loves me.' Sarah blushed. 'He kissed me, Celia, once upon the terrace in the rain, and then again when he proposed. It was . . . exciting. Do you think it wicked of me to think so?'

'It would be most depressing if you found it boring.' Celia squeezed Sarah's hand. 'I am so very, very pleased for you, and for Lord Deben, who is the nicest of men. He has always treated me in a sisterly way, and never put me to the blush over my limp. You will be very happy, I am certain, and I nearly joined Marianne in applauding how you bested the awful Miss Darwen. At least I will not be married because of an accident, not because I am such a ghastly female, at least I hope not.'

'I still think you will be married, Celia. Lord Levedale has devoted so many hours to teaching you to drive, and I am sure you must have been proficient long before now. He must have a liking for you.'

It was true that he rarely advised her upon her handling of the reins now, but Celia resolutely told herself he saw that it was giving her opportunities to converse, which would not be so when she was accompanied by a groom, and so was being, like Lord Deben, kind. She did not believe it, but it was a good lie, because she had little doubt that it was to Marianne he would offer his hand, if not his heart.

'Your happiness inclines you to look upon everything in the most positive light. I do not blame you for it, but doubt its veracity. Now, about you and Lord Deben. Is he taking you home to Stratford, or going ahead to see your papa?'

'I would dearly like to be there, to introduce him. I am not sure he would choose to knock upon the door and simply announce himself as the man who wanted to wed the daughter of the house. He has said he will hire a post-chaise to convey me home, and he will accompany the vehicle in his curricle, since accompanying me in the chaise would be rather too daring. He will set about making preparations in the morning. It means I must break up the party, although some will not notice my departure, and others be glad of it.'

'I shall be glad only because I know it is for the most felicitous of reasons, and you must promise to write and tell me all about the response of your mama and papa. Now, off to your bed, lest there be bags under your eyes in the morning. Lord Deben would not like that.'

'Oh, I shall not sleep a wink, Celia.'

Sarah fell asleep almost as her head touched the pillow, and with a smile upon her face.

CHAPTER NINETEEN

Celia awoke with the feelings she associated with waking from a pleasant dream into depressing reality. This often occurred when she dreamt of dancing – dancing with a handsome, witty partner whose features were never recalled the moment she surfaced. In the last few weeks she had had such a dream twice, and knew exactly with whom she had danced. Lord Levedale's tall person, and his smile which compelled one to smile back, lingered after the music and steps were forgotten. This morning her feelings were not consequent to a dream, but the awareness that her friend Sarah, who had seemed doomed to a future as the wife of a man she did not love, and barely liked or respected, could now look forward to a future with the man she loved, and who loved her. She did not resent that, and was very happy for them both, but it contrasted starkly with what she herself faced. She had become reconciled to her single state, frustrated by her limitations but accepting that they held her back from the aspirations of her peers, that is until Lord Levedale had come into her life.

Now she was no longer reconciled, no longer accepting. She was consumed by negative emotions – anger, misery, despondency – and was conscious that the more they took control of her, the less there was for him to like. He had been attracted to her, she was sure of it. That first moment on that first evening, she had encountered a look she had never received from a man before, and felt as though something intangible but strong drew them together. To her total mystification, and growing dismay, the following days had seen him behave as if two different men. He was paying court to Marianne, although she would swear he did so without feeling. At the same time, having avoided her own person for several days, he had put himself in a situation where he was alone with her, and when they were together it was as if there was nobody else in the world. Their physical proximity, the occasional touch of gloved hands, a bumping of knees in the little pony cart, was as nothing to the feeling that in spirit they were so close as to meld into one being. When their eyes met it was as if she was in his arms, and yet he still attended Marianne in the manner of a suitor. It could only be that he was fighting his heart, and that his head told him that marriage to a cripple would be unthinkable. He might even assume that her injury prevented her, for some reason, bearing him an heir. Celia told herself it would be far better that he went away soon, and ended the torment, but at the same time she could not bear the thought of not seeing him again.

Lord Deben rose even earlier than his normal hour, and wrote a hasty note to the nearest posting inn, which was in Cirencester, requesting a vehicle in which to convey his beloved to her parents. He had debated whether departing before luncheon might seem impolite to his host and hostess, but came to the conclusion that arriving at Colonel Clandon's door just as he sat down to his dinner would not endear him to that gentleman. Therefore leaving before noon, and taking a little refreshment upon the road, was a better idea. Being naturally modest, it did not occur to Lord Deben that the arrival of a young man of title with unimpeachable manners and excellent prospects, seeking to marry their daughter, might put thoughts of food from the heads of both her parents.

Whilst most of the preparations for their joint departure did not affect the young couple, they spent a considerable time in making their farewells and thanks. Sarah ensured that Marianne Burton had her address, although Marianne cogently noted that it would not be many months before she must be sent a new and different address, and name. Sarah smiled at this, and confided that the idea of being called Lady Deben as yet felt alien.

'You will become used to it in a trice, and I shall write you lots of letters, but I expect replies.' Marianne's pleasure was unaffected and she did not for one moment regret that it was not her hand being sought first.

Secretly, Sarah thought that from what she had heard of Marianne's writing style from Celia, and her own knowledge of the young lady, interpreting the letters might delay any replies, but she promised to be a faithful correspondent.

Mr Mardham said goodbye to his friend with a degree of melancholy, being of the opinion that marriage would mean Deben never coming to Town, and being surrounded in short order by a plethora of children. Lord Deben's assurance that it would probably be Christmas before the knot was tied, and that he had every intention of bringing his new bride to London for the Season in the spring, did little to solace him.

'It is more likely that you will become sick of the sight of us, dear fellow. What with Mi . . . my Sarah being a connection of yours, and now a friend of your sister, we shall most likely be under your feet here at Meysey to the point where you think we haunt the place.' Lord Deben did not want his friend feeling dismal when he was in alt.

This improved Mr Mardham's mood to a degree. Celia was saying something quite similar to Sarah.

'You must, absolutely must, come and see us when

you are making bride visits, and if you can spare us the time from the whirl of Society you will always be welcome here. I shall miss you.'

Sarah still thought that Celia herself would not be living at Meysey by the following year, but forbore pressing the point.

Having waved the couple off, rather more as though they had just been married than were going to request permission to marry, the party adjourned for luncheon feeling a little flat.

The only person to take active pleasure in the departure of Sarah Clandon and Lord Deben was Miss Darwen, who went about with a smug look as if she had driven them away with intent. The only problem of which she was aware was a marked disinclination upon the part of all the other guests to listen to her pearls of wisdom, which was one way of looking at the fact that they ignored her. Of course her own situation had not materially improved, since Lord Levedale had proved such a disappointment to her. In fact the more she thought about it the more his disaffection rankled. What had been her aim became, in her mind, her right. He would have come about and paid court to her, and it was a combination of his own gullibility and the devious nature of Celia Mardham that had brought about what Mama might see as failure. The Cripple, unable to attract a man by honest means, had played upon her disability to make Levedale pity her, like some bird with a broken wing, and, like a fool, he had fallen into the trap. Well, if he was that foolish, he was unworthy, and she regretted wasting her time upon him.

Lady Mardham was relieved the young couple had gone, though she was conveniently coming to believe the self-deception that it was down to her that the romance had blossomed. However, their presence was a depressing reminder that poor Celia was not yet betrothed. The fact that she had received an offer that Lady Mardham had generally encouraged, and refused it, was set aside. Overall, her ladyship was tending to the pessimistic, and in such a mood needed an outlet for her feelings.

She found one conveniently in Mrs Wombwell. That lady was herself increasingly low-spirited, since she was watching her son making every effort to achieve a disastrous marriage, and for no better reason than the chit was uncommonly pretty. It was incomprehensible.

The two ladies retired to one of the smaller saloons after luncheon and reminisced about their own successes as debutantes, which solaced them both. However, after a while, Lady Mardham sighed.

'My poor Celia,' she murmured. 'When you think what Cora Clandon's daughter has achieved, it is most unfair. Not that Celia's hand has been unsought, but she has not received an offer that I could consider suitable.'

'Sir Marcus Cotgrave?' Mrs Wombwell was fairly certain, but it was nice to be sure.

'Alas, too old. I told Celia so. But if the Burton girl

can attract suitors with her background, you must be able to understand that I find Celia's lack of success most trying. I mean, she is really rather a beautiful girl, if one does not see the . . . so sad. I really ought not to tell you, but you are such a close friend, and I know you will not breathe a word, but Mardham's papa made the most peculiar stipulation in his Will.'

Lady Mardham then revealed the worry, indeed dread, that Aurelia Blaby's daughter would claim the inheritance, and make her mama even more insufferable. Since Mrs Wombwell had no liking for Lady Blaby, she could concur wholeheartedly that it was 'an Awful Thought'.

'And thirty thousand, you say?'

'Yes. Not that one would wish to attract fortune hunters, of course, but if it could be known I am sure many gentlemen could overlook poor Celia's problem for the sake of thirty thousand pounds.'

'Quite.' Mrs Wombwell, herself comfortably off, could still sympathise, and be impressed at the figure.

'I mean, if Deben could ignore Sarah Clandon being as poor as a church mouse, and that her ears had a tendency to stick out a little, did you not notice, and calling her "passable" is generous, Celia ought to be a great success still.'

Maria Wombwell's sympathy was very soothing.

Mr Wombwell found himself less than well disposed towards Lord Levedale. Whilst he was no longer chasing

The Money Pot, he appeared to have made the girl very cautious. There was thus, at this very late stage, still no sign that she had any inclination to succumb to The Wombwell Charm. It hurt his pride, and with Quarter Day upon him, Mr Wombwell knew that his return to London would be marked with a shower of insistent, and increasingly threatening, letters from his creditors. As a mark of his desperation, he had even started drawing up a list of wealthy widows who might lap up his flattery, and be forthcoming with the readies, even if he could avoid having to actually marry one of them.

He encountered his parent mid-afternoon, and his expression of discontent made her heart bleed for him.

'My poor boy.'

Mr Wombwell enjoyed being the object of maternal pity as much as having a peal rung over him. His frown deepened.

'Really, Mama, there is no need . . .'

'But there is. I am so distressed at the way you have, despite my strongest recommendations, continued after the Burton girl. If only you had done as I hoped.'

'Which was?'

'Given consideration to poor Celia Mardham. You would now be thirty thousand pounds to the better, not that it ought to signify, but even so . . .'

'Thirty thousand pounds?' Mr Wombwell's eyes nearly started from their sockets.

'Oh, I ought not to tell you, in one way, but . . .'
It did not stop her for a moment, and it left his brain

reeling. Miss Burton was worth more, in the long term, but thirty thousand, assured and without delay, would fund his pressing debts and make other creditors turn a blind eye to his dilatory payments in the hope of future custom. That limp was truly repulsive, but he would not have to live with it much. He could settle his bride with his mama, pop home occasionally, and otherwise carry on as normal. It had potential. The problem lay in time. As he saw it, the party would be breaking up by the end of the week, and Levedale's interest, which he had previously seen as an advantage, put the man once again in his way. What he needed was to remove Levedale as a rival and impress Miss Mardham, swiftly.

His frown remained, but now it was one of deep thought.

In blissful ignorance of the degree of antipathy which their relationship aroused, Lord Levedale suggested going out driving as a way of cheering Miss Mardham up, after the departure of her companion. He did not actually mention the word 'lesson', however.

'Oh, you must not think I am less than delighted for Sarah, and indeed for Lord Deben, sir. They are so well suited, and it is only that I will miss Sarah which occasions my slight lowness of spirits.' She thought it also an excellent cover for the true reason.

'There is Miss Burton.' He was thinking of her being unhappy at having Miss Darwen as a companion.

'Yes, there is.' Celia was still in two minds about

Marianne. There was nothing that the poor girl had done which would jeopardise their friendship, except attract the man sat opposite her in the pony cart. It had not been something of her making, and Celia felt guilty at her own cool feelings towards her erstwhile schoolfriend. Lord Levedale saw the slight crease between Celia's brows.

'Is there something troubling you, Miss Mardham? If there is any way in which I might help . . .'

Celia shook her head. She could scarcely say 'fall in love with me, please'.

'I think perhaps also I have, despite the Awful Miss Darwen, enjoyed having guests here, and the anticipation of the party breaking up, with two members already gone, is not conducive to high spirits, sir.' It was as close as she could get to the truth.

'Yes. I too will be sorry, very sorry.' He wanted to speak up, but without having cleared himself with Miss Burton it felt wrong. Tomorrow, yes, tomorrow he would be free to make his feelings known. At the moment, however, it was better to change the subject. 'You note, Miss Mardham, that I am not giving any criticism or advice upon your handling of the ribbons.'

'Yes, sir, I had noticed. That may of course be because you have decided it is a lost cause.' The dimple indicated that Miss Mardham did not consider this likely.

'There is that,' responded Lord Levedale, his face

impassive. 'Is this the point where you think I may beg you to deny even having driven out with me, and claim it was with Mr Wombwell?'

She dimpled further, and asked if he would be brave enough to complete three circuits of the park with her.

Miss Burton, keen to avoid Miss Darwen, went to write another letter to her papa. She thought perhaps it would be the last before sending a note that she would be coming home. There was much to say, what with the fire, and the strange incident with the pendant, and the Romance.

My dearest Papa,

I do not think it will be long before you have me once more at your side because the visit seems to be coming to an end. Two people have already departed but I will tell you about that later. We have had quite an exciting time these last few days and not entirely nice. I do not know if you suffered from a thunderstorm three nights past but it was awful here and Lady Corfemullen fainted and Miss Darwen had hysterics and Lady Mardham hit her which was a very good thing. A tree close to the house was struck by lightning and split right into two parts of which one fell onto the billiards room roof and we were so lucky. The gentlemen all went out with Lord Mardham and the servants to prevent the fire from spreading by using a ladder. Mr Mardham and Lord Levedale got upon the roof and pulled the top of the burning tree so that it fell onto the ground. Mr Mardham fell off the roof too but it was not far and he had a sprained ankle and buckets of water were thrown at it. Lord Deben was also very brave in rescuing Mr Mardham and so Celia and Sarah Clandon and I became nurses and got water and cloths and things and all the little injuries were cared for. It was very frightening but exciting at the same time.

The next day Miss Darwen thought her pendant had been stolen but nobody would want to steal such a dismal jewel I promise you. Lord Deben thought it was ravens. She was most unpleasant about it and hinted that Celia was the thief which was silly because Celia could not climb a drainpipe.

In the end Lord Levedale found the pendant under a plant stand by Miss Darwen's chamber and everyone was happy except I think Miss Darwen. This must be because of the slap in the face disordering her wits. Lady Mardham came to dinner I mean old Lady Mardham from the Dower House. She is most formidable and everyone is afraid of her I think but she was very gracious and nice to me because she did not say anything cutting.

Lord Deben has gone off with Sarah Clandon. They are very much in love and he wants to speak to her papa so they went away before luncheon which was very nice but also a bit sad. I liked Sarah even though she was quiet and poor. It just shows that money and beauty do not guarantee that love will be forthcoming which I find in fact Papa quite heartening.

Mr Wombwell has been quite persistent and I am becoming annoyed at it. I hope he goes soon. His mama has been quite unpleasant and I am sure she does not like him chasing after me. Lord Levedale is very friendly and funny but he is not at all in love with me and I do not mind because he would suit Celia very well even with the limp. I am not so old that I need to be afraid that I shall not receive an offer from some nice gentleman. In the meantime I shall be coming home to be happy with you my dearest Papa.

I remain your loving

Marianne

PS I will write to say I am coming home so that the bed is aired.

Thinking that this would provide her parent with much entertainment, Marianne went to find Lord Mardham so that he might frank the letter. She was already imagining being back at home with Papa and spending several evenings discussing all that had gone on in the last few weeks. She almost walked straight into Lord Levedale as he returned from driving with Miss Mardham.

'Oh! I am so sorry, my lord. I was wool-gathering!' She blushed, prettily.

Lord Levedale saw his opportunity, and seized it.

'Miss Burton, might I beg the honour of a few minutes of private conversation with you.'

'I . . .' Marianne was not sure how to proceed. She trusted Lord Levedale, but being closeted with a gentleman sounded dubious. His look, which was intent, but not passionate in any way, made up her mind for her. 'Yes, my lord, a few minutes.'

He opened the door for her into the yellow saloon, and found it thankfully empty. He invited her to sit, but remained standing. Neither had observed Miss Darwen as she entered the hall, or followed to place her ear to the door.

'Miss Burton, I have a confession to make.'

CHAPTER TWENTY

Marianne took a deep breath.

'My lord, if you are about to tell me that you are not intending to make me an offer, I can only say that it is not in any way a surprise to me. You are very nice, and entertaining, but . . . why do you pay so much attention to me when it is my friend for whom you have a decided preference?'

'Ah.' Lord Levedale gave a rueful smile. 'Ah' was the best he could come up with in the circumstances. He had no idea what to say. It was Marianne Burton who eased the situation; she whose openness had caused awkward moments.

'I have to confess, my lord, that I am a frequent correspondent with my papa, who has disclosed to me that you came to Meysey thinking to find, perhaps, a partner in life. Yet at first I did not think that could be the case. Over the past weeks, however, it has seemed to me that my dear friend Miss Mardham has come to entertain tender feelings towards you, and that they are reciprocated. I fail to understand why you see the need to use me as a diversion. Surely, you are not testing her affections? And you cannot believe that Lord Mardham would not be happy to see Celia established.'

'Miss Burton, I can do nothing but apologise to you.' Lord Levedale looked most discomfited. 'There are reasons – reasons which I am not at liberty to disclose – why I came to Meysey, why I . . .' He halted. How could he tell this innocent young woman that he had been sent to woo her for her dowry. 'You had been described to me as a very nice young lady, and very beautiful. I came, forgive me, to see if perhaps we might suit, and with not the slightest idea that my heart would become engaged elsewhere.'

'That does not explain why you have persisted in paying attention to me, sir.'

'No. It does not.' His collar felt too tight, the room suddenly oppressively hot.

Miss Burton looked at him, candidly, but with sadness.

'Will gentlemen only ever pay attention to me because I am an heiress, sir?'

He had thought her a beautiful, guileless ninny, and perhaps in some ways she was, but Marianne Burton had learnt a surprising amount during her stay at

Meysey, and among a set of people from whom, just occasionally, she felt set apart. Men liked to look at her. She had known that since she was sixteen, and she simply accepted it. She was not a vain girl, and did not preen herself over it. Her Papa, she knew, had ambitions for her to be a titled lady, but not to the exclusion of her happiness. He thought the wealth she would inherit would assist her, but she was coming to the conclusion that it would be a burden.

Lord Levedale shook his head.

'Miss Burton, you are a very beautiful young lady, and unlike some beauties, do not "demand" adoration. I hope I may be as frank with you as you have been with me. Some men will seek you out because of the money you will inherit, and they will charm you, but I think, since you have been so perspicacious in seeing how things lie between myself and Miss Mardham, that you will not be taken in by charm alone. Some men will admire your beauty but find your, forgive me, lack of "lineage", an obstacle. However, I am certain that there will be gentlemen who will disregard it, for you are most ladylike in all respects, and among them you will find one worthy of your affections. I cannot promise he will be titled, of course, and a title does not guarantee that a man is of good character, I assure you.'

'Thank you. It is perhaps now a case of being where I might meet gentlemen.'

'You have made good acquaintanceships here. I do

not doubt you will receive other invitations to visit friends.'

'So no invitation from Miss Darwen then.' Marianne dimpled, and he laughed.

'No, for which you may be truly thankful. You might find a sojourn in Bath "useful", if Sir Thomas were to lease a house for some months, and employ a lady to chaperone you.'

'He has vowed never to take the waters again, having tasted them, my lord.'

'I do not blame him for that, but there is more to Bath than taking the cure. You are very young, Miss Burton, still unfurling your petals, so to speak. Do not feel crushed that this foray into Society has not brought forth your "knight in shining armour".'

'I shall not. This does not, however, make all well between yourself and my friend Celia.'

'No, but it salves my conscience in one part at least. I had feared that my attentions might have led you to anticipate that which I could not, in any honesty, offer you. I may now go to Miss Mardham and try to explain . . . beg her forgiveness . . . and hope she forgives me being a prize idiot.'

Try as she might, Miss Darwen could not catch every word, but she heard enough to be outraged. Lord Levedale was obviously intending to make The Cripple a declaration, and he and The Ninny had laughed at her, Lavinia Darwen. Well, the laughter was past changing, but Miss Darwen's lips lengthened in a most unpleasant smile. She might yet get her revenge upon him, and ruin his chances. It was all a matter of timing.

Lord Levedale made a valiant attempt at shaving himself before dressing for dinner, but was all of a doo-dah. He managed to nick his chin to add to the slightly disreputable look that his visage, as yet not fully healed, conveyed. It was not, he admitted to himself, the ideal face for making a proposal of marriage. He had not seen Miss Mardham between the end of their drive and coming upstairs to change, and realistically, there was no possible opportunity of requesting an interview with her alone before dinner.

When he did go down and joined the others, she was listening to Lord Pocklington and her brother. Richard Mardham was seated, since standing upon one leg only was exceedingly tiring. Lord Pocklington was in discussion with him about whether he would be fit to join him for some cubbing with the Quorn.

Lord Levedale thought Miss Mardham still had a vague air of preoccupation. Although Miss Clandon had been very quiet, and Lord Deben emollient, their absence seemed to have changed the dynamic of the party. There was an air of dissatisfaction, a feeling that the party must break up. The Corfemullens were together, talking to Lady Mardham, but close together as if for silent but mutual support.

Miss Burton was being lectured by Miss Darwen,

and seemed resigned to her fate, and Mrs Wombwell was engaged in a very desultory discussion with Lord Mardham and Sir Marcus. Mr Wombwell had not yet deigned to make his appearance. When he did so he had an air of arrogant boredom on his face, but immediately placed himself so that he might engage Miss Mardham in conversation, and Lord Levedale thought that he glanced at him and smirked as he did so. Having rather better manners, Lord Levedale, who had been on the point of extricating himself from the Corfemullens and his hostess, moved on without looking towards Miss Mardham, and nobly attempted to rescue Miss Burton by putting himself next to Miss Darwen. She had recently become a little less of a burden to him, but this evening her glance was remarkably cool and supercilious, if not downright antagonistic. He could only assume that his action over the pendant had at last broken her idea of attempting to ensnare him.

'How is your face, my lord?' she asked, not with sympathy, but, he felt, rather as if she hoped he would say it was giving him continued discomfort.

'Oh, much as you see, Miss Darwen. Shaving is a trifle awkward, but healing takes longer than one would hope. I shall be in the pink of condition in a few days, rather than red of face.'

Her smile could have curdled milk.

'I am very glad we ladies never have to shave,' said Marianne Burton, with a slight shudder. 'I would hate to have to wield the sharp blades for fear of cutting myself, and to have to do it daily . . .' She pulled a face.

'Ah, but we are spared curling papers, or hot metal tongs, or whatever it is that keeps ladies' hair so nice, and there is little time wasted upon dressing our hair. A good brushing, and perhaps a little oil, and we are set.'

'But having one's hair dressed in different ways is quite fun,' Miss Burton smiled, rather more genuinely than Miss Darwen.

'Only for ladies, Miss Burton, I assure you.'

She dimpled, and Celia noticed, and then felt guilty for her jealous feeling. It did not improve at dinner, because Lord Levedale was so light-hearted. Being relieved of the concern that Miss Burton, sat next to him, might be taking his advances seriously, and anticipating making a declaration to Miss Mardham, he was plainly happy. He and Miss Burton were at ease, and Miss Darwen smiled all the way through her mushroom soup, even though she was not fond of fungi. Miss Mardham barely touched her food, and was glad when the ladies rose to withdraw. This feeling did not last long.

Miss Darwen was trying to judge her moment. She did not want to make a scene so early that Miss Mardham disappeared before the gentlemen joined the ladies, but she had to make her move prior to that arrival. She therefore appeared to listen to Lady Corfemullen's tale of a tipsy cook and an ensuing dinner disaster before going to sit near Miss Mardham and Miss Burton.

'So, Miss Burton, are you going to keep your secret, or tell us your news?'

'My news?' Marianne looked surprised.

'Come, come, do not tell us you have none, or are you waiting until your dear papa has been informed?'

Celia's mouth felt suddenly dry, and her heart beat too fast.

'I do not know what you mean,' declared Marianne, but she blushed.

'You were closeted with Lord Levedale some time, and alone. Do not tell us you were discussing the weather,' Miss Darwen gave a peculiar titter, 'we really would not believe you.'

Marianne was in a dilemma. She could not reveal the true conversation, for how could she say 'We discussed him not wanting to marry me but marrying my friend', with that friend before her and unaware of the imminent proposal.

'It was nothing important,' murmured Marianne, looking at the floor.

'Yet both of you seemed very happy this evening,' purred Miss Darwen. 'You really cannot disguise a man in love, can you.'

'No, I suppose not, but . . .'

'Then you have given us our answer.' Miss Darwen looked triumphant, as well she might.

Marianne Burton fumbled to find the right words.

'It is not as you imagine. We—'

'Ah, that lovely term "we", indicative of a couple. How romantic.'

Celia wanted the floor to open up and swallow her.

She felt a little sick and rather faint. Although she had feared that he would offer for Marianne despite, she was sure, having some form of tendre for herself, he had pushed it to one side. Her own feelings for him had become so strong it had to be unthinkable, and yet he had done so, straight after their afternoon drive together when he had seemed so concerned about her agitation of spirits. She could not look Marianne in the eye and say 'congratulations', but nor did she blame her for what had happened.

'Are you quite well, Celia?' Marianne saw her friend's colour drain from her face.

'Yes, yes. I mean, my leg is somewhat more uncomfortable than usual this evening, that is all.'

There were sounds from the hallway, male voices, and then the gentlemen entered. Lord Levedale was first, and his eyes went towards the sofa where Celia and Marianne were seated. He smiled. He might not be able to speak to Miss Mardham tonight, but should be able to at least arrange to speak with her in the morning, and she would be in no doubt as to the reason for the interview.

Celia saw Lord Levedale's smile, and in that moment all Celia's misery became anger. Just so had he smiled at her, not once but each time they went out driving, each time their eyes met. How could he be so perfidious as to positively encourage her to lose her heart to him, and do the same with Marianne Burton? Mr Wombwell had a reputation as a ladies' man and made no real pretence to be otherwise, but he, he had played the decent fellow all the way through, and she had believed him. He was coming towards them, still smiling. She could not bear to be close to him, and so rose, gripping her stick firmly, and turned away. Lady Mardham was speaking to Lady Corfemullen, but not in any great discussion. Celia said the first thing that came into her head.

'Mama, might I order the carriage tomorrow and go into Cirencester? I would like to buy a pair of gloves for when I drive my new phaeton, and I have gone through the heel of one too many stockings. The patten really increases the wear.'

Lady Mardham looked up at her daughter. There was a brittleness to her voice at odds with the mundane nature of her words, which confused her.

'Well, Lady Corfemullen is coming with me to visit your grandmama in the morning, so it could not be then, but if you could wait until the afternoon . . .'

Lord Levedale was immediately behind Celia.

'If you wish to go to Cirencester in the morning, Miss Mardham, I would be honoured to drive you. I am sure with a little care you could manage to climb—' He got no further.

She turned on him, pushing away the arm he extended as she wobbled. Her face was white, not with shock, but fury.

'I would rather . . . hobble to Cirencester, my lord.' Her voice was low, but throbbed with passion. He froze.

'If I could be of any assistance, ma'am? I would be immensely honoured to put myself, and my groom, of course, at your disposal.' Mr Wombwell saw his chance. There had clearly been some rift between Levedale and Miss Mardham, and he was keen to exploit the opportunity it offered.

'Thank you, Mr Wombwell. I shall be delighted.'

'Then let us be away betimes, ma'am. Shall we say nine of the clock?'

'An excellent hour.' With which Celia grasped her stick firmly, and, casting Lord Levedale a look which combined loathing and defiance, stalked out of the room as best she could. He was left looking after her with such a look of patent astonishment upon his face that Miss Darwen positively beamed at Sir Marcus and invited him to tell her about his orangery.

There was nothing Lord Levedale could do, and in any case he was at a loss to understand what had just taken place. As he had entered the drawing room he had smiled, thinking to go over to Miss Mardham, and knowing Miss Burton would understand what he was about. He had seen that Miss Mardham's face was marked by an absence of colour, and she had then flashed him an intensely angry look, but he could not for the life of him think why. It occurred to him that Miss Burton might have revealed something of their afternoon conversation in some addle-brained attempt to pave the way for him, and it had been misconstrued. Perhaps Miss Mardham felt that he was using Miss Burton as an intermediary and was, quite understandably, annoyed that he was not brave enough to declare himself without the assurance of her friend smoothing the path for him. However, a swift glance at Miss Burton had shown her startled in the extreme.

Besides, any irritation at his being pusillanimous about making her an offer would not have made her as patently incandescent with anger as she had shown herself to be. There was no logic to it at all, and all he could do was intercept her in the morning, and make things right. It was far from ideal, but it was all he could do.

He had intended to rise early, but slept fitfully, and finally woke late. He came down to breakfast just after nine and found Miss Burton in possession of the breakfast room. She had hoped to speak with her friend before her expedition, but had just missed her departure.

'Good morning, Miss Burton. Breakfasting alone?'

'Yes, my lord.' She paused, then asked what was in her mind. 'Lord Levedale, what happened last night?' Marianne was curious, and having had such a frank interview with him the day previously, felt she might ask.

'I am not entirely sure, Miss Burton. No, let me be honest. I have no idea at all.'

'I am not sure why Celia agreed to let Mr Wombwell drive her to Cirencester.'

'You recall, I am sure, that I described myself as "a prize idiot"? I think, Miss Burton, that was to show me that I am indeed a prize idiot.'

'Oh. I see. At least I think I see. But Mr Wombwell is not driving her to Cirencester.'

'He is not?' Lord Levedale spoke sharply, and Marianne dropped her slice of toast.

'No, for I overheard him telling his valet to have his evening clothes all laid out in readiness, because he might not be back from Bath until shortly before the dinner hour. Had I seen Celia, I would have warned her. '

'Bath! Good God, has the man no sense? Miss Mardham could not travel to Bath in his phaeton, especially not at the pace he would have to take to get there and back in the day, let alone with any time for Miss Mardham to complete her shopping. He is either mad, bad or a mixture of both. Miss Burton, I must leave you immediately. If I can catch them I may be able to bring Miss Mardham back before she has sustained any harm.'

'You think it that serious, sir?' Marianne paled.

'I do.'

'Oh dear.'

Lord Levedale did not bother sending to the stables to prepare his curricle, but simply went to his bedchamber taking the stairs two at a time, shrugged himself into his driving coat, grabbed hat and gloves, and went to order the vehicle prepared as he waited. Rarely had Lord Mardham's stable worked so fast as they did with his lordship clearly so keen to be off, and looking at his watch before them. Knook climbed up behind as the horses were set in motion, and the curricle swept from the yard at a very brisk trot. The pace was increased to a canter until the main gates of the estate were reached, and there, perforce, they were brought to a brief halt until the gates were opened. The curricle moved off and turned immediately to the left, and was set once more to a cracking pace. Lord Levedale did not, therefore, see the carriage that turned into the gateway before the lodgekeeper had time to shut them, nor the crest upon its doors.

CHAPTER TWENTY-ONE

Celia had regretted agreeing to travel with Mr Wombwell from the moment his groom climbed up behind and he set his horses in motion. He did not do so with the tidiness of Lord Levedale, but rather a swaggering bravado that clearly put his animals upon the fret. Before they had even left the park he had looked at her, grinning, and declared, 'How about at little excitement to blow the fidgets away', and set his pair to a canter which was not in the least comfortable. He slowed, with reluctance, for the gates. They turned in the direction that would take them to the Cirencester road, but again the pace was unnecessarily swift, and Celia protested.

'Mr Wombwell, we are not attempting to arrive in Cirencester, make purchases, and be back by noon.'

'Cirencester? Why, ma'am, a lady such as yourself is

wasted upon the meagre shops of Cirencester. For today you are in my hands, and I would have so fair a lady make her purchases in Milsom Street. We are going to Bath, for I have kidnapped you on an adventure, and I shall have you back in time for dinner too, laden with bandboxes.'

Celia went white.

'It is a poor jest sir.'

'No jest, I assure you. Fie, Miss Mardham, do you have no adventure in you? Bath. Think of it in comparison with Cirencester.'

'I am thinking that the distance is too great, Mr Wombwell.'

'Not if I spring 'em,' he laughed, and dropped his hands.

The phaeton bowled along, but at a pace neither safe nor at all pleasant. Miss Mardham closed her eyes as they swept past a gig with the crown of a bend before them.

'Please, I beg of you, sir, ameliorate the pace and let us go to Cirencester only.'

'Scared, Miss Mardham? You will become adjusted. Levedale is but a mere whipster who dares not handle his cattle at pace. He has got you used to creeping about when the open road is for speed.'

For a moment Celia wondered if the man had been drinking late into the night, and was thus still drunk, but there was no breath of spirits upon him.

'Why are you doing this?' she cried.

He looked at her. He had thought perhaps to entrance her by his spontaneous act and dashing conduct, but the little fool was just a scared girl. Well, if he might not win her over by charm and daring he would at least be revenged upon Levedale. For all that the girl had given him the cold shoulder last night, the man was clearly besotted, and imagine his horror when he found out that she had been transported to Bath and back.

'It pleases me to do so, Miss Mardham. I wish it.'

'It is madness.'

'It is escape from stultifying boredom, ma'am. Now, if you are a good girl, and do not bleat forever at me, I will myself purchase you a nice bonnet in Bath.'

Celia was stuck. Even if they had to halt at a toll gate, she was incapable of dismounting from the phaeton without assistance. All she could do was cling on, and pray. In addition, she at first mentally berated Lord Levedale for his driving her into the lunatic arms of Mr Wombwell, but then honesty made her accept that it was her own pride that had committed the folly. She had wanted to prove she did not need or want Lord Levedale's company. She had lied to herself – lied because she was hurt.

The bouncing about, and the need to grip the handrail for dear life, soon took its toll. She felt physically sick, and her leg ached appallingly. The speed was ameliorated a little in Cirencester itself but increased once more as they turned onto the post road towards Tetbury. She knew it well enough. The Bath road through Malmesbury would turn from it in a few miles. She must endure hours of this, and how thereafter she was meant to travel home by the same method she could not imagine. She tried to think clearly.

At this pace he must surely change horses at The Old Bell in Malmesbury. She wondered if she might request assistance to alight upon some pretext there, and refuse to continue. The coin in her purse had been for gloves and stockings, but would surely cover the cost of sending a post boy home to Meysey with a note for Papa. How she was to account for her being with a gentleman so far from home and so desirous of parting company with him that she would face sitting alone and unchaperoned in a posting inn, she did not know, but her body could not possibly endure such a shaking all the way to Bath.

It did not have to do so. Some miles short of Malmesbury, Mr Wombwell overtook a laden waggon, and upset the oxen pulling it. As they tossed angry heads, his horses spooked, for a moment he lost control, and the next his large rear wheel had gone onto the roadside and they were veering into the ditch. He hauled upon his horses' mouths, and they jibbed. The phaeton teetered at a precarious angle, and the carman, having settled his beasts, ambled past with comments that were not fit for a lady's ears. Celia did not hear them, for she was sat, paralysed by fear that the vehicle was about to tip onto its side, and she would be in the ditch with it upon her.

* * *

Lord Levedale was not a man who drove recklessly, not in normal circumstances. These were not normal circumstances, and Jeb Knook was both shocked and surprised at the pace, and his lordship's willingness to overtake other vehicles at speed. He suppressed a remonstrance the first time, but was favourably impressed by his employer's skill. Besides which, his lordship was usually a pleasant and well-tempered gentleman, and the look upon his face now was one of grim determination and anger. Knook said nothing. They negotiated Cirencester at a necessarily curtailed pace, but once upon the straight road of the old Fosse Way Lord Levedale dropped his hands and for a few brief miles his team had their heads. Contrary to Mr Wombwell's belief, he did know how to handle his horses.

He judged that they were good to last until Malmesbury and he had every hope of catching Wombwell before that point. He paid attention to the road, but his mind was full of tumultuous thoughts. What was Wombwell thinking, trying to get Miss Mardham to Bath and back in a day? Even assuming a ridiculous pace it was the best part of four hours and the thought of her at risk from Wombwell showing off his driving skills sent a chill down Lord Levedale's back. He told himself that the man would not be so foolish, but did not fully believe it.

Just after crossing the Thames & Severn canal the post road to Malmesbury turned off the Tetbury road.

By now his right hand was hurting, and the glove felt slightly sticky inside.

It was perhaps no more than three miles before he saw a vehicle ahead of him, precariously situated with one wheel in the ditch, and the driver struggling to control his horses. He wanted it to be Wombwell, even though he knew Miss Mardham, who must be the female figure leaning at a desperate angle, must be terrified of the phaeton toppling over. He pulled up his team a little to the rear of the accident, with a curt command to Knook to stand to his horses' heads, and came up to the carriage on the near side. He stepped down into the ditch, which was comparatively dry, ignoring the risk that the equipage might yet fall sideways upon him. Miss Mardham, her face white, her lips compressed, was clinging on to the side of the vehicle.

'Miss Mardham, you will be quite safe. Loosen your grip and let gravity have its way. I will not let you fall.' She stared at him, her eyes wide. 'Celia. It is alright. Trust me.'

She did trust him, but she had spent every mile since Cirencester gripping the thin rail as if it were her hope of salvation, and now that grip had become vice-like, and she could not move her fingers.

'I cannot. My hands . . . are fixed.' Her voice was a whisper of distress.

'Look at me. You must relax them. All will be well now. I will take you home.'

'My leg hurts.' She was frightened, frightened of what

might happen, and of what might have already happened. Her words frightened him also, but he applied logic.

'You have been jostled about and jarred by the accident. It is no wonder that it hurts, but I am sure no worse has occurred. I will take you back to Meysey and your doctor can be summoned.' He spoke calmly, ignoring the imprecations Wombwell was still directing at his groom, struggling with the frightened horses, ignoring too the movement of the phaeton. 'Trust me, Celia. Let go, my love.' The endearment sprang naturally to his lips. She was looking at him intently, willing herself to be able to obey the instruction, and those two words made the difference.

She had accepted Wombwell's offer in a fit of pique, wanting to show she did not need Lord Levedale, did not care if he offered for Marianne – but she did need him, did care. He called her 'his love' and look and voice confirmed the truth of the words. She wanted the security of his arms about her. She shut her eyes, focused upon loosening her own grip and, with a gasping cry, slipped from the seat and into his arms.

He stood firm, almost, staggering only very slightly as he was put off balance, and held her close. She was trembling. The phaeton lurched as the disposition of weight changed, but did not slip further into the ditch. He stepped carefully along the inequalities of the ditch bottom to where the slope was less steep and he could see a likely foothold. He did not want to relinquish his burden to Knook, nor take the groom from his horses' heads. He trod with care, and if Celia gave a little cry as she felt their balance teeter, the manoeuvre took but a moment, and then they were upon the road. He smiled down at her, encouragingly.

'You see. I told you I would not—' He stopped. She was looking at him, and there was so much more than trust in her eyes. Knook had his back to them, and Wombwell and the other groom were likewise engaged in other things. Nobody would see. He kissed her; in one lingering kiss he conveyed his love, that her ordeal was over, that her safety was assured. 'Celia, oh my dear girl.' He pressed his cheek to hers. 'If anything terrible had befallen you . . .' The thought drew him back to an awareness of Wombwell. 'I would have killed him, I swear it.'

'He is of no matter, now.'

'No, of no matter. You must trust me further, my love, and let me lift you into my curricle. Arms tight about my neck, yes?'

'Yes.' She gave the tiniest of smiles, and gripped him tightly. He took the step without lingering, so that they were not balanced upon its narrowness for more than a second, and set her upon the seat. Then he went round to climb up and take the reins.

'Good girl.' He sat beside her and called Knook to stand away from the horses's heads and climb up behind once more. Then he began to manoeuvre carefully past the damaged phaeton. Mr Wombwell cast him a scowling look.

'Here. Take me up instead of the groom and I can get a fresh turn-out in Malmesbury, Levedale.'

'It is probably no more than five miles, Wombwell. The walk will do you good. You can use the time to consider your foolhardiness, and your lack of consideration for Miss Mardham's safety and wellbeing. You may also consider how close you have come to me knocking you down, here and now. Oh, and by the by, two of the spokes of your nearside wheel are broken.' With which Lord Levedale set his pair to an easy trot, and looked to the road ahead.

Celia was still trembling, and he glanced at her pallor. It was the jarring and the shock, nothing more, surely.

'I am going to change horses in Malmesbury, for mine are best part blown, and a fresh team will give an easier ride.' He raised his voice. 'Jeb.'

'Yes, my lord.'

'I would have you wait with the horses, and bring them back to Meysey at an easy pace, this afternoon. They ought to be rested enough by then.'

'But that means we shall be alone, my lord,' murmured Celia. 'What of the proprieties?'

'To be frank, my love, the proprieties can go hang in a situation that is an emergency such as this, but you are right. As an honourable man, I shall of course repair immediately to Lord Mardham and offer for your hand.' He managed to keep his voice steady.

'You must not think that . . .' Celia saw his lips twitch. 'It is not fair to roast me, sir, for I am in no condition to think.' She sighed. 'I just wish that I might cease to shake. It is most demeaning and unpleasant. I have always despised "die away airs" and look at me now.'

He looked.

'Very nice, though I prefer you with more colour.'

In more normal circumstances she would have blushed fierily, but only the slightest change was visible upon her cheek.

The remainder of the journey into Malmesbury was conducted in near silence, Lord Levedale concentrating upon making their progress as smooth as possible, while Celia tried to set her thoughts in order. They reached The Old Bell in Malmesbury, where Celia declined an offer of tea, and preferred to remain seated in the curricle during the change of horses rather than be lifted down.

'If you feel too knocked about, I can secure a chamber for you here, drive back to Meysey and have a more comfortable carriage come for you with your mother to attend you.' Lord Levedale was worried by her looking so unwell.

'Thank you, but I want to get home, to my own bed, and if Dr Stour might be called . . . I would feel the easier for knowing there is nothing really wrong.'

'You know, were that not so, your condition would be far worse. Once a bone is mended I believe it is no weaker than before, and you were not, thank God, thrown from the phaeton. You have been jolted and frightened and bumped about frightfully, but the discomfort will pass. You need rest.' He squeezed her gloved hand.

'All set, my lord. I'll have the chestnuts rubbed down and watered, and bring them back nice 'nd easy like you said.' Knook looked quite unperturbed, as if they had merely gone for a morning's jaunt.

'Thank you, Jeb.' Lord Levedale handed him coin to pay for whatever was needed at the inn.

'My lord, since you are not about to drive at a ludicrous pace, might I suggest the route back via Cricklade, which is not as straight, but shorter, and a quieter road?' suggested Celia, diffidently.

'Of course. You will have to direct me in the lanes after Cricklade, however.'

'I know them well enough, sir.'

He turned his new pair about and took the road as directed. The horses were pretty evenly matched, and had, he was relieved to find, a good, even pace.

'You are not too uncomfortable at this speed?' The trot was steady. 'I should have you back to Meysey in an hour and a half at a guess.'

She shook her head, with a ghost of a smile.

'That's the spirit.'

It was another mile or so before she spoke.

'This is, of course, all my fault.'

'I would like to hear how. You goaded Wombwell into driving to Bath at breakneck pace?'

'Of course not, but I ought never to have accepted his offer of taking me anywhere. I dislike and distrust the man.'

'So why did you?' He had a fair guess as to the reason

but wondered if she would admit it openly.

'Because . . . because I wanted to show you I did not care, and I did, I do. I did not want you to marry Marianne, and I did not understand how you could behave that way with her and make me fall in love with you at the same time.' The words tumbled out.

'My darling, I do not think the word "make" ever entered into our falling in love. I even tried not to do so, and have failed "miserably".'

She leant very slightly against his shoulder.

'I tried too, because I thought it was not possible that you should love me, but when we were together I felt as never before. When you took me out driving I had no doubts, and yet, at the house, you . . . you flirted with Marianne.'

'I shall explain, later. Suffice to say, it was not from any natural inclination to do so, Celia, my love.'

'And when you said you would speak with Father, it was from "inclination" not a feeling that you ought?'

'You know that. You must know that.' He slowed the horses to a walk. The road was empty. He slid an arm about her shoulders, and she held up her face for his kisses. When they parted, she slipped her arm through his as he drove on.

'It seems so strange that you do not mind me being . . . as I am.'

'Oh, I mind, Celia,' he said, his voice still a little husky. 'I mind an awful lot, but not because you are crippled, but that the injury "cripples" your enjoyment of life, curtails what you want to do.'

'It appears it will not curtail me from doing what I want most of all, and becoming your wife.'

'And I want to make as many things possible for you as can be achieved. There will always be limitations, Celia, but life can still be a delight.' He could not say what filled his mind at that moment, that the thought of her as his wife conjured up those thoughts most unsuitable for a public road. When he had kissed her her response had been inexperienced, of course, but innocently eager, and in his arms he had been aware of the soft femininity of her. It had heightened his desire for her.

Celia felt otherworldly, her body at odds with heart and mind. Her leg ached abominably, all her muscles felt overwrought, and the shaking, at last diminishing, was exhausting. She had barely the strength to sit upright, and yet her heart beat strongly. Her mind, which had been fogged with terror, had cleared only to be filled with such delicious and happy thoughts it could still not function at a pragmatic level. He loved her.

The journey back to Meysey was one which both parties wanted simultaneously to last forever and be over as soon as possible. Being alone together transcended mere pleasure, though the irony was that in a situation where they might talk unreservedly of their feelings, they were too overwhelmed to say much. At the same time Celia was frightened that some damage might have been done to her leg, and Lord Levedale, despite being more sanguine, wanted the reassurance of her doctor.

When they drew up outside the house, Celia sighed with relief. Lady Mardham came out in a flutter of agitation, but Lord Levedale barely acknowledged her, dismounted, and came round to look up at his beloved.

'Safe home, as I promised.' He smiled gently at her, set one foot upon the step, and lifted her from the curricle, settling her more securely in his arms to carry her into the house.

'Miss Mardham has been badly shaken, and it would be advisable, ma'am, to send for her doctor, just to alleviate any qualms.' He spoke calmly to Lady Mardham, seeing a woman who might dissolve into tears, if not hysterics, and strode to the front door. Copthorne held the door wide as he stepped within. He was about to carry her up to her room, but then realised that to do so would imply a knowledge of her bedchamber that might raise embarrassing questions. 'Direct me to Miss Mardham's bedchamber, and have her maid attend her immediately, please.'

'Yes, my lord.' Lord Levedale was clearly in charge of the situation, and Copthorne obeyed without demur.

Lady Mardham fussed behind, suggesting everything from possets to hot bricks and laudanum. Lord Levedale carried Miss Mardham up the broad staircase in Copthorne's wake, and along the passageway to her chamber, where the butler held the door wide. His lordship stepped over the threshold and laid his burden tenderly upon the bed.

'I will leave you now, Miss Mardham,' the words were formal, but his smile was intimate.

'Thank you,' she whispered. Her hand reached for his. He clasped it, removed the glove, and kissed the back of her fingers. 'I do not know what else to say.'

'We do not need mere words. I know that I have your "yes".'

'You do.'

'Rest, and do not worry. I shall go and find your father.' He turned, a little too quickly for Copthorne, whose normal impassivity had been replaced by a beatific smile, and for Lady Mardham, for whom his final words had cast any worries about her daughter aside. Her handkerchief was clutched to her bosom, but her face was a picture of relief and joy. Lord Levedale nodded to her ladyship and withdrew before she could assail him with questions, congratulations, or anything else.

CHAPTER TWENTY-TWO

Lord Levedale's desire to speak immediately with Lord Mardham was disrupted. At the foot of the stairs Mrs Wombwell was wringing her hands, and turned an ashen face towards him.

'My poor boy! What has happened to my poor boy? You are returned, but he . . .' She dissolved into gulping sobs.

'Your "poor boy" ma'am, is perfectly well, except perhaps for a blister or two.' Lord Levedale did not sound in the least sympathetic. In fact he sounded as if he wished Mr Wombwell was indeed lying lifeless at a roadside. 'That is far better than he deserves, and if I encounter him upon his return I may yet ram his teeth down his throat.'

Mrs Wombwell's eyes widened in horror. 'Villain!' She

exclaimed, and stepped forward to drum her fists upon his chest.

'Oh, take a damper, ma'am.' Exasperated, Lord Levedale thrust the lady from him, and made for the library, which he knew to be Lord Mardham's favourite bolthole. He entered with the grim look still upon his face, which was rather unusual for a man about to solicit a young lady's hand in marriage. Lord Mardham was already gazing towards the door, wondering at the high-pitched commotion beyond it. He regarded Lord Levedale with a questioning look.

'Mrs Wombwell, my lord, and needless hysteria.'

'Ah. I do not hear the more familiar tone of my wife in the same state, I note.'

'No, my lord. She is with Miss Mardham, who has sustained, I believe, no lasting hurt, but has been rather shaken and is laid upon her bed until her doctor can assure her all is as it should be.'

'What happened?' Lord Mardham poured himself a glass of claret, and proffered one to Lord Levedale, who shook his head, and described the accident upon the Malmesbury road.

'Wombwell's a damned fool,' grumbled Lord Mardham.

'Yes, sir. He is.'

'And I owe you a debt of gratitude for rescuing my daughter.'

'There is none, sir, but if you believe it to be so then it is easily repaid. I would ask that you permit me to make Miss Mardham a formal offer.'

'I assume that, informally, there is an understanding between you?'

'Yes, my lord, there is.'

'I see. Well, I cannot deny it is something I dared not hope for, in the circumstances, and you appear to be a decent and level-headed fellow. In fact, I would go so far as to say I am delighted, my boy.' He smiled, and came forward to clasp Lord Levedale firmly by the hand. 'I take it, of course, that you can support a wife?'

'I have an income of some five thousand a year from my estate in Devon, and land in Leicestershire, sir, and I have been ploughing much of the profit back into the estate these last two years, since I inherited. Thus far I have put away three thousand in Funds, which is not, I admit, a fortune, but I have enough to live very comfortably if one does not spend the Season in Town.'

A crease appeared between Lord Mardham's brows. He was reminded of the stipulations of his father's will. For himself, he thought that seeing Celia married, and to an excellent young man who would cherish her, was far more important than an inheritance, but he was not sure that his lady would see things in the same light. The repercussions might be unpleasant, and he disliked unpleasantness.

'I see. Look, Levedale, I know this must sound unfair to you, but I feel I must consult Lady Mardham before making you an answer.'

'Before . . . ? Is there some doubt as to my suitability

because of my income?' Lord Levedale's frown matched that of his host.

'I cannot speak of it until I have consulted with my wife. You may be sure that I will give you my answer after dinner.'

Lord Levedale, perplexed, and somewhat affronted, bowed, and withdrew to spend a very uncomfortable few hours in limbo. He did not want company, and therefore strode off into the park, where nature would give him solitude in which to contemplate his future, which he hoped would be bright.

Celia lay upon her bed, with a body as jumbled as her mind. Every bone and muscle felt jangled and disordered, and at the same time she felt an enormous lethargy, as if lying down was too much effort and she ought to simply melt into the mattress. She hoped Dr Stour would be able to come without delay, and remove the barrier of concern that held her back from total happiness. She dared not let herself be so happy, for fear that some awfulness would stand between her and the joy of being loved as she loved.

She had tried telling herself that she was being silly, and that Lord Levedale – her own beloved Lord Levedale, was eminently sensible. What she was suffering now was the result of being tense and frightened and bounced about for miles, not a fall that might cause a break, but having discovered the fragility of her own bones she was more aware than most that they were not invulnerable.

Her mama did not seem concerned, as she had been upon her arrival, but was flitting about the room in an agitated manner, and coming out with disjointed phrases about winter weather and fur trimmings. Horley eventually turned upon her ladyship and requested that Miss Celia be left in peace until the doctor arrived.

Dr Stour arrived an hour later, having been out attending Lord Bathurst's butler at Cirencester Park, who had tripped and broken his wrist.

'Now then, Miss Mardham, what have you been up to?' His first glance assessed, and he already guessed that his fee would be one for affirming health, not confirming a problem.

Celia did not want to give the truth, but Horley had no such qualms.

'She's been jangled and jumbled something terrible, Doctor, by a very silly man who thought that driving like a madman would impress her.'

'Ah.'

'I had to grip on so tightly, Dr Stour, that at one point I could not make my hands let go,' Celia was still bemused by this spasm of muscles. 'And after that I could not stop trembling.'

'But there was no accident?' The doctor lifted her wrist and measured her pulse, which was a little fast for one who was recumbent.

'Almost. A wheel went into a ditch, but the vehicle did not topple over, just tipped at an angle.'

'I doubt there is anything seriously wrong, Miss

Mardham, but you were wise to call me out. Now, if I may just check your left leg . . .'

He pressed and moved the limb, asked questions about sensation, and smiled at her in an avuncular way.

'Well, Horley has the correct diagnosis, Miss Mardham. You are indeed, er, "jangled and jumbled". An excessively unpleasant experience has had your frame very tense, and this is the very natural reaction that follows. I know how you dislike taking laudanum, but would say that if the discomfort persists tonight, a few drops would help you sleep, and a good night's rest will see you back to normal. I would recommend that you let Horley tuck you up comfortably in bed, and that you remain there until tomorrow. By all means eat well, if you have the appetite, but do not be concerned if you are not very hungry. What you have is a shocked system that will take a few hours to calm itself.'

'Thank you, Dr Stour.'

She looked so relieved he patted her hand. 'I am always pleased to give encouraging news, Miss Mardham, and to good patients who obey my instructions.'

With which he went to assure Lady Mardham that there were no serious consequences to 'the incident'.

Celia was so relieved that tears pricked her eyes, and she closed them to conceal her emotion. By tomorrow she would feel perfectly well, and everyone would be happy for her and . . . She completely ignored Miss Darwen, Sir Marcus, and Mr Wombwell in the tableau she imagined in her head, and from which she moved to Sarah opening the letter which announced that her friend was as happy as she was herself. She sighed.

'There now, Miss Celia. You just close your eyes awhile and rest like the doctor said. I will go and arrange for tea and biscuits to be brought up because you have missed your luncheon, or would you prefer a posset?'

'Tea would be nice, Horley, thank you,' murmured Celia, rather dreamily.

Left alone, she permitted herself a broad smile.

'He loves me,' she whispered, and because saying it sounded so good, she repeated it several times, louder.

Welney was already laying out his evening clothes by the time Lord Levedale returned. Having seen Lord Curborough's man below stairs, and who had revealed, most unprofessionally, that they had come very much in a rush, Welney was well aware of the earl's arrival. Since his master did not mention the fact, he thought it unlikely that he knew of it and decided it was not his place to inform him. His lordship therefore went down to dinner in blissful ignorance of his father's unwelcome presence. He stepped into the room and came up short.

'Good God!' As a greeting it lacked warmth, but more than made up for it in surprise. Lord Curborough was in conversation with Lady Corfemullen. He looked at his son, coolly.

'Good evening, Levedale.' He sounded almost bored, as if the encounter had been planned weeks before.

Lord Levedale advanced into the room, and bowed self-consciously to his sire.

'I had no idea you were coming to Meysey, sir.' He did not sounded overcome by delight.

'Nor had I until I read your letter, Levedale,' responded Lord Curborough, cryptically, which made Lady Corfemullen prick up her ears. Much to her annoyance, however, the earl then changed the subject entirely.

'What happened to your face?'

'It had an altercation with a tree.'

Lord Curborough appeared to think this was not the real reason at all, and looked huffy, and Lord Levedale excused himself as soon as he was able and went to ask Lady Mardham how Miss Mardham fared.

'Oh, Dr Stour said that she had suffered a nasty shock, but that all she required was rest. He recommended that she remain in bed until the morrow, but that rest and quiet are all she needs, my lord.' She smiled at him, but it was a tight smile, and she gave no further information. It gave him food for thought, and the thought was not encouraging. A lady who had just agreed to her daughter receiving a gentleman's addresses would surely have been more forthcoming and effusive towards that gentleman.

Lord Mardham entered, and the feeling of impending gloom increased. He look preoccupied, and at Lord Levedale's low voiced request to be given his answer, replied with a hasty 'not yet'.

* * *

Dinner was a strained affair, at which the negative emotions of the majority depressed those unaffected, namely the Corfemullens, Miss Burton and Lord Pocklington. The table was, perforce, uneven, with only four ladies present, and Lady Mardham had placed Lord Curborough next to herself, but with Levedale on his other side, whom he rather pointedly ignored. Lord Levedale was lost in some deep cogitations of his own for much of the meal, and spent the rest looking angrily at Mr Wombwell sat opposite him.

Mr Wombwell looked sullen, which was an understatement. He had had a very bad day. Miss Mardham, instead of being excited by his 'abduction upon an adventure' had shown every indication that she was loathing every second, and was obviously responsible for his veering off the road, with her alternate pleadings and caustic comments. He had been forced to walk five miles upon the public highway with all those passing him from behind well aware of why he was on foot. He had been subjected to very insolent comments from persons of inferior rank, who had laughed at him. His phaeton had sustained such damage that it would take at least two days to repair, even though he had offered the wheelwright an excessive sum to see to it as a matter of urgency, and had driven back in a vehicle that he was ashamed to be seen in. The wheelwright, disliking the gentleman's high-handed tone, and seeing that the wheel would require the removal of the rim and two felloes to insert new spokes, decided that Mr Pye's cart wheel would take precedence over this unknown dandy's fancy vehicle.

As if all this were not enough, Mr Wombwell had returned to find his mama in mild hysterics, throwing herself upon his bosom and behaving in a most embarrassing manner. None of what had occurred had been his fault, and his nemesis, Lord Levedale, still looked as though he would dearly love to knock him down. Whilst enjoying boxing as a spectator, Mr Wombwell had never enjoyed participation in the Noble Art, and was not at all sure that he could adequately defend himself if Lord Levedale chose violence.

All in all, he simply wanted to leave Meysey as soon as possible, visit his own friends as cheaply as possible, and think up some new scheme to restore his fortunes. A wealthy widow still sounded the best bet.

Mrs Wombwell's nerves were, like Celia's bones, 'jangled', and she was aware that her beloved son had acted in a most thoughtless manner towards her friend and hostess. He could be, she decided, such a silly boy. It ruined her appetite and made speaking with Lord Mardham embarrassing.

Sir Marcus Cotgrave was wallowing in a rather enjoyable gloom. Feeling sorry for himself was in some ways rather consoling, especially when he lacked anyone else to do so. However, he had resolved to go on to Bath, where ladies of a delicate constitution were prone to gather, and where mamas might yet hope to find husbands for daughters who had not quite 'taken', or those who were not sufficiently wealthy to have essayed London for the Season. He had been undervalued here, but ultimately, after these disappointments, he would find a young bride.

Miss Darwen's annoyance with Mr Wombwell was profound. He had ruined an excellent opportunity, and in fact thrown The Cripple almost literally into the arms of Lord Levedale. That Lord Levedale did not look in alt this evening, did not penetrate her justifiable wrath. She would make her excuses to Lady Mardham, who was a foolish woman, and go home to regale her mama with the tale of three pointless weeks among persons of poor intellect and worse manners.

The ladies withdrew. Lord Levedale could do nothing but sit and drink his port and make part of what was a less than convivial grouping. Lord Mardham, giving up after the decanters had been round the table but twice, suggested that they join the ladies. It was Lord Levedale's opportunity, and he fell in beside his host.

'Well, sir?'

'I am sorry, my boy, damned sorry.'

'I see. I think, my lord, I am at least due some explanation, in view of your apparent pleasure at my declaration earlier.' Lord Levedale felt as if the bottom had just fallen from his world.

'Yes, I can see that you would. Not now though. We will speak of it in the morning. I am sorry.'

That was all Lord Mardham felt that he could say. He had endured a very fraught half hour with his wife, who had been all but making out the guest list for the wedding breakfast until he had revealed the state of Lord Levedale's finances. Her face had fallen.

'Can he not simply transfer some of his income into Funds immediately?'

'My dear, he has put that money back into his estate. It is not accessible.'

'But he has to do so, my lord.' There was an edge to her voice, one he knew well. It meant that whatever he said she would stick to her assertion, regardless of it being impossible.

'My love, he is a fine young man of good breeding, and Celia will be far happier living the life of a country lady where she may entertain at home, and her neighbours will soon be used to her infirmity. A month ago you would have been delighted to think that she would receive a good offer, and moreover it appears she is delighted by the arrangement.'

'Well, I am not. To think of That Woman gloating as Jane claims Celia's inheritance, it is too much. I will not have it, I tell you.'

'And how otherwise are you going to conjure up a husband for Celia? Put an advert in the papers?'

'Of course not. You must Do Something, my lord.'

Short of kidnapping some wealthy man, he could think of nothing, and so he told her. Tears ensued. Deep down he knew he ought to be firm, but Lady Mardham was quite capable of making his life a misery for weeks, and he disliked that intensely.

He had therefore capitulated, but felt he was being unreasonable and unfair to Levedale, and, more importantly, his daughter.

Lord Levedale entered the drawing room with beetling brows, and was clearly not in the mood for conversation. He spoke briefly to Mr Mardham and Lady Corfemullen but requested permission to withdraw before the tea came round. Small talk eluded him.

As he reached the stairs his name was called, and he turned. Lord Curborough was staring at him.

'I wish for words with you, in private, Levedale.'

Lord Levedale did not want to say anything to anyone, least of all his progenitor, and put his foot upon the first stair, but then sighed and turned about. He led the earl to the book room. He did not look in the least filled with filial affection when he shut the door and looked at his sire.

'Well, sir, and to what do we owe this pleasure?' he enquired, sarcastically.

'That is no way to speak to your parent,' grumbled the earl, hoping to gain the moral high ground from the start. He failed.

'It is when you only show an interest in me when it affects yourself. I say again, why have you come?'

'To prevent you making a fool of yourself, my boy, and ruining us into the bargain. Had I even a suspicion that you would show such a complete lack of sense . . . the young woman is a harpy, there is no getting past it. I have encountered her for but a few hours and that much is clear. You have been presented with a beautiful, biddable and wealthy girl, and only by some act of self-destructive lunacy could you have preferred the Darwen chit. The family will not be able to settle more than five thousand upon her at best, and in my view it would take three times that to make her worth the misery.'

Lord Levedale was rendered speechless for a full minute.

'You think that . . . Miss Darwen?' Lord Levedale laughed rather mirthlessly. 'If you had spent more than "a few hours" in her company you would realise that all the money in the Royal Mint could not make it worth marrying her.'

'But . . .' Lord Curborough looked blankly at his son, and then a horrible suspicion dawned upon him. 'There is only her. Good God, my boy, you cannot count Mardham's lame filly.' Hs voice rose in volume and register. 'But she's a cripple.'

Lord Levedale's expression hardened.

'For Heaven's sake keep your voice down. For your information, Miss Mardham suffered a near fatal fall from her horse, and as a consequence has endured, still endures, much pain and discomfort. Her left leg is shortened, and stiff. She is not incapacitated in her faculties, nor in any other physical form. A broken leg is not hereditary.'

'She is abnormal.' Lord Curborough snorted. 'One may pity her, but it is unthinkable that you would . . . breed with such a female.'

Lord Levedale had spent several if not many, very

pleasant daydreams thinking about just that, and had had recourse to splashing his face with very cold water to cool his ardour.

'She is the young woman I love, and my feelings are reciprocated, fully. I have, for reasons not yet explained, had my suit rejected by Lord Mardham. If I find that you have interfered, sir . . .'

'I have not.'

'I shall lift not even a finger to save you, or Silvertons.'

'Well, if you married The Girl With the Limp, you would not be in a position to help, so that is no threat.'

'I am meeting again with Lord Mardham in the morning after breakfast. It appears Lady Mardham is the one to have taken my offer badly, and I will attempt to make my case with his lordship once more. If that fails, then all I can see is the prospect of waiting until Miss Mardham comes of age, and may marry whomsoever she likes.'

'Without a penny to come with her.'

'If needs be, yes, and I would settle all I possess upon her and any children, should I predecease her. Not a penny would go to you.'

Lord Curborough's reply involved loud and unpleasant words, which left Lord Levedale untouched. They parted at odds, and each departed to his bed where they neither fell asleep quickly, beset as they were with worrying thoughts. Before he rang for Welney, however, Lord Levedale wrote a very short note, and pushed it under the door of Miss Mardham's bedchamber. It contained but the two words 'Permission refused'.

CHAPTER TWENTY-THREE

Celia awoke to find her dream was reality, and lay in bed too happy to even open her eyes and start the day. Eventually she rang for her maid, and stretched, cautiously. Her leg felt a little stiffer than usual first thing in the morning, but otherwise she felt quite well.

Horley entered, and picked up the folded note from the floor.

Celia's happiness evaporated.

'Which gown would you be wishful to wear, Miss Celia? Miss Celia?'

Celia tried to think. Nothing happened. There was a terrible void.

'I do not understand,' she murmured to herself.

Horley cast her a thoughtful look and did not repeat the question.

She tried again, but thoughts came slowly. Why should Papa turn down her one chance of happiness? Had he not even encouraged the situations in which the romance had developed? Then the truth dawned. It must be money. Lord Levedale did not look poor, but if his investments came below those stipulated by Grandpapa Mardham's Will . . .

'Pass me my dressing gown, please, Horley.'

Horley did so, and helped her mistress rise from her bed. She was always a trifle unsteady getting up.

'Thank you. I will return shortly. I must see Mama.'

With which Celia took up her stick and hobbled to the door.

Lady Mardham was enjoying her morning chocolate, but upon Celia entering her room, she spilt it upon the counterpane, and went 'Oh' in a worried voice.

'Do you hate me, Mama?"

'Of course not, my poor child. Do not be histrionic.'

'Then tell me why, after repeatedly saying how marriage is important, frees one, you have prevented my chance of marriage?'

'You have had two offers, my love, which shows you are marriageable after all.' Lady Mardham did not look her daughter in the eye.

'No, Mama, it shows one man was desperate and the other the only man to ever appreciate me for who I am, not how I look and walk.' Celia suppressed a sob.

'You do not understand. A marriage is not "freeing" if one is impoverished.'

'Are Lord Levedale's coats patched? His stockings darned? Does he look "impoverished"?'

'Appearances can be deceptive, my poor Celia.'

'Not to that degree. Look at his horses.'

'That would tell me nothing.'

'No. Perhaps not to you, but to me, and Papa must know. This is about the Will, is it not?'

'You cannot marry a man who has no money, dear.'

'I would rather marry a man with "not enough money to please you" and be happy, than remain a spinster, dependent upon the family.' She stopped, as an idea occurred to her. 'And if I am not permitted to marry Lord Levedale then I will wait until such time as I am of age. I will not marry anyone else.'

That Celia might consider actually waiting for Lord Levedale had not crossed Lady Mardham's mind.

'You speak in heat. When you have had time to consider . . .'

'I love him, Mama.'

'You think you do, but in only a few weeks . . .'

'I love him, and in keeping us apart you wound my heart.' Celia cracked, and had she been able, would have run from the room. Instead, her tears flowed as she left, slowly, her limp more than usually pronounced.

Back in her room, Horley was waiting.

'There now, Miss Celia. You sit yourself down and compose yourself,' urged Horley, comfortingly. Celia sat, and blew her nose, and sniffed. When the tears had ended she took a deep breath, and with the inhalation came a thought. Her voice was firm when she spoke.

'I am driving to the Dower House, Horley. A morning dress, if you please, and my grey pelisse and lilac bonnet.'

'Yes, miss. But her ladyship may not be up early, miss. You will go after breakfast?'

'No. I would rather await her in the Dower House.'

Thus, half an hour later, Celia was assisted into the little pony cart, with the faithful Pom between the shafts. She declined a groom, and drove alone, not wishing for company on the way there, nor other ears to hear her upon the return. If she had to wait a year to wed Lord Levedale, then if he would wait for her also, she would do so, but oh, how she considered it a waste of life. If anyone could help her in her predicament it was Grandmama. She thought that the old lady had rather liked Lord Levedale, and if she had, then woe betide Papa, or Mama, if they tried to stand in Grandmama's way. Celia only hoped her grandmother would see matters in the same light as herself.

The shutters were still drawn across the reception room windows when Celia arrived. There was nobody to hold Pom, or help her down from the cart, so she looped the reins about the brake, and descended cautiously. Then she went to the pony's head.

'Now, Pom, old fellow, I am depending upon you. Be a good boy and do not think of leaving.' She patted his neck, and went to ring the doorbell firmly. She heard it resounding through the quiet house. It was a maid, with duster in hand, who opened the door, as Chorley emerged from the the servants' quarters, still pulling on his coat.

'Miss Celia! Her ladyship is still taking breakfast in her room, miss.' He sounded rather shocked.

'It is alright, Chorley. I will await her in the morning room. I would not have her rushed, but it is imperative that I speak with her.'

Chorley, with the wisdom of over three times Celia's years, considered these statements contradictory. If he told his mistress that Miss Celia was downstairs and it was 'imperative' that she speak to her ladyship, then Lady Mardham would of course rush. If he did not say anything, he would be berated later. He sighed.

'Yes, Miss Celia. I will have Jane open up the morning room for you in a trice.' He nodded at the waiting maid, who was all agog.

'And can you have someone sent to the stables so that the pony can be attended to, please?'

'Yes, miss.'

So Celia waited, rehearsing all that she wanted to say. It was nearly half an hour later when the dowager entered the room.

'Well? What on earth can have you on my doorstep at dawn, miss?' It was some three hours since the dawn, but Celia was not going to argue. Grandmama did not sound pleased to see her.

'I had to come. Grandmama, only you can help me in this fix.'

Lady Mardham, reading her granddaughter's face better than she could have guessed, sniffed, and sat down upon a sofa, patting the seat beside her.

'Best you tell me about it then.'

Celia's sentences melted. Grandmama might sound frightening, but this was Grandmama at her most understanding. Celia took a breath, managed 'You see . . .' and buried her face in her grandmother's rather narrow bosom.

Lord Curborough did not enjoy his breakfast, being too concerned that his son and heir might eschew it altogether and closet himself with Lord Mardham without him being able to be a third at the interview. He feared the boy could be too damned persuasive, and a night's repose might well have brought Mardham to the realistic conclusion that any offer was better than none, and the girl was scarcely likely to receive another. That interfering to dissuade Lord Mardham from changing his mind was entirely contrary to his only remaining son's fervent wish and future happiness did not concern him a whit. The boy was young enough to get over it. He sat in silence with Sir Marcus, who approved of such behaviour at the breakfast table.

Lord Mardham had come, eaten, and departed some time previously, before Lord Curborough made his appearance. Lord Levedale entered, and halted upon the threshold.

'Has Lord Mardham breakfasted?'

Sir Marcus nodded, and waved a forkful of roasted beef in the general direction that would indicate the library. Lord Levedale did not even acknowledge his father's presence.

'Thank you.' He withdrew, and Lord Curborough, muttering, cast down his napkin, made an excuse to Sir Marcus, and stomped after him. He had to ask a footman for the direction of the library, and entered without knocking. Lord Levedale, who had not taken up an offer to be seated, turned, and glared at his father.

'This does not concern you, sir.'

'It does, by Heaven, and I am honour-bound – honour-bound I say – to ensure that Mardham is fully aware of the facts, the unpleasant facts.'

Lord Mardham blinked, and wondered what on earth these facts might be. Levedale had at no time given any inkling of being less than an honourable man, and indeed Lord Mardham felt very guilty at refusing him, in the light of his actions upon the night of the fire and the previous day.

'I beg you will not wash our dirty linen in public, sir.' Lord Levedale was thin-lipped with anger, and the request sounded more of a command.

'I must be honest,' declared the earl, giving what his son thought was a poor impression of an early Christian martyr.

'Might we all three sit down, my lords, and speak plainly but without heat?' Lord Mardham was now fully aware of the antipathy that crackled between father and son. Both looked at him, and sat, very upright, in chairs as far apart as possible.

'I am seeking to find out why Lady Mardham, and I can only assume it is her wish, objects to me as a husband for your daughter, sir.' Lord Levedale was trying to remain calm. 'I can see no reason why she might think my character deficient.'

'I can assure you that there is no reflection upon your character, in any way, in the decision, Levedale.' Lord Mardham felt acutely embarrassed.

'Then is it simply that I am not wealthy enough? My income is steady, and my outgoings likewise. I do not think that Miss Mardham seeks to live at great expense in Town so . . .'

'Of course, by the time he inherits, the earldom will be but a name only,' interjected Lord Curborough, with a peculiar mix of gloom and satisfaction.

Lord Mardham looked stunned. It was hardly normal for a man to advertise the imminent financial ruin of his house.

'Er . . .' he managed.

'Through no fault of mine. I live within my means, and—' Lord Levedale got no further.

'Through every fault, sir, because you have failed to do as you were told.' Lord Curborough's tone was biting, and his complexion became choleric.

'I have every intention of making the likely future of the estates known to Miss Mardham. If she is content to live modestly . . .'

'Penny-pinching, he means,' murmured Lord Curborough in the voice of a Cassandra. 'And if Silvertons remains, devoid of its treasures but still in our hands, she will be faced with leaking roofs, perished plasterwork and a great deal of damp and mildew which must be harmful to a delicate creature. You would not be a caring parent if you exposed your only daughter to that.'

'My lord, my father is trying to put you off simply because he desires me to play the fortune hunter and drag him out of the River Tick.' Any pretence at speaking 'without heat' was gone. Lord Levedale's voice was raised.

'And that is a son's duty,' cried Lord Curborough. 'Would not you expect the same, Mardham?'

Lord Mardham could not even begin to envisage such a scenario. He therefore said nothing.

Celia did not say much during the short journey back across the park, focusing on her driving so that her grandmother should not be jolted. The pony cart was, after all, not the well sprung and deeply upholstered vehicle in which she was used to travel. Lady Mardham sat very straight, and silent not through displeasure but because she was thinking. Eventually she did ask one question, though she was certain of the answer.

'Your heart is engaged, patently, but I have to ask, child, if you have encouraged it to be so because Levedale is the one man who is likely to offer you the chance of marriage and a household of your own?'

'I love him because he sees Me, Grandmama, not the limp, but the real Me, and loves Me. He is my chance of happiness. I have had another offer for my hand, but that was Sir Marcus Cotgrave.'

'Cotgrave? But he is nigh on Mardham's age, and a bore to boot.'

'He is, dear ma'am, but offer for me he did. I refused him, because I would rather remain single to my dying day than be his "replica" wife, and he wanted to prevent me doing anything without him, as though I were a vase that might smash. He wanted me to be totally dependent upon him so that he could feel powerful, I suppose. Well, I would not, could not. Papa would have agreed to my marriage to Lord Levedale. It is Mama who has forbidden it, and she is thinking of the inheritance, not me.'

'And you would marry Levedale with his meagre however many thousand a year.'

'Yes, ma'am, for I do not want a Society life, an expensive life. How could I function in Society? No, I would be more than happy in Devon, living quietly as he does, with him, the man who has my heart.'

'Then we must ensure that you get the future you deserve and desire.'

'Can you persuade Papa to let me marry and ignore the inheritance?'

'Leave things to me, my dear.'

Celia bit her lip. The pony cart swung in front of the

house and came to a halt. Copthorne, his normal butler's impassivity broken by the sight of his old mistress in so lowly a vehicle, called out the footmen to assist her.

'I am not a piece of furniture,' announced Lady Mardham, eyeing the footmen as they approached. They were circumspect in their aid, and as soon as she had dispensed with them, one went to help Miss Mardham. She followed her grandmother into the hall.

'No need to announce me, Copthorne, nor direct me.' Her ladyship was in control. 'I can hear where the gentlemen are, perfectly clearly.' With which she lifted her head and strode imperiously towards the library, her stick rapping upon the floor. Copthorne bustled to open the door for her. Unannounced she might be, but her arrival stopped the argument in its tracks. The three gentlemen turned their heads and stared at her.

'Good morning, gentlemen. Do not let me stop you. I am sure there are parts of Gloucestershire as yet unaware of your disagreement.' Her tone was acerbic.

She stepped further into the room. They rose automatically, and Lord Levedale, the first to make a recovery, pulled forward a high-backed chair.

'Good morning, ma'am.'

'Hmm. I do not consider having to leave the comfort of my own home to sort out foolishness a good morning. However, one patently cannot leave a sensible decision to mere men.' She conveniently forgot her daughter-in-law's part in the mess. Her basilisk gaze alighted on Lord Curborough as she sat down. 'And among "mere men" few are more "mere" than you, Curborough. I can only say that if Levedale took after you and not after his mother, I would not countenance my granddaughter marrying him.'

'Mama, this is . . .'

'Be quiet, Mardham. I thought I had only brought one ninny into the world, but it seems I was wrong. Your only daughter receives an offer from an unimpeachable young man, and you cast her happiness at nought.'

'Mama, you do not understand the complexity. Lord Curborough has disclosed the depths of his family's financial embarrassment and . . .'

'He has, has he?' She turned on the earl. 'You really are a most unpleasant specimen. I do not wish to view you any longer. Leave the room.' Curborough blinked at her. He was certainly not used to being treated like a schoolboy. 'Leave the room, sir. I wish to speak to Mardham and Levedale only.'

Lord Mardham made apologetic noises in his throat, but did nothing. Reluctantly, Curborough withdrew, and Lady Mardham pursed her lips and settled herself more comfortably in her chair.

'You do not understand, Mama.'

'Poppycock. I understand the terms of the Will very well.' Mardham opened his mouth to speak but she raised a hand to halt him. 'Yes, I know the rules also. But the situation is simple. The only reason you have refused Levedale is that he has not got the required capital, correct?'

'"Required capital"?' Lord Levedale frowned, confused, and looked from one to the other, but Lady Mardham ignored his interjection.

'If he has five thousand in Funds, the stipulation is fulfilled. Levedale, what is your income?'

'I count on a little over five thousand pounds a year, ma'am, from my estate in Devon, and I have some three thousand already put by, in Funds. It is not much, but my lifestyle is not exp—'

'So you need a minimum of an additional two thousand. Well, I can have my man of business advance you three thousand and then there is no problem. Mardham can give his permission for you to marry Celia, and can rejoice in the fact that she, rather than her cousin, inherits the bequest.'

Lord Levedale still did not understand.

'You cannot give me three thousand pounds, ma'am.'

'I can do what I like, young man, and you will say "thank you", nicely, and make my granddaughter very happy.'

'But—'

'"But" nothing. I can do what I like with my money. I am nigh on eighty, and it won't be long before what I have will be divided between my grandchildren anyway, and the majority to the girls. This is just pre-emptive. The problem is solved. Mardham, you give your permission, that's it, nod wisely, and Levedale, tell your father to go home, and then find Celia. I won't tell you what to say or do. I think it is fairly obvious.'

'Yes ma'am. And thank you.' He raised her hand to his lips and kissed it.

'Hmmm, keep that sort of thing for my granddaughter. Off with you.'

Lord Curborough was pacing outside like an expectant father. He looked up as his son came out of the library.

'Well?'

'Very, thank you, sir.'

'Do not be facetious, Levedale.'

'After your actions today, I shall be as I like. You have flaunted our pitiable situation in front of others as if it were a badge of honour, and why? To try and ensure that I do your bidding. I will not do so.'

'Damn it, sir, you turn not a hair whilst telling me you would ruin us? I declare I ought to turn you off without a penny.'

Lord Levedale achieved what in a less agreeable man would count as a derisive sneer.

'Firstly, our ruin has been achieved without any interference by myself, and secondly, this whole unfortunate situation appears to be founded upon the fact that you no longer possess a penny, with or without which to turn me off.'

'You are insolent and disobedient, Levedale, putting your own wishes above the needs of the family.'

'And squandering a healthy inheritance was with "the needs of the family" to the fore, was it, Father?'

'I forbid you to enter my house again until you have

come to your senses. All I asked was that you marry well.'

'Miss Mardham's lineage is unimpeachable. What you mean was that you demanded that I marry money, which is not the same thing, sir.'

'I as good as promised Sir William Burton that you would offer for his daughter.'

'I would not have offered for Miss Burton were she the last girl in the world, and as for crossing your threshold, I do not care if I do not do so ever again, and if our circumstances force its sale that will be the case. However, if I am in a position at any time to salvage house and land, I shall do so, upon the condition that you remove to the Dower House and hand over the finances to me.'

'You would have me your pensioner.'

'If necessary, yes. Now, I have more important matters to attend to.'

'What are you going to do?'

'I am going to tell Miss Mardham that her father has agreed to our betrothal. Good day to you, sir.' Levedale did not wait to hear what his sire's reaction to this might be, but caught the attention of Copthorne. 'Where will I find Miss Mardham?'

'In the small parlour, my lord,' answered the butler, with an encouraging smile which, as he later explained to the housekeeper, was a lapse, but one in exceptional circumstances.

Lord Levedale did not quite run to this room, but

his steps were urgent. He opened the door, and found Celia alone, gazing out into the garden, but clearly not 'seeing' anything outside her own misery, for she still dared not hope. She turned, and he could see her cheeks were damp.

'You know, my love, were it not for the fact that I have just offered for you and been accepted, I think I would offer for your grandmother, because I am half in love with her after the last five minutes.'

He was smiling, his eyes alive with joy and something more.

'Papa changed his mind?'

'He did not get much option.'

'Grandmama can be—'

'Unstoppable? Indeed she can, for which you and I, my beloved Celia, must be eternally grateful.'

'But how?' Celia gazed at him, still more confused than delighted. He noticed how some of her eyelashes had matted together where she had shed tears, how one brow arched very slightly more than the other, and for a moment he could not speak, because he was overcome with the intense delight of realising that the future was one in which he would see the little details of her every day.

'Apparently I had to possess five thousand pounds in the Funds in order to be "acceptable" and fulfil some stipulation for an inheritance. Your grandmother is writing me a draught upon her bank for three thousand, more than I actually require, which means that my previously rejected offer is now accepted, and I may now pay you my addresses. I have, by the by, also had a very frank exchange of views with my far from esteemed parent, which means that you and I, my darling, will not be making bride visits to Silvertons. In fact, I doubt very much if you will ever get to set it to rights, since it is highly likely the bank will foreclose upon it. Father said I had "ruined" the family but . . .'

'Did Papa disclose my inheritance to you? The amount, I mean.'

'No, for it is immaterial to m—'

'I will inherit thirty thousand pounds.' She enunciated the figure slowly.

'Thirty thousand . . .' repeated Lord Levedale as slowly, before letting out a crack of laughter. 'Oh my Lord! If only he had known!' He took her hands, and smiled down at her. Celia smiled back. His voice trembled very slightly, and it was not with merriment. 'I want you to be my wife because I adore you. You know that.'

'Yes, I know it.'

He let go of one of her hands and slipped an arm about her waist, pulling her closer still, then bent his head and kissed her, firmly, deliberately, a kiss founded in his right to kiss her, not in nervous supplication. Celia made a small sound, and reached up her free hand to touch his cheek. For a few minutes they gave themselves up to the intoxication of mutual desire, and when they parted, just a little, each felt shaken. Celia blushed, but he shook his head at that.

'We are betrothed, and very soon you will be my lawful wedded wife.' He lifted her into his arms, and carried her to the sofa where, most reprehensibly even for the newly betrothed, he sat with her upon his knee.

'I never dreamt this would happen, that I would fall in love, nor even more that the man I loved should love me,' whispered Celia, leaning her cheek against his shoulder. 'I am sorry if it has made you break with Lord Curborough.'

'I am not, unfilial as it sounds. Besides, he will come round when he finds out that, whilst not an heiress in the same league as Miss Burton, you have the advantage of inheriting now, not at some distant future. He will be coming cap in hand, you can wager upon it, but I would rather deal with the bank and redeem the mortgages. It would be nice to restore the house, but logically, other than vital repairs to the fabric, it would be better to get back the land and its income. I fear, my love, that when you see the ancestral home, you will be horrified, for it has had no lady to oversee its care since my mother died, and for some years before that her ill-health meant that, like her, everything "faded".'

'I would live in a cave, if it were with you,' she said, simply.

'It is not that outmoded.' He laughed, and bade her lift her head from his shoulder and look at him. 'I do not live a life in the social whirl, and have never sought to do so. I would be happy in the little Devon property, but the Curboroughs have had a house on the ground upon which Silvertons stands since they obtained the barony in the fifteenth century, and part of me would regret letting it go. I cannot offer you riches or a grand mansion, just a competence and the prospect of a tired house and estate.'

'We will have each other. There is nothing more to say.' Celia sighed.

'Oh yes there is.' His lips twitched.

'What?'

'Bless thine inheritance.'

SOPHIA HOLLOWAY read Modern History at Oxford and also writes the Bradecote and Catchpoll medieval mysteries as Sarah Hawkswood.

@RegencySophia
sophiaholloway.co.uk